17.99   3 RB   FOL

Donated by the
Friends of the Lake
County Library
with a grant
from the
Lake County
Wine Alliance

THE
EMPIRE OF
GUT AND BONE

THE EMPIRE OF GUT AND BONE

THE NORUMBEGAN QUARTET, VOL. 3

M. T. ANDERSON

SCHOLASTIC PRESS
NEW YORK

Library of Congress Cataloging-in-Publication Data available

ISBN 978-0-545-13884-0

10 9 8 7 6 5 4 3 2 1
11 12 13 14 15 16

Printed in the U.S.A.   23
First edition, June 2011

The text was set in 11-pt. Excelsior.

Book design by Steve Scott

To N.
in the House of Haunts

THE
EMPIRE OF
GUT AND BONE

ONE

A staircase led to nowhere. It stood in the middle of a rough, broken plain.

A stocky boy sat on the stairs, sagging low, his elbows on his knees. Dim blue light shone from jagged cracks in the black sky. It faintly lit ruins.

Brian Thatz raised his head to look out across the murky horizon. Arches below him supported nothing. Columns stood with no roof. Cellars sat naked beneath the low, dark sky. And beyond all this, there was only a flat sea of ooze.

Brian uncurled, reached out to lift the singed leg of a broken chair, and stirred the ashes of his fire. The ashes glowed faintly. He slid across the step he sat on to get closer to the warmth.

At the top of the ceremonial staircase, a few steps up, stood a black slab, a gateway to another world.

Brian was cold — chilled to the bone — and tired. He had not eaten for a day. At least he thought it was a day.

Time was difficult, for there was no sun, no night, no day — just cracks in the sky and a reflecting glimmer in far marshes of stew.

The ruins covered a square mile or so. They were all built of rough-hewn brown stone. Hardly anything stood. Chimneys. A few walls. The staircase was the tallest thing in the city. It was a broad staircase, and had a twist to it. In an earlier age, all the refugees of lost Norumbega had fled down these wide steps, coming to this world to make a new home.

Now a dull silence lay over the fallen metropolis. Occasionally, the wind stirred, shuffling over the desolate marshes.

Brian could hear the bickering of his friends as they returned to the camp.

"This is dumb."

"*You're* dumb."

"I am not dumb."

"I didn't mean you were actually dumb. I just mean it's dumb to say that things are dumb."

"You're not even — don't even argue with me! You're not even real!"

"So I'm fake, and you're dumb. We're even."

"You're dumb *and* fake. You're programmed to be dumb."

Brian was exhausted, and wished they'd stop fighting. They had all spent the last twelve hours or so searching the ruins for life or clues. Before that, they'd spent an awful day crawling around under a mountain, dodging silver tentacles, defending a kitchen against alien invasion, and vanquishing an undead real estate developer.

Brian's friends came trudging up the steps to nowhere. One was a blond boy with a burned hand wrapped in a piece of cloth. The other was a troll in Renaissance armor.

"We didn't find anything," said Kalgrash, the troll.

"We found *something*," said Gregory, the boy. "A bureau. We found a smashed-up bureau."

Kalgrash held out a wooden drawer. "For firewood." He tossed it down on the step. It cracked and slid down a few stairs.

Brian stood up and looked out over the sinkholes and slime. "What are we going to do? Where have they all gone?"

The three had risked everything to come in search of the Norumbegans, the elfin race that had raised this city in this weird plain. Back in the pleasant valleys of Vermont, the tricky, wicked Thusser had been arranging an alien settlement, stealing into dreams and corrupting time. The Thusser's invasion had been slowed, Brian hoped, by the destruction of their agent on Earth — but it had not been stopped. Even as Brian stood helplessly on this staircase to nowhere, the Thusser might be marching through a gateway onto the green lawns of Brian and Gregory's world.

Brian whispered, "What happened to this place?"

"No bodies," said Kalgrash, squinting. He clanked over to the side of the staircase and looked down at the cellars. "No sign of a battle or fire."

3

"The bureau was almost okay," said Gregory. "Just missing one leg. It was, you know, the kind of bureau that has legs."

"Maybe," said Kalgrash softly, "maybe the city was never destroyed."

"What do you mean?" Brian asked.

"I don't think the city was ever finished in the first place."

Brian and Gregory thought about this. The wind picked up. It blew Brian's black hair into his eyes, and he raised his hand to push the mess of it back.

Kalgrash said, "Maybe it's not ruined. Maybe it's unbuilt. Like the Norumbegans abandoned it. They got here, started to build — *tinka-tonka, tinka-tonka, tinka-tonka* — and then they moved on. Nothing looks like it was ever finished. I mean, the stonework. In the City of Gargoyles, they did all this fancy carving. Here, nothing's carved. It's like they were just starting. And I think some of these aren't even cellars — they're quarries. Where they were cutting out the rock. Yup." He nodded and looked around at the pits and columns. "Yup, yup, yup. That's what I think."

Gregory sat down wearily by the fire. He rubbed his roughly bandaged hand.

"I think you're right," said Brian. "Yeah."

Kalgrash mused anxiously, "I wonder what made them keep going . . . or . . . you know . . . wiped them out."

"It doesn't matter," said Gregory. "The thing is, we're trapped, right?"

4

"Yeah," said Brian. "Prudence and Snig can get us through the portal on their side, but we need someone to open it from this end, too. I don't know how."

"Right. Bingo," said Gregory. "So it doesn't really matter whether the Norumbegans were wiped out or they left. Because either way, we're stuck here in the middle of nowhere with nothing to eat and nothing in any direction except an ocean of goo." He flapped his hand at the glistening swamp.

"Better goo than gunk," said Kalgrash.

"What?" Gregory said, exasperated.

"Gunk's grimier than goo. Goo's . . . gookier, but not grimy." Kalgrash looked to Brian for support. "Am I wrong?"

Brian didn't answer. He was looking up at the obsidian portal, which just twelve hours before they had walked through like it was a pool, but which now, if they tried to pass back through, would be hard as marble.

Gregory glared at them both. He picked up the broken drawer and snapped it across his knee. He fed the pieces into the failing fire.

The black smoke went up, curled like the staircase, rising high above the shattered landscape and disappearing into the gloom.

✳ ✳ ✳

The boys slept while the troll kept watch.

They imagined that night had fallen, but the light

5

didn't change. The cracks in the sky still shone lurid blue. The wind blew bitterly across the marshes, through the half-built arches.

Gregory awoke. Someone was whispering something. He raised his head up.

The fire was still going. Kalgrash must have gone down and grabbed another bureau drawer. Brian was sleeping with his head on his arm.

Gregory looked down the great staircase.

The troll was twenty feet below them. Gregory rose carefully. Kalgrash stage-whispered, "Hey! Yoo-hoo! You two! There's something moving down there!"

Gregory shook Brian awake. Brian was startled, and blinked behind his glasses. He smeared his eyes and was about to ask something when Gregory shushed him and pointed down at the troll, who leaned forward, gripping his battle-ax.

"There's something in the city," Gregory whispered. Even as he said it, he felt a chill down his back.

They crept down the stairs to stand beside Kalgrash. Now they could see what he'd seen — an indistinct shape passing through the unfinished basements near the foot of the steps.

"What is it?" asked Brian. "Is it a person?"

"Maybe a person in a cloak or a robe," Kalgrash reported. "But lumpy, lumpy, lumpy."

"Lumpy's not good," said Gregory.

They paced down another few steps, the boys hanging back behind their armored friend.

"I'm going back up to get the musket," said Brian, and he loped back up to their campsite.

Kalgrash bobbed his head back and forth. He lifted his hand to his visor, which was pulled back on his forehead. He muttered, "It's gone."

"Gone's not good, either," said Gregory. He crouched, weaponless. His hand was still burned from a dumb stunt with an all-purpose cleaner.

Something leaped at the bottom of the stairs and began to swarm upward.

It was like a spiked burlap sack. It rolled and scraped up the steps, its skin clawed.

Brian was running down toward them, the musket held clumsily in his arms.

Kalgrash raised his battle-ax above his head. "Smite the bag!" he cried, and rushed the beast. He clanked as he descended, arms held high.

Brian came to Gregory's side. "I can't shoot with Kalgrash in the way." He sighted down the length of the musket, lowered it, shouted, "Kalgrash!"

But the troll was already smacking at the angry sack with his ax. It leaped at him. Its nails scraped across his plate mail.

He swung the ax again. The thing clung. He clawed at it. It fell.

It surrounded his feet, its clawed hide clamping on his greaves.

"Get away from it!" Brian shouted from up a few flights. "I can't shoot!"

Kalgrash tried lifting his feet — one, the other — but the thing held on. It bunched and rattled, its spikes or teeth rasping along the metal shoes, catching on the plates.

Kalgrash swung his ax.

It cleaved the bag in two.

The bag stopped moving.

He prodded its pieces. It kept still.

He turned and said triumphantly, "We should have known. Where there's goo, there's things." He grinned.

"Kal —!" screamed Brian, but it was too late. Already, more of the things were leaping up the steps — a ravenous pack of spiked bags flapping.

Brian sighted the musket. He thought of the portions of the Cantrip of Activation that had to be kept in the mind. He spoke the trigger words, and the musket flared. One sack flailed and dropped. Three more still crowded Kalgrash's knees.

Gregory didn't know whether to run down and help or run back up. There was nowhere to flee. They were stuck on the stairs. The portal above was tough as rock. And he had nothing to fight with. The creatures' teeth would shred him.

Brian kept trying to fire. He wasn't hitting much. He had to be careful so he didn't blast the troll.

Kalgrash was overwhelmed by the things galloping all around him, clawing at his metalwork. He swiped back and forth, but hit nothing. He was losing his balance.

He was near the edge of the stairs, and there was no banister.

He teetered, hacking. They clamped on to his armor. Another was rippling up the steps past him, heading for the boys.

Brian fired.

Kalgrash screamed.

There were dark shapes rising all around them, scuttling out of the ruins. Gregory looked around desperately. There were fifteen or so, all crawling toward them now, attracted — who knows? — by noise or scent or the heat of warm flesh.

The steps were crawling with them. Some were scratching their way up the thick Gothic supports. Gregory yelped as one flung itself over the edge and bunched toward him.

Panicked, he clattered back up the steps.

He and Brian were forced up — up — while Kalgrash was ringed below, hacking and crowing battle cries.

Brian fired again, but the creatures were too close to his ankles. He couldn't think — couldn't clear his mind to fill it with the Cantrip of Activation, the triggering images.

He and Gregory were almost back at the top, the landing, the dead end, the slab of unopened gate, the drop.

Kalgrash was crawling with toothed bodies. He tried to dislodge them through calisthenics — swinging his torso, kicking, flailing.

"Oh no, oh no — no!" said Gregory as one slithered closer. It clacked on the pink stone.

And then an aroma filled the air.

They didn't notice it much at first.

Gregory lashed out at the thing with his foot. He kicked it. It reared. It wavered sluggishly.

Brian was sniffing, looking around.

"While I'm being eaten," said Gregory unkindly, "you're sniffing out bacon." He stomped on the bag, then swore. A tooth had speared the rubber sole of his sneaker.

"There's something . . ." said Brian vaguely, holding up his hand. He waved his fingers in front of his nose.

Gregory shook the dead bag loose.

He looked around.

The things were getting sluggish. They were still rippling and heaving, but more slowly.

And the air was filled with sweet vapor.

Kalgrash, down below, was peeling off beasties and hurling them over the edge.

There was a light, burning and orange.

"What's going on?" said Gregory.

Then a voice called out of the gloom in a language that had not been heard on Earth for generations.

TWO

The man strode toward them over the broken terrain through clouds of gas as thick as powder. He wore some kind of ribbed jumpsuit and a hooded coat that sprouted white, bristly hairs. On his back were strapped two crossed planks — skis. In his hand, he held a contraption: a tin cylinder punctured with holes, in which something orange burned and gave off smoke. A fan behind it blew the smoke forward in jets and darts.

The man asked them questions in a language none of them understood.

He stopped and cocked his head. He gestured at the dead bags. He spoke again. He shrugged.

"I'm sorry," said Brian. Clearly and deliberately, he asked, "Do you speak English, sir?"

The man shut off the fan. The thick smog, no longer driven forward, bunched and dawdled. The man spoke again.

"Sorry," said Gregory. "We don't speak jumpsuit."

The figure grimaced, put down his gadget, and took out a short, curved knife. It was stained brown.

Kalgrash hefted his battle-ax and looked resolute.

The man took out a cigar and cut off the end. He lit it in his tin lamp and stuck it in his mouth. He had a black goatee, and looked wiry and sure of himself.

Keeping his knife out, he walked over to one of the toothed sacks. He began splitting it open. He separated the skin from some dry, red lining. Brian, appalled, watched as the man seized on to a dry mat of nerves and tugged them free.

Once the tangle of nerves dangled from his hand, he tossed the rest of the carcass aside. He moved on to the next sack. He paid no attention to the troll, who was only a few feet away.

Brian and Gregory descended the staircase, stepping gingerly over the dead bags. When they reached the foot of the stairs, Brian said to the man, "Norumbega?"

The man glanced up from his work, now interested. He pointed at the portal at the top of the steps. "Norumbega," he said. He jabbed his finger again up toward the black slab. Then he indicated the boys. "Norumbega?" he asked.

Gregory turned to Brian. "Do we say yes to that, or no?"

They did not answer. The man went about his work without further interest in the boys, tearing out the nets of nerve and gathering them in a skin. When he was done, he rose and looked inquiringly at the three who'd watched

12

him gut sacks up and down the stairs. He asked them a few questions, which they could not understand. He touched his skis, then indicated he wondered where the boys' skis were.

Brian shrugged. He shook his head and swiped his hands back and forth to show they didn't have any.

The man looked irritable. He gestured for them to follow him.

They picked up their few things and walked through the ruins. They passed under incomplete arches and down hallways that had never been built.

At the edge of the ruin, the sticky, yellow marsh began. Only a few feet from shore stood the man's sleigh. It was huge, with a little cabin, windows lit, and the chimney of a woodstove. It was drawn by three beasts of burden — headless, it seemed, mainly folds and flaps of skin, but with six or seven legs apiece. They idled in the saffron muck.

The man hauled his wide skis off his back, fastened them to his boots, and slushed out to his sleigh. He clambered aboard and returned with a little goo-sled and a paddle. He fetched the three of them one by one.

In a few minutes, they were all sitting aboard.

"I guess he's friendly," said Gregory.

"I guess." Brian wasn't sure. The man didn't smile or talk any more. He pulled back his hood. His ears were pointed.

Far above them, against the cracked, black sky, spidery birds lolloped into dusk.

For hours, they slushed over miles of muck. It was two or three feet deep. Quite quickly, the unbuilt city disappeared behind them, and then all that was left were the sharp veins of light in the sky, and the dim plain. Occasionally, they passed a metallic stem rising out of the goo, a single, crooked finger glinting dully, bloated at the top with some kind of pod.

"I hate the sky," said Gregory. "It looks like lightning got lazy."

"I think," said Brian, "that it's not a sky. I think it's actually a surface."

Gregory grimaced. He didn't like any of it.

The place was too empty. The landscape looked, somehow, like defeat.

They spent some time below, in the cabin. The stove was warm, lit with something like coal, and Brian and Gregory huddled close to it, trying to get the chill out of their hands. Most of the cabin was crammed with appliances. The boys couldn't tell what the gadgets did. They had cranks and revolving chains and (in one case) four sets of little riveted wings.

The troll sat up above, watching the sticky tundra pass. The goateed man saw that Kalgrash's arm was damaged, and, clenching his cigar in his teeth, went below for tools. As the troll sat and watched the three lumbering beasts pull the sleigh, the man carefully soldered his arm, slashed back on Earth by the crystalline kreslings. It was not a complete fix, but it improved the break.

They passed an islet of dull green rock. There was nothing else for miles.

Later, as Kalgrash and the two boys sat near the stove, Brian said glumly, "It's not like I expected here."

Gregory snorted in agreement. "Yeah. I thought it would be like when we traveled into the past. The palaces and all the noblemen in wigs. I thought there would be more fanfares, and the Emperor would be here —"

"Remember him?" said Brian warmly. "The guy you stole the crown from? And the Empress? And that bishop? The ones we saw on the barges and in the Haunted Hunting Grounds."

Gregory grinned. "Right. Exactly. The long coats and all the silk stuff. That's what I was expecting." He waved his hand with repulsion. "Not so much sludge."

The boys were getting hungry. Brian said he'd go ask the man when they were going to eat. He clambered up the little staircase to the bench where the man sat, holding the reins of the three ruddy steeds.

Their host was talking into a speaking-horn. He growled into it, then held it up to his ear to listen. He seemed testy. Brian quietly went back down into the cabin.

"He's on the phone," he told Gregory.

"I could eat a horse."

Kalgrash cautioned: "Hooves."

Brian mused, "It sounded like he was arguing. I'm worried. Where do you think he's taking us?"

Gregory flopped backward on the cot. "A Chinese buffet," he groaned, his arms trailing backward over his head. "Spring rolls. Pot stickers. Chicken lo mein. French fries. Five Vegetable Pleasures."

He stood and went up to reason with their host.

"French fries?" Kalgrash muttered. "What kind of Chinese buffet do you people go to, anyway?"

Gregory shut the door to the cabin. Their host was off the phone. He leaned forward, smoking his cigar, watching the dark, wet terrain. The beasts yanked them untiringly across the waste.

Gregory pointed to his mouth. He clapped his jaw open and shut.

The man mistook his meaning. He apparently needed no food himself, and perhaps did not understand eating at all. He assumed Gregory wanted a bit and a bridle to help pull the sleigh. A little mystified, he went below and got one, handed it to Gregory, and pointed down at the sloppy tundra before them in invitation. He signaled that the bit should be gripped in the teeth. Gregory, in despair, held the bit dangling.

So there was no food, and it took what might have been days to cross the marsh. Brian had a headache and lay on his side near the dead, cold stove. Gregory's stomach rattled. Kalgrash usually only ate food for show — he didn't need it — but he was worried for the boys, and kept watch over them while they slept.

Above, the cracks in the sky turned from blue to white. And the sleigh for the first time switched direction, according to some knowledge or agreement of their host. It crossed miles toward some uncertain destination, its ski tracks and wake ebbing behind it, dimming in the sludge.

THREE

An elf was in the soups.

He chose chicken and stars — hurled three cans in the cart. He had the veg already, and baggies of sliced meats.

Wee Snig was at the Halt'N'Buy. It was his turn to buy provisions. It was hard to get enough to eat, with time passing so strangely, so quickly, within the barriers of the Thusser settlement. In the few hours it took to walk from the base of Norumbega Mountain to get groceries, a day passed beneath the mountain and in the haunted suburb on its slopes. For whichever of them stayed behind, watching the portal in the catacombs — Wee Snig or Prudence — it felt like forever.

Snig selected bread. He was not doing well at looking unobtrusive among the humans. He looked a little crazy. His vest was open, his shirt collarless and dirty from imprisonment. His pants were rolled up above the shins and patched like a clown's. He wore an orange, knit ski hat — though it was eighty degrees out — to hide his ears.

He quickly scanned the cart. Every moment counted, amplified. He had what he needed. He got in line. The line was intolerably long. He stared impatiently at the glossy magazines in the rack — *Chic, TV Guide,* and *Me.* He thought of Prudence crouched there in that infernal darkness, amidst the blackened scabs of long-burned monsters.

In the line, it was his turn. He didn't know exactly how checkout worked, but he figured that he couldn't go wrong if he approached the whole process in a lordly and commanding manner.

He threw his items onto the conveyor belt. He handed the cashier Prudence's card. "Madame!" he said to the girl. "Make money come out of this card to pay for these foodstuffs." He waved his hand.

She stared at him.

"Make — make the money happen!" he said. "She told me a number! I tell you the number, and you make the money happen! Why do you look at me as if I'm insane?"

The girl gave him the keypad to type in the PIN. As he jabbed with his finger, he berated the boy bagger: "My friend, I wonder if you would be so good as to stop staring at me as if I were your day's gift of lunacy and just deposit those bananas in that fine paper sack. Come! Stop gawping. Don't you have opposable thumbs, child of Eve? Use them. Pinch. Lift. While you dawdle with my dinner, empires fall. Generations of moth spring forth, flourish, and die. My gums recede, my flesh shrivels! Time passes, children! Your pink face pales, young woman — old woman! Beneath it lies the skull, awaiting its moment to burst out and show its teeth!"

The kid with the bags said, "This is your dinner?"

"Indeed. Bag it, bagger!"

"It's dog food."

"Horse," said Wee Snig proudly, "can be perfectly succulent." He grabbed his bags by their handles and swept out.

Wee Snig was in a snit, so he did not notice the photocopied pictures taped on the door — photos of two boys missing for four days.

He tramped behind the Halt'N'Buy and headed down a path through the woods. It was late summer, and the sun was bright.

In another forty minutes or so, he reached the perimeter of the Thusser settlement. There was no marker, but he could feel time slither differently as he passed through. It moved faster. Five minutes later, and he was walking through fall. The leaves were browning.

He climbed an outcropping to see Rumbling Elk Haven. ("Where Nature Meets Class! Affordably!") He gazed through the branches.

He swore. It had gotten much worse since he had left for groceries.

There was no longer any semblance of order. Cars were deposited on lawns or in ditches. The doors on some were open. The batteries had died days before. No one moved in the houses. People were hiding or had already been absorbed and were dreaming. They were the surface on which the Thusser would settle, the medium through

19

which the Thusser would move. Some lay asleep on their lawns, slumped as if discarded.

The webbing of Thusser construction was spreading from the center outward. Houses wobbled in the wind, becoming more like the filmy nests in which the Thusser roosted.

There was one spot of human motion. It was near Prudence's old place — a little sixties ranch house in the midst of the new construction. Kids rode in slow, hypnotized circles in front of it. They did not stop or speak. They looked very thin.

And then Sniggleping saw someone else.

A door opened. A man came out on the front stoop. He was dressed in sneaks, Dockers, and a cardigan. He walked down the brick path that led from his door to the street. On the way, he stepped on the hand of the house's previous owner, who now slept sprawled out on the drive.

All at once, Snig saw that the man's ears were pointed, and there were dark rings around his eyes.

The Thusser had arrived. They had taken possession while he was out getting dog food and soup.

The man paused by his new mailbox — hesitated — and looked up into the hills.

His eyes met Snig's.

And Sniggleping ran.

He thrashed through the bushes down the rock face, along the path toward the hidden door to the roots of the mountain.

He had not gone thirty feet when he came upon a new

lawn. A new house. Its rooms were still empty. It was built across the path, and had appeared in less than two hours, according to the time that the rest of the world kept.

The settlement was spreading.

Snig crouched low. The plastic bags rattled. He ran around the lawn. He didn't touch it with his feet.

The path continued, though interrupted by new construction.

He reached a door in the rock. He opened it and shut it behind him.

Down through the dark passages into the City of Gargoyles, he ran.

In the city, there was light.

It was dim, but lanterns were lit all up and down the avenues. The fleshy bulbs that grew on houses glowed from within. They were Thusser nests, and they were occupied. Thusser walked the streets. They had thrown caution to the wind. They had come through from their world.

Snig pulled off his cap. His ears sprang free. He stooped near mud, ran his finger through it, and smudged it around his eyes. He needed to look like one of the Thusser.

Carefully, he walked through the streets.

Not many had come yet. Those who'd arrived were still settlers, exploring the ruins, setting up shop. A few businesses were open, wares still in crates. At a sidewalk café, two Thusser in nineteenth-century morning coats and cravats relaxed at a table, discussing real estate. Both had drinks in metal flagons hung from hooks near their heads. Long tubes ran from the bottom of the flagons to needles that pierced their throats. They drank directly, without the use of their mouths. It allowed them to talk more freely as the rich vermouth of alien worlds drained directly into their gullets.

Snig, alone amidst his enemies, was in a panic. He tried to walk like nothing was wrong. He strode like a Thusser.

Poor Prudence, he thought. *Time must be going even faster. She hasn't eaten for what — two days, then? Three?*

He hurried to get to her side.

The drawbridge of the castle was guarded by Thusser in military smocks. They did not pay much attention to Sniggleping as he crossed the square. He passed by them, bustling as if he had business.

The boys must have reached the Emperor by now, he fretted. *The Rules must be invoked. This is all in direct violation.* He wondered where they were, how they were faring — they and his dear troll.

He slipped into St. Diancecht's Cathedral. It was dark. He raced for the back, where the door to the crypt lay.

Behind him, he heard the great doors open.

A soldier entered with a torch. In the language of the Thusser, the soldier called out, "Sir? Sir? There's no one allowed in the cathedral."

At once, Sniggleping turned, startled — and one of his plastic bags split. The food tumbled out across the flagstones.

He turned off his lamp.

"Sir?"

The soldier approached, his footsteps echoing in the dark nave. He pulled out his saber. He shone his light around. It picked out faces — angels, devils, saints on bikes, souls smiling as they left behind their bodies. The pool of light from his torch sloshed across cans of dog food and a bundle of celery lying on the cold stone floor. They cast steep shadows across the pews.

The soldier arrived at the shell of the torn bag. He glanced around nervously, looking for the intruder. No sign. The air itself was white with ancient dust. With his elbow, the soldier adjusted his shako . . .

. . . and was clobbered by a Famished Lad™ Beef Stew.

Sniggleping stepped from behind a pillar. He had, in his day, been a crackerjack pitcher for the Norumbega team.

He rushed forward to gather the cans in his remaining bag and descend into the crypt.

When the guard awoke, there was no sign that anyone had been there at all.

FOUR

We changed course while you were sleeping," Kalgrash told the two boys. "We're headed for something."

The day looked no different than when they had gone to sleep. They were incredibly hungry. They were thirsty. They did not bother to stand up. They stared out the window at the featureless plain.

Kalgrash went up and tried to make signals to their host. He paid no attention to the troll.

Down below, Gregory, looking haggard, said to his friend, "I had a dream. The Thusser are everywhere. We've lost. Tell me we haven't already lost." His voice was husky.

Brian shook his head solemnly. "I'm telling you," he said. "The Thusser tried to colonize your dreams back in the suburb. It's not real, whatever you're thinking."

"You're sure."

"I'm sure."

"I remember them. Come on. You must, too. The Thusser were always there, right? They were at my house.

24

One of them used to sit in my room, staring at me all night. It was awful." He held on to one of his arms with his other hand. He looked weak and pale.

Brian insisted quietly, "It's not true, Gregory."

"I remember it."

Brian wrapped his thick fingers around the padded edge of the seat. "No . . . you can't let them fool you. They tried to force their way into your head. You've got to stop thinking they're already in Boston. They're not. They never have been."

Gregory closed his eyes. "I know you're right. But I can see them. They were everywhere. They directed traffic. They were . . ." He squeezed his eyes till the lids wrinkled.

"You're going to be okay," Brian said. "They're not there yet. We can still win. Honest."

Gregory stared out at the plain of slime. The two of them watched the dull light and the galloping shuffle of the headless beasts of burden.

The sleigh mushed past gray outcroppings and into a deeper, thicker mire.

Kalgrash came down below. He shook his head. Brian watched Gregory toy with the dead appliances.

In another few hours, they discovered where their host was heading. He was meeting someone. They saw another sleigh approaching. It was larger, with some huge cargo shrouded in burlap tied onto the top, bulging out of the sides.

The two sleighs pulled up alongside each other. Their host laid a gangplank across the space between them. He

25

hailed the other captain. He signaled for the boys and the troll to sit tight, and then picked up his bag of nerves — which bristled like coils of thornbush — and clomped across the plank to do business.

The two captains saluted each other. They both took off their coats and, in some kind of greeting ceremony, inserted keys between each other's shoulders and wound each other up vigorously.

"He's an automaton," whispered Gregory. "That's why he doesn't eat."

Kalgrash pointed out, "I eat."

"But you don't have to."

"I *choose* to. Just like you don't *have* to be a jerk."

The captains were making a trade that they had evidently discussed on the speaking-horn. The boys' host pulled out ten of the cluttered bundles of nerves, shook them to disentangle them, and laid them in a row on the deck of the other sleigh.

The other sleigh's captain attached some alligator clips to one of them and ran some electric current through it. The branching nerves shone bright blue. He seemed satisfied.

In return, he presented a little canister with rivets and a kind of periscope on it. The boys' host nodded, asked some questions. For a while, the two men talked. Then the host turned his head sharply away from the other captain and held that pose. The other captain tinkered with small tools, pried open a panel in the side of the host's neck, and inserted the canister. He made a few adjustments and shut the neck.

They shook hands.

Ten minutes later, the boys' host returned across the gangplank, drew back the bridge, waved, took up the reins, and began slushing again across the endless monotony of the marsh.

"What was that all about?" asked Gregory.

"I wonder where we're going," said Brian. "We've got to try to get him to understand we have to find the Emperor. This is . . . We're just wasting time while the Thusser are spreading."

"I wonder how close to winding down I am," Kalgrash said. "Snig winds me usually."

"How are we going to tell him we need to see the Emperor?" Brian persisted.

"Hand signals," said Gregory.

"Charades," Kalgrash suggested, touching his own long nose.

"Just tell him," said their host. "Say what you want to say, kid." He put his cigar back in his mouth.

"You speak English!" Brian exclaimed.

"Just had it installed."

"What?" Gregory protested. "What's going on? What is this? Where are we?"

"You're in Three-Gut. The Fields of Chyme. We're headed to Delge. A trading station near a valve. Unless you tell me who's paying me to take you someplace else."

"Who are you?" Gregory demanded. "What's going on here?"

Brian said, "Where are the Norumbegans?"

"You want the Emperor? So I hear?"

27

"Yes," said Brian. "He's a blond man. With a beautiful wife. They're very . . . very fun."

The captain shot a murderous look at Brian. He spat off the edge of his sleigh. "Fun," he said. "Sure, kid."

"We need to see them. Do you know about the Thusser?"

"I've heard of them. Ancient history. Not around since I was made. Look, the Emperor's at New Norumbega. It's a different system. Circulation. It's in the Dry Heart. Huge palace up there. Turrets and buttresses and battlements and sentinels all over the place. You have to approach it through the flux." The captain surveyed their three faces. "He going to pay for me to deliver you?"

"He'll be grateful," Brian said. "We're bringing him important news of the old Norumbega. Back through the portal. The one they came from."

"You from there, too, right?"

"Yeah."

"What's it like?"

"Dark, now," said Gregory. "But it must have been really cool. Back in the day."

"Snazzy," said the captain without much interest.

"So can you take us to the Emperor?" Kalgrash asked. "To New Norumbega?"

"Why are you along for this ride?" the captain asked Kalgrash. "This side of the portal, automatons, we wind each other."

"We're all together," Kalgrash explained, pointing to his friends.

"Mechanicals shouldn't get tied up with breathers.

28

Eventually, they'll just tell you to start lifting stuff." He jerked his thumb at Brian and Gregory. "Look at these two. Sick because they haven't put other breathers into a hole in their face for a couple of days. They haven't cut off something's hind legs, shredded it with little metal claws, and stowed it under their nose." He shook his head. "What kind of way to live is that?"

Gregory said, "You've clearly never been to a Chinese buffet."

"Kid, you're in the belly of the beast." The host gestured to the sky, the plain, the dim walls they could make out in the gray half-light. "Of course, we don't know it's a belly, and we don't know it's a beast. I'm no theologian. But —"

"You mean," said Gregory, "we're inside something? In its stomach?"

"Stomach, lung — no one really knows. We just use names. Who knows how the thing works? Whether it breathes or eats? No one. It fills everywhere. It's everything. The Great Body. It's huge. We just know stuff washes past. Or used to. Not so much any more. A few hundred years ago, there was more stuff. More fluid. Now it's dead or between meals. You have names?"

They introduced themselves. Their host was called Dantsig. They asked him what he did. He said he rode around, picking up waifs in ruins.

"Ha ha," said Gregory.

"I'm a trapper. A hunter. And I scavenge when I need to."

"So where are we going now?" asked Brian.

"I told you. Delge. It's a trading post near a valve. We'll figure out what to do with you there." He frowned and scratched at his goatee. "Have to check in with the Mannequin Resistance. See what they want done with you."

Brian didn't like the sound of this. Gregory asked about the Mannequin Resistance.

Dantsig explained, "Mechanicals. All of us. Who absented ourselves from the marble and alabaster halls of the overlords. The breathers. The Norumbegans. We got tired of being told we weren't real, we'd never know love or the beauty of a baby's laugh or a puppy with a single tear in its eye. We got sick of it. Lift this. Carry that. Go dig in the mines. So we all left." He looked quickly at them. "Respectfully. You know, bowing. Walking backward." He pointed at the kids. "You *always* have to back out of the Imperial Presence. Got it? Protocol. Got it?"

"We got it," said Gregory.

"I don't know how they bring up kids these days," said Dantsig, shaking his head. "In a stable or a shooting arcade or something. No one has any manners."

"You're just jealous because we start little and stupid, but then grow," said Gregory.

Dantsig looked at him with honest dislike. "Wow," he said. "Wow. You really will get along with the Emperor." With a sense of menace in his voice, he said, "I hope you get a chance to meet him."

Gregory and Brian didn't know what he meant by this. They fell silent as they slid through the waste.

30

Hours passed. The two boys didn't know what to do with themselves. The cabin of the sleigh was cozy, once the stove was lit, but Gregory and Brian were incredibly hungry, and it didn't sound like there would be any food at a trading post for clockwork people. So they shifted uncomfortably from side to side, holding their stomachs.

Eventually, Dantsig decided to try to catch them something to eat. He sat with a harpoon across his knees, watching for movement on the horizon. In another hour or so the sleigh careened back and forth a few times, and he clambered down the steps with a repulsive, leggy thing with lots of cords and breathing holes.

"Fry it up?" he asked.

They looked at it. It dangled from his mitt.

Brian was the first to speak. "It was really nice of you . . . to . . . it was just really nice," he said. "But I'm not sure we should eat something from this world without knowing what's in it."

"There could be poisonous glands," said Gregory.

Still, Kalgrash said he'd give cooking it a try.

Forty minutes later, Gregory and Brian ate triangular pieces of it. They kept their eyes closed. As they chewed, Kalgrash recited lists for them: "Fried chicken. New York strip sirloin. Potatoes au gratin. Asparagus with hollandaise sauce. Mac and cheese. Fried shrimp. Hush puppies."

"No puppies," said Gregory, mouth full. "Ban on puppies."

After they'd eaten, they could fall asleep.

Outside, the monotonous landscape went on and the twilight went on without change. Half-light. The slick, glistening plain. The dredge of the sleigh through sludge. Its clammy wake.

When the boys woke up, the light was just the same. The veins still glowed faintly in the dome of the gut.

Brian asked Dantsig, "What makes the veins glow?"

He half shrugged. "Lux effluvium. The gook in the veins. I don't know why. It gets real bright if you run electricity through it."

Brian asked, "Is it the blood?"

Dantsig seemed uninterested in the question. "We call things blood and stomachs and hearts, but no one knows what all the equipment does. There's a whole bunch of hearts, a cluster of them, but they aren't shaped like your heart or a Norumbegan's. It's just, they look like they pump fluids. So people call them hearts. And there's a bunch of organs filled with a different goo, and we call them stomachs, and there are other places we call lungs — fifteen or so, scattered around, we've found so far — but we don't know much except that they get bigger and smaller. I'm telling you, no one knows. No one understands. It's just the Great Body."

"What's outside the Great Body?" Gregory asked, and Kalgrash added, "Has anyone ever gone out the mouth? Through the teeth and over the gums? Et cetera?"

"Some of the rich Norumbegans — Varsity men — they fund expeditions sometimes to find mouths. Try to see if there's anything out there. They head off into the

32

wild gray yonder. Lots of equipment. Big fanfare." He smiled. "None of them ever come back."

Gregory asked joyfully, "What about the butt? Anyone ever gone out the butt?"

"They've been saving that for a special boy like you."

Brian did not like any of this much. Anxious, he watched the dull miles pass.

✳   ✳   ✳

In a while, they came to Delge. The first thing they could see through the gloom of Three-Gut was the derricks — tall, spindly arms and gantries reaching up out of the goo.

"Mining," said Dantsig. "They extract ore from the blood fluid. Valves go through to the capillaries."

The sleigh passed through heaps of slag. There were huts strung with electrical wiring.

They didn't see any people.

Then came houses — shacks on stilts. They were high above the Fields of Chyme.

Something was wrong. Several were burnt. They looked desolate. Piers stuck up out of the marsh, their tips blackened. No one crawled up and down their ladders.

Huts had been pulled down and lay on their sides. The windows of one were smashed, and some red polka-dot curtains trailed out into the sludge.

Doors were off their hinges.

Dantsig was muttering in his own language. He slowed down the beasts. He stood up and surveyed the village's wreckage.

On an island, surrounded by docks, there had stood a little town. There was not much of it left. Houses were in ashes. The embers of the commissary still glowed. A few small flames flickered in the ruins. Goods — barrels, stoves, some metal sinks — could be made out, soot-blackened, beneath the fallen beams.

Around the town there were large, round holding tanks. Holes had been blown in the metal. They were empty.

Dantsig went below and brought up a rifle. He looked grimly from side to side.

"I'm going to look around," he told them. He said to Kalgrash, "Get your ax. Stand guard. Breathers: below." He pointed down the hatch.

Brian and Gregory looked at each other. They didn't want to go below. They wanted to keep an eye out, too. It just felt safer.

Dantsig dropped a gangplank and crept ashore. He told them to pull the gangplank up. They did. He motioned them to go below. They stayed put and watched him creep behind a building.

They sat on either side of Kalgrash, staring at the little huts on little islands. There were bridges and steep roofs and torn nets hanging between telegraph poles. Punctured tanks stood on high pedestals like statues of some robot god.

"I do not like this. Bad, bad, bad," said Kalgrash. The gloom seemed particularly dense. Brian wondered how much was darkness and how much was smoke.

Off in the ruins, where Dantsig had stalked off, there was a cry.

"What was that?" hissed Gregory.

Neither of the other two bothered to answer him.

Crouched forward, they waited. Occasionally, they heard something crack or splash. The fire popped. The air smelled of burning diesel.

Forms shifted in the dark . . . Kalgrash rattled, stepping into battle position.

"Hey!" he said. "Who goes there?"

Dantsig appeared in the midst of the smoke. "Me, Kalgrash. And one of the miners." Beside him was a man bent with trouble, dressed in a padded, grease-smeared miner's suit.

Gregory and Brian lowered the gangplank and the two men came aboard.

"He's the only one they didn't get," said Dantsig. "We're taking him with us."

"What happened?" Gregory asked.

Dantsig didn't bother to answer him. He spoke to the miner in their language and sent the man below. Then he goaded the beasts into motion. The sleigh pulled away from the dock. Dantsig still kept his eye on the ruins they passed. He still kept the rifle by his side.

They were heading back out into the plains.

Gregory asked, "Where are you taking us?"

"Pflundt."

"Did you just hawk a loogie?"

No one laughed. Kalgrash rolled his eyes.

"Who destroyed the town?" Brian asked.

"The Norumbegans. They wanted samples for study. They came in and captured everyone. Took them away."

Brian asked what he meant by "samples for study."

Dantsig said, "They've forgotten how to do a lot of things. A lot of them died when they got here, to the Great Body. And they're lazy. I mean, they have other interests. For generations, mannequins had made mannequins. Suddenly, we wouldn't make any more for them. They don't recall how to put us together. They don't have any more of us. We left. For their own good." His jaw twitched to the side and locked, tic. He closed his eyes and fiddled with his goatee. "Their own good." He opened his eyes and mashed his mouth around to loosen his jaw. Then he said, "Last few years, they've been raiding. When they can be bothered. When there isn't a concert or a whiskey tasting. They come down here and destroy a village. Hunt the people who escape as they struggle away through the muck. Chase them across the plains. It's a sport. Tickles their lordships' fancy." He surveyed the horizon from side to side. He said, "This is the worst raid I've ever seen. They came in, he said — came in and just grabbed everyone. No one could stand up against them. When they order you . . . it's . . ." He shook his head. "Doesn't matter that they've forgotten so much. They're descended from gods. They're like nothing else. But they can be —" He stopped speaking, as if he couldn't say more.

Finally, he concluded, "The old guff thinks they disassembled everyone before they took them away."

"Disassembled?" Kalgrash said, fear in his voice.

Dantsig didn't answer, but a few minutes later, he nodded and pointed.

They saw bodies mired in the goo. Jumpsuits and calico dresses. Hands coming out of sleeves. Feet with boots.

"The memory is in the head," said Dantsig. "All the delicate stuff." He tapped his own temple. "That's what they can't get anymore. Without our craftsmen. They can't design thought. They have mechanicals now — they call them drones — just machines. No thought. No emotion. Just simple commands. Standard format. Hardly any grammar."

He looked at the dark horizon. "They want to build more of us. They want servants who they can hurt." And then he blinked slowly, and finished by saying, "May they have long lives, of course, and may the veins of heaven shine upon all their endeavors."

And Brian realized that Dantsig couldn't say much that was bad about the Norumbegans. Because he was built to serve them.

Brian was horrified. He couldn't stand the thought of all those mannequins being disassembled by their former masters. Maybe having to watch, standing in lines, while others before them were taken apart.

"They can be put back together again, can't they?" asked Kalgrash. "I mean, someone has taken off my head before and put it on a different body, and I feel like a jillion bucks."

"Sure, that's beautiful, troll. But you need the heads."

Brian suggested, "If you take us to see the Emperor, maybe we could petition for the heads to be returned. So the people can be reconstructed."

Dantsig looked at him evenly. "Sure, squirt. That's just what the Norumbegans will do." He glared off into the belly's dark evening.

"That's great!" said Brian. "We have to see him about alerting the Rules Keepers that the Thusser are cheating in the Game. So if you could take us to him, that would be . . ." He realized a second too late that Dantsig was being sarcastic, and he felt stupid. Like he was chirping in the dark. Like he was an idiot, whiffling away. He fell silent.

As soon as possible, Brian, Gregory, and Kalgrash went below.

The miner was curled on the floor. He did not look well. He gripped his own arms and stared into the tangle of mechanical junk.

"We need to do something for him," said Brian. He asked the man if he was okay. If he needed anything. If there was anything they could do. The old man didn't speak English — just the language of Norumbega. He shook his head and laid it back on the floor.

Gregory sat with his arms crossed on the bunk. He looked irritably at the stove.

"That was awful," said Brian softly. "I can't believe they just came and took the whole town."

Gregory shrugged. "They're the Norumbegans' autom-atons. So the Norumbegans can do whatever they want with them. And plus, the townspeople can be put back together again. Dantsig said so. What's the big deal?"

Brian glanced quickly at Kalgrash.

The troll was clearly angry.

Gently, but with incredible rage, Kalgrash said, "I could take you apart. And see how well you go back together."

Gregory did not laugh. He didn't make a joke. They glared at each other. There was anger in their eyes.

And the sleigh carried on, dragged over the slime, pulled through the stomach's dim night toward the fortress of Pflundt.

FIVE

A day later, they reached Pflundt. The terrain rose into an infinite gray slope, rough and cut with channels. Coursing down the cliff was a fortress like a floe of ice, a waterfall of wax. It might have been built, or features might have been carved into some ancient deposit there — a weird citadel of blobby towers cut with windows, deep hollow gateways, and cannons mounted on frozen sluices.

The sleigh sped through the great arch and into a vast stable, a cavern soaring with Gothic pillars made of something that looked like it once had been molten, now gray, translucent, and lit with crystal lanterns. There were wooden stalls for the beasts of burden. Dantsig pulled up beside a stall and dismounted. He unharnessed his steeds so he could wash them down and curry their pimpled flesh. The stall was filled with gravel. Dantsig's beasts hunkered down in it and covered themselves, delighted.

When he was done, Dantsig led the boys and the troll into the fortress and its stone town. Hungry and thirsty,

40

they were overwhelmed with Pflundt's activity. Men in black frock coats rode along the rutted avenues on bicycles with baskets of old gears and cranks. Peddlers offered robotic hands, slim and beautifully carved, inlaid with brass and mother-of-pearl. One old woman at a bench sold only springs. An optician sold eyes.

The keyhole could not be seen on all of them, but on many it was planted clearly between their shoulders. Some of the people were simplified, their faces a series of smooth planes with black, crystalline eyeballs. Some were built like harlequins, some like knights, and some had extra arms for heavy lifting. Most were dressed soberly in dark clothes of bygone eras.

Gregory and Brian were dazzled by all the automatons climbing up staircases and bustling through courtyards. Dantsig smiled. "Pflundt," he said. "Carved right out of the living phlegm."

He led them to the headquarters of the Mannequin Resistance, which was in a tall, gray house that towered above the metallic bustle of the streets and alleys. He told the boys and Kalgrash to sit, and headed off to speak to some official. They waited for a while on a wooden bench.

A secretary appeared in a black coat and bid them follow him. He took them to a long table, where they were served food. Though no one in the city ate, many had cooked for centuries before they'd left the service of the Norumbegans. They knew how to whip up a dinner. The food — steaks of some three-legged animal — was delicious, seasoned to perfection. The boys took a long time eating, cramming their mouths with salad and squash.

"At least," said Gregory, stopping his gorging long enough to be repelled, "I *hope* it's squash. And not something carved right out of the living phlegm."

They lay down to sleep on the benches. An hour and a half later, they were called into the presence of someone named General Malark.

The general was upstairs, in a cold, whitewashed chamber high above a courtyard. He waited with Dantsig. The general was a thin, glowering automaton, once built to look like a lined old man — now disfigured by thick slices hacked out of his head in ancient battles. His workings were visible through the cuts. As he spoke, the boys could see the gears within him spin, the spindles reset and retract to pucker his brow or give him dimples.

Those dimples were friendly as he shook the boys' hands and bowed to the troll.

Behind him, on the wall, was a banner with a message in the Norumbegans' runic language. Beside it, another, smaller, which read: NON SERVIAM — I SHALL NOT SERVE.

"You came through the portal in the Ruins of Entry," he said to the boys.

Neither of the boys knew what to say to that.

"You came from Old Norumbega. From the City of Gargoyles."

"Yes, sir," said Brian.

"You wish to see the Emperor."

"Yes, sir."

"Regarding the Game."

42

Brian and Gregory nodded.

"The Emperor has abdicated. He has been replaced by his child." The general sat behind his desk. "You are strangers."

Brian said, "Yes, sir," as politely as he could.

"Breathers," the general said.

Gregory pinched the skin on the back of his hand and showed it to General Malark. "Look. It's real."

The general said, "You might simply be convincingly designed. We can eat, if designed to eat. We may be pinched. We can even feel pain at pinching."

Kalgrash nodded fervently.

The general asked the troll, "You, sir, are an automaton?"

"Yes indeedy."

"Welcome. I am General Malark of the Mannequin Resistance. I was constructed several hundred years ago during the Third War of Thusserian Aggression. I defended Old Norumbega from the invader. Until," he said sourly, "my masters decided to give up and flee."

Brian asked eagerly, "Was that when they started the Game?"

Malark grimaced. "The Game. Yes. The Game. We forfeited the kingdom for a Game." He picked up the stapler from his desk. "You know that we here are now in a state of revolt against our former masters."

"The Norumbegans, right?" Gregory clarified. "You're fighting against the Norumbegans?"

"The Norumbegans of *flesh*." The general smiled tightly. "For we are all Norumbegans. Whether organic or

43

mechanical." He looked down at the stapler in his hands. He rubbed his thumb against the two fangs of the staple that projected from the carriage, as if caressing a cobra to charm it. When he pulled his thumb away, the skin was white where the tines had pressed.

"There are only rarely open hostilities with our masters," he said. "Over the last century, we have all abandoned their capital and spread throughout the Great Body. We will not go back to serve them. They are angry that we have deserted them, but they cannot do anything about it. Occasionally, they send out a force to try to reclaim us, but we resist them. They stew in their palaces alone.

"But. As you have seen . . ." He idly opened the stapler and closed it, the spring twanging as he shut the cover. When he continued, he said, "Delge Crossing. They shut off and kidnapped everyone in Delge. This is new. Descending on a larger town like that. Openly. It calls for a new strategy. This," he said, smiling, "is where you come in."

He sat forward.

"We are considering whether we might trade you in exchange for some of the heads of the citizens of Delge. We do not know yet whether you and your message will be considered important enough by the Emperor to merit a trade." He sighed and put down the stapler. "For one thing, the Imperial Court will not pick up the phone."

Brian asked, "Did you say that the Emperor isn't the Emperor anymore? The blond man? With the beautiful queen?"

"He abdicated. Gave the crown to his son."

44

"Why did he do that?" Brian asked.

The general frowned. "Emperor Fendritch wished to be at leisure. Emperor Fendritch likes his leisure — his golf, his tennis, the foxtrot, downhill skiing. Emperor Fendritch . . . one cannot say anything against Emperor Fendritch — no — one cannot say a word against one's former master — one cannot — one cannot say a thing against Emperor Fendritch because we all have been designed never to —" (Here the general's mouth flapped shut, and he grimaced.) "We cannot . . . so let me say instead that the Emperor was so variously gifted with talents and enthusiasms — quite splendid, really — that he did not find it convenient to reign. So he abdicated in favor of his child." He quivered, then added, "Long may he live."

"So his kid's Emperor now," said Gregory. "So it's his kid we need to talk to."

General Malark and Dantsig exchanged glances. "Not precisely," said General Malark. "The boy is too young to reign. He has an elected regent who rules in his place. But this is immaterial. We need to hear your story so that we can convey to the Emperor's Court who you are and try to arrange an exchange."

So Brian, Kalgrash, and Gregory told their story. They explained how they had, the year before, played the Game, not knowing what they were part of, traipsing through the woods and encountering puzzles and elves and trolls. They told the general that it had turned out that Brian was playing for the Norumbegans (though he didn't know it) and Gregory for the Thusser Horde, which waited to spill out across the landscape. They explained that Brian had won, scoring a victory for the Norumbegans.

Brian said, "I realized at the last minute that we weren't both playing for the same team. Without knowing it, we were rivals."

"So I let Brian win," said Gregory. "He was being held down by a Thusser assassin at the time. So I could have just won, but we made an agreement that I would let him win."

"I see," said the general. "To confirm: The Norumbegan side *did* win?"

"Sure," said Gregory. "Because I let him win. Really, either one of us could have won. I mean, either one of us, except that I was the one who wasn't being strangled by the assassin. So I could have won more easily, technically. If we'd been playing fair." He shifted on his seat and stuck his hands between his knees. "But Brian won. As it happened."

"He won for the Norumbegans," said the general.

The boys nodded.

They told how they'd gone home, back to Boston, and how Brian, as the winner, had been designated to make up the next round of the Game. They explained that Brian had started to work out a whole story about gangsters and detectives that some players would stumble into, in a few years' time.

And then everything had gone wrong. Gregory's cousin Prudence, the last winner, had disappeared. The Thusser had tried to kill Brian. Brian and Gregory had traveled up to Gerenford, Vermont, where they'd played

46

the Game the year before, only to discover that the forest where they'd had their magical adventure was now an interdimensional suburb waiting for Thusser invasion.

Kalgrash said, "The Thusser might even be there by now. They're bad, bad, bad. I don't like them at all."

"But if the Norumbegan side were to win, the Emperor and his Court would be able to return to Earth," said the general.

Brian shrugged and nodded. Gregory said, "Sure."

"That might be an unexpected boon," said the general. He smiled. Gears turned behind his eyes. He and Captain Dantsig spoke in Norumbegan.

"Now," said the General. "We must call the Emperor's Court again."

He went to a worn wooden cabinet and lifted out an old Edwardian phone with a speaking piece and a whole complicated tree of dangling mouths on wires. He brought the contraption over to his desk and set it down. Pulling the speaking piece to his lips, he made a demand for a call to be put through and waited while the mouths all whispered, "Ring ring. Ring ring. Ring ring."

After a long time, one of the mouths perked up and drawled some alien greeting.

General Malark and the mouth spoke for some time. His eyes were guarded, careful, waiting to see whether the mouth would barter.

He turned to the boys. "It is the Regent. He wishes to speak to you directly."

"Where are the little cubs?" said the mouth in English. "Tell them to talk."

"We're here, sir," said Brian. "We've come —"

"From the old kingdom, is it? Grand. Just grand. We miss the old place. I suppose it's all Thussery now."

"They're breaking the Rules of the Game," said Brian. "You've got to stop them. They're settling in your —"

"Yes, plenty of time for that, little chap. Malark, might you adjust the loupe so I could get a gander at the squirts? Be a good fellow."

General Malark pulled out a small lens on a retractable cord and pointed it at the boys. There was a brief interchange where the mouth made demands and Malark responded, occasionally translating orders to the boys: "Put up your arms. Turn around. Pull down your lips and show your gums.

"The fat one in the armor isn't human, though, is it? Rum thing, but I recall humans being less spiky and green."

"I'm not fat," said the troll. "I'm big-boned."

General Malark confirmed, "He's an automaton. Built as a troll."

"I see."

"I come with the other guys," said Kalgrash. "We're a package. Three for the price of two."

"Bully for you," said the mouth lazily. "Now, Malark, why don't you send them up here? You've no use for them."

General Malark pulled himself to his full height. "We have a list of noncombatants recently captured at Delge. We demand their release in return."

"You have the names?"

"I do."

"Blast. I don't have a pencil handy. Well, you just tell me and I'll try my level best to remember."

Malark delivered a list of thirty names, all of them unpronounceable.

He and the mouth continued to haggle.

Eventually, he hung up.

He turned to Dantsig, the boys, and the troll with a tight smile.

"It is agreed," he said. "A trade. Ten of the automatons for each one of you. The Court is anxious to hear your story." He lifted the phone and mouth-tree from his desk and replaced it in the cabinet. "You are on your way to New Norumbega and the palace of the Emperor!"

SIX

The capital city was far, far away, in a clutch of hearts that hung in the distant reaches of the Great Body. The sled was too slow, and in any case, the ducts that led to the capital never connected directly to the gut that cradled Pflundt. The boys were told they would have to travel through the flux. They were given a picnic hamper for the ride.

Surrounded by a set of guards in metal helmets, Dantsig led them deep into a cavern. Lanterns lit the walls of a great shaft that dropped straight down beneath the city. A platform was suspended by ropes. When they stepped on, Dantsig pulled a lever, and they all descended.

"There's a valve," he explained, "so we can get into the flux."

"Flux?" said Kalgrash. "What's flux?"

"There are seven major fluids in the Great Body," said Dantsig. "Ichor, yellow bile, the hard aliment, the sublime aliment, flux, lux effluvium, and brunch.

"No one knows what any of them are or what any of them do. Some of them might be food. Some of them might be blood or saliva. I don't know. Who cares? The flux doesn't move anymore. People say it used to. Maybe because the Great Body is dead. Or we might just be between heartbeats. Or flux might not be blood at all." Dantsig shrugged and spat over the edge of the descending platform.

"Adding your own fluids to the mix?" Gregory said.

Dantsig smiled lazily. "I generate liquid," he said. "It condenses in my mouthbox. Design flaw."

Brian asked politely, "What were you made for?"

Dantsig shrugged. "Exploration. What about you?" Dantsig grinned wolfishly at the boy.

Kalgrash offered, "I was made to ask riddles and smite."

"Crazy."

The platform had reached the bottom of the pit.

They'd come to rest next to a huge brass dome — the valve into the flux. They entered the dome through reinforced doors.

They were in an air lock, a docking bay for submarines. The walls were riveted together. Small capsules with propellers and rudders hung from brackets. Men and women in old diving suits clanked around by hatches. Portholes looked out into some green mess in which the beams from electric lights slowly bumbled.

The guards accompanied them to a gangway. It led down through a tube and into a sub: a cramped space filled with tanks and pipes and spigots and dials and nozzles. Marines, frowning, took up positions around the cabin. Dantsig offered the boys benches upholstered in torn red plastic. A few of the crew, dressed in blue body-suits and finned helmets, ran past calling unintelligibly to one another.

In a few minutes, there was a jolt, and the submarine moved out into the flux. The deck hummed.

"Whoa," said Gregory, pressing his palms against the metal wall. "It tickles. The vibration." He put his hand to his mouth. "It makes my teeth itch."

Kalgrash offered, "I could remove them for you."

"Naw," said Gregory. "What would you do without my winning grin? It would be like the sun had gone out in your heart."

Dantsig asked Brian over the din of the engine, "What's with them?"

"They fight a lot." Brian was too embarrassed to explain that Gregory made fun of Kalgrash for being an automaton. He didn't want Dantsig to know and to hate Gregory.

The sub nosed through the darkness of the vein, its lights picking out growths and shy, slithering things.

Brian pointed at something finny doing backflips to escape the illumination. "Are they part of the body? Or are they like parasites?"

"Uh, yeah, kid, we're all like parasites. Hey, will you let me spit in here?"

Gregory said, "Let's keep the liquid outside."

"You're the one who's seventy-eight percent water, squirt."

52

"But the other twenty-two percent is charm."

"He can add," muttered Kalgrash in surprise.

Brian was worried that his two friends no longer even pretended to like each other. It made him miserable. He wanted everyone to work together. Everyone should be a unit. Like superheroes. Each with his own power. One can turn things into ice, another can melt them with his thermal fist. As a gang, they're unstoppable. That was how it was supposed to be.

Instead, he thought of the detective novels he loved, in which everyone was always double-crossing each other. They were always telling each other lies out of the corner of their mouths and hiding things from each other in train lockers. They were telling women they'd love them forever and then turning them right in to the police for fraud. That wasn't how he wanted his friends to be.

Even worse: He knew that Gregory was really the problem. Kalgrash was incredibly nice — well, when he wasn't smiting. It was Gregory who persisted in baiting the troll.

Brian wondered why.

He had a long time to wonder. The submarine whirred through miles of duct. It followed hidden routes up veins or down arteries. Once, it passed a huge domed city in the flux, lit with a thousand little brass lanterns.

"When we get to the capital," said Dantsig, "and you're in the presence of the Emperor and the Regent, try to class yourselves up a little, got it?"

"What do you mean?" said Gregory. "Brian is already

53

stunningly debonair. Look at those track shoes, that bowl cut. . . ."

"The track shoes are kind of dirty," said Brian, kind of miffed, "because I wore them while I was crawling through the dungeons of Norumbega, trying to free you."

"Hey — hey! None of that, for instance," Dantsig demanded. "This is the Emperor you're seeing. There are rules. You can't turn your back to him. Even if he's . . . surprising."

"What's surprising about him?" asked Brian.

Gregory said, "He's a kid, right?"

"Never speak until you're spoken to," Dantsig said. "Wait to be presented to people. You're lower in rank, so you'll be presented to the nobility. Not the other way around."

"What're you talking about?" Gregory said. "I thought you hated the Emperor's Court. Why are you suddenly getting all Emily Post on us?"

Dantsig looked strained. "The Emperor," he said, blinking rapidly, "is due some respect."

"Who's Emily Post?" asked Kalgrash.

"She wrote about manners," said Brian. He asked Dantsig, "Can't you say anything bad about the Emperor? Is it because you're programmed?"

Dantsig leaned forward. "I can say whatever I want! You got that?" he answered angrily. "I'm just telling you, the palace is a tony kind of rig, and you can't act like you've just stumbled in from the snot-fields of Cheln."

"Kalgrash did," said Gregory. "He's a banjo-plucking hick from the dark side of the gallbladder."

"I *like* the banjo," said Kalgrash. "In reality."

"Gregory," said Brian, "we should probably . . . you know . . . stop making jokes . . . with . . ."

"What? Does Emily Post have rules about this, too? In her chapter describing what you can talk about with a troll in a submarine in someone's artery? 'Bluegrass music is never a suitable topic for trolls, in or out of submarines.'"

And then the troll was shouting and Gregory was laughing and Dantsig was threatening to put out his own eyes with a screwdriver if they didn't shut up.

Finally, they just turned to the windows and all stared out at the passing duct. Gregory had a slight smile on his lips. Brian looked anxious.

The sub hummed on toward New Norumbega.

✻ ✻ ✻

The boys were asleep when the submarine docked. It was many hours later, and thousands of leagues of dull green had smeared past the portholes.

Clamps locked down the sub. The boys could feel the sound of screws and winches through their feet. The hide of the sub rattled.

"New Norumbega," said Dantsig, draped casually over some oxygen tanks. He rose. "Time for the exchange, kids. Put on your best smiles and your bow ties."

Sailors in finned helmets pulled down a ladder and released the hatch. They led Dantsig, Gregory, Brian, and Kalgrash up into a clammy circular stairwell. The stairs were rusted. The little party ascended.

"Prepare yourselves," said Dantsig. "Keep your cool. Sure, New Norumbega's fancy. But they want to hear what you have to say. Hold your chins up high and keep your hands in the open."

At the top, there was another hatch. Dantsig unscrewed it and raised himself up into brilliant light. The others followed.

It took some moments for their eyes to adjust. They were standing on a bright, salty plain. The overwhelming light came from seams in the sky shining whitely. Distantly, several figures labored toward them across the granules.

There, beneath the harsh light of strange veins, was a shantytown made of planks, old iron, and what looked to be clippings of flesh. Rising up in the middle was a great lumpy tower the color of beef jerky, with wooden gantries hanging on the side of it and uneven turrets sprouting out of the top. It looked like a potbellied stove with five chimneys.

"There it is," Dantsig announced. "New Norumbega. Home of the Emperor. Capital of the Empire of the Innards."

SEVEN

That's the *palace*?" Gregory protested. "Looks more like a slum."

Dantsig snorted. "If that's a slum, I'd like to see the cities back on Earth."

"Pflundt is nicer than that," said Brian. "Your own fortress."

Dantsig looked at them, unbelieving. "You two are feeding me the biscuit, right? Because that place is stumendous."

Brian was about to say something further when trumpets began to play a fanfare. The Imperial delegation was approaching.

Two ranks of armed elfin soldiers accompanied several royal carts pulled by several of the headless, seven-legged beasts that had drawn Dantsig's sleigh. The beasts were marked with tribal paint in broad stripes of white or spots of earthen red. The carts they lugged were adorned with golden canopies and symbols of power jutting up on staves. Strings of beads hung from their rigging, glittering in the brilliant light.

On the foremost cart rode the heralds, blowing their trumpets and ghoul-snouted trombones. In the next cart rode a crowd of sullen, imperious courtiers, jostled by the uneven terrain. The men wore navy blazers. The women wore suits with matching skirts and little jackets in coral pink or powder blue.

Then came another cart with an oldish man on a throne. And behind him finally, a cart with racks of immobile heads — the dismantled prisoners, Brian guessed, who would be exchanged for him and Gregory. The mannequin heads stared sullenly in front of them. They were surrounded by guards.

"There they are," whispered Dantsig. "Everyone wins. You get to talk to the Emperor. We free the heads. The Court hears your spiel about the Thusser Horde."

Brian held his hand above his eyes to cut down on the glare. The carts were pulling up in front of them. He was excited, but anxious. He couldn't believe that, after all this time, he was finally going to meet the Norumbegans. He examined them closely — these mysterious eldritch beings who had, in ancient days, created the Game and the City of Gargoyles.

A herald climbed down from the cart and approached Dantsig. He asked a question in the language of the Norumbegans. Immediately, Brian, Gregory, and Kalgrash could feel images and traces of language sliding across their minds, the psychic residue of Norumbegan speech.

Dantsig responded. The herald nodded. Dantsig pointed to the kids and explained something. He and the herald spoke briefly.

Then the herald turned toward the throne cart and cried in English, "Dantsig, Explorer, calling himself Envoy of the Mannequin Resistance, requests permission to approach the cart of His Excellency the Imperial Regent, Duke Telliol-Bornwythe."

The man on the throne said something to a page boy in a parti-colored tunic who stood up and repeated in a high, girlish voice, "His Excellency, the Imperial Regent graciously grants Automaton Dantsig's supplication for an audience and demands said Dantsig to approach the Glory Float accompanied by the two children of Earth."

"Showtime," muttered Dantsig. He bowed and stepped forward.

Kalgrash began to follow, but the Regent quickly whispered something to his page boy, who announced, in his piping tremble, "No such audience has been granted to the automaton troll champion, who shall remain motionless until such time as he is granted permission to stir."

"Oh, I'll stir," muttered Kalgrash. "A big cauldron of butt-kick." Still, he remained behind.

Gregory, Brian, and Dantsig approached the throne on its float. The noblemen and women watched this pageant silently, drinking mint juleps.

Now that the carts were close, Brian could see that the glittering ornaments were not all of great expense. The poles were strung with rickrack. The beads that flapped along the canopies were cheap baubles for dress-up.

59

He was surprised, too, by the figure on the Glory Float, Duke Telliol-Bornwythe. The old man wore a silver wig and a velvet frock coat, but the frock coat was worn, the gold braid rubbed almost white near the buttons. One knee of his silken breeches had been scraped on something long before, and was almost worn through.

The page boy engaged Dantsig in a long conversation in Norumbegan, prodded by the Regent on the throne. At last, the Regent himself spoke.

"Still in English, hmm?" he said. "Very well." He clicked his tongue in his mouth, as if getting used to the language. He took out a pair of round sunglasses with scratched lenses and put them on. He asked, "You are Dantsig?"

Dantsig bowed. "Your Excellency is gracious to admit me into your august presence. I come as an envoy from General Malark of the Mannequin Resistance."

"There is no Mannequin Resistance."

"I am myself a member of the Resistance, Your Excellency."

"I proclaim there is no such thing. There cannot be."

"There is."

"No. There could never be. Automatons cannot rebel. So we recognize no Mannequin Resistance. There is no General Malark. There is, I believe, a *Mr.* Malark, automaton. He has no rank."

"He is our general, sir."

"He has no rank. There is only one army — the Imperial Army of Norumbega. Mr. Malark is no longer part of it, having fled into disgrace."

60

"I come, sir," Dantsig insisted, "from the Mannequin Resistance, and —"

"I have said there is no such body. You will not contravene my word, automaton."

Dantsig bowed his head and frowned.

The Regent looked at the two boys. "My lads, you are Gregory Stoffle and Brian Thatz? You have the misfortune to be human?"

"Yes, sir," said Brian. "We're human."

"Ah well," said the Regent delicately. "Nothing we can do about that now." He turned to Dantsig. "You did the right thing to bring them to us. Thank you. You are a good little servant."

Dantsig smiled suavely — though Brian could tell the man was livid with anger. "I didn't bring them on your account," Dantsig said. "I brought them for the exchange of prisoners."

"As I say, you are a perfect little servant. You've done exactly what you should."

"We didn't bring them so you could —"

"You know your master's will."

"With the respect due your title, sir, you aren't my master. I just —"

"Am I not? Well, you've done exactly what I wanted. And you are an automaton."

"But I didn't . . . I'm here for *them*," he pointed at the heads on the cart.

"Them?" said the Regent. "They're nothing. They're heads. Shut off. They're going nowhere."

"We'll check them for damage when we get them on

61

the sub," said Dantsig with a hint of defiance in his voice. He no longer looked directly at the Regent. He looked at the dark shadow on the salt beneath the Regent's cart, as if he couldn't meet the Regent's eyes.

"You won't be getting back on your submarine, Mr. Dantsig. Those machines are going nowhere. And neither are you."

Dantsig looked, shocked, at the Regent. "You wouldn't break your word!" he protested. "A Norumbegan nobleman never breaks his word!"

"You can't make a promise to an automaton," said the Regent. "Any more than you can pledge something to a toaster. Saying something to an automaton is like speaking in an empty room."

Dantsig roughly grabbed Brian and Gregory by their collars and was about to haul them backward toward the valve. Gregory and Brian exchanged a look: panic.

They heard the whistle as Kalgrash started to swing his blade.

The marines in their finned helmets raised wands.

Dantsig pulled the boys back from the cart. They stumbled over the mounded ground toward the valve.

"I've got your back, Dantsig," called Kalgrash. "Just tell me when you want the smiting to begin."

"You won't take the humans," the Regent demanded. "You are my servant."

"I am not your —"

"Perhaps I may say something that shall convince you."

"I cannot listen to you, sir."

62

"Hush, hush. Hush, my boy. In the base of these carts that surround you are electromagnets. If my page activates them, you, your cronies, and your quaint troll will collapse with all memory erased and your workings irrevocably garbled. So freeze. Release the children. Let them come to me."

Dantsig stood defiantly. *"Breathers!"* he swore. "You *never* keep your word. You *never* follow your own rules!"

"Guards, get the children away from the rogue."

"If I could curse you . . . ! If I could curse you . . . !" Dantsig kept yelling. He did not meet the Norumbegan Regent's eyes.

"But you can't. You can't say a word against me."

Guards stepped forward to guide Gregory and Brian away from the automaton. Dantsig yanked them back.

Suddenly, Dantsig raised his head and looked right at the Regent. "If you're a danger to the Norumbegan nation, I can. Then I can eliminate you." He nodded. "And maybe you are. And if that's the case, then it's my duty to protect the other breathers, the other Norumbegans. I'm allowed to do that. I'm required to."

"Careful," said the Regent. "He appears dangerous."

"It would be my duty to remove you," said Dantsig.

"Dangerous and boringly talkative."

"It would be my duty to destroy you, just like you shut us off. I could challenge you to a duel. I could fight you on the battlefield. I could kill you while you slept."

The Regent said something to his page boy, who rose with a dial in his hand. He turned the dial slightly. There was a hum.

Dantsig swayed. He looked terrified.

With a clank, Kalgrash fell to his knees.

"No!" Brian screamed. "No! Don't!"

Gregory ran toward the Glory Float. "Stop it, please!" said Gregory. "We'll come with you!"

"Please!" said Brian, running to Dantsig's side.

The Regent didn't smile. He didn't alter his face in any way. He simply muttered a command, and the boy turned off the current.

Dantsig sat on the hot granules beneath him. He was breathing heavily. His hands fluttered near his heart.

"So, Mr. Dantsig," said the Regent. "I am afraid you shall be detained at our pleasure, along with your troll champion and your guards. The children shall be presented to His Sublime Highness, the Emperor of Old Norumbega, New Norumbega, and the Whole Dominion of the Innards, Elector of the Bladders, Prince of the Gastric Wastes, Sovereign of Ducts Superior and Inferior, Lord of All. And he shall determine what shall be done with them."

Having said that, the Regent clapped, and his soldiers moved in to do his will.

EIGHT

An hour later, the boys were dragged to cocktail hour in the Grand Hall of the palace. Brian could not think, he was so worried about Kalgrash and Dantsig, who had been dragged off, bound. And now Gregory and he were surrounded by noblemen and duchesses, all of them eating cheese, drinking white wine, and talking at them.

"Dear children, it is too, too lovely of you to come by."

"Must have been ghastly, being squeezed through the flux with those chitchatty *appliances*."

"*Oh!* One cannot *bear* them prancing around the blood, calling themselves a Resistance."

"Skidneys! Something must be done."

"Who'll do it? Too *dull*, old fish. It's just too weary-making."

"I agree, your lordship. One can't dash off to war in a special hat every time a tin clothespress starts barking speeches about the rights of all to run through fields, hand in hand."

"Still, it must have been terrible for you boys. Being their prisoners and whatnot."

"Someday, we'll bestir ourselves and give them a good, solid brass hiding."

"That's what they need: taken across the knee. Walloped till their eyes juice up."

"Darling," said a duchess, "I'm not sure a mannequin's eyes juice."

"We'll install ducts. They should ruddy well drop a tear with the rest of us."

It was almost impossible for Gregory and Brian to understand everything that was being said. One of the Court magicians had cast a spell of translation so they'd understand Norumbegan. Now it sounded like everyone was speaking English with an accent stranded halfway across the Atlantic between Britain and America, like someone who'd spent a year abroad and come back pretentious, or those actors from black-and-white 1930s films about rich New Yorkers dressed in tuxes and velvet who fall in love and end up tripping into bathtubs filled with champagne. With the help of the spell, the boys could tell what was being said, but they could also feel how much Norumbegan still slid past them in the ether, all the alien thoughts flowing across their brains like oil over a walnut.

The Court was gathered to celebrate the boys and the news they brought from the Old Country. Nonspeaking robots with birdlike heads — much simpler automatons than any the boys had seen yet in all the catacombs and organs of the Empire — served little sandwiches on trays.

They wandered stiffly through the crowd, their goggling glass eyes unseeing, offering party napkins and goodies on toothpicks. They wore long tabards of cheap felt in the colors of the Empire.

The Grand Hall was built of huge curls of dried flesh, pink and strong as granite. The ceiling, however, was covered in acoustic tiles, most of which were webbed with brown water damage. A row of sliding glass doors jammed into bare plywood led out onto a veranda that looked down the slumping belly of the palace and over the city of New Norumbega.

The boys had seen enough of the city as they'd rolled through to be depressed by its squalor. The Norumbegans were living in huts — brightly painted, but ramshackle. The streets were narrow and dirty. Broken chairs and chests of drawers leaned against walls. Men in swallow-tailed coats and muddy spats ducked through doorways made out of old windows. Girls in torn ball gowns sat on roofs eating apples and hurling the cores over alleys. The whole city smelled like garbage.

It had been hundreds of years since the Norumbegan refugees had arrived, but it seemed like they had never bothered to make themselves a true home.

"You are wondering," said an old, frowning man in a brocade frock coat, "why this city is so sunken in grime, when we were, in ancient days, such a noble race." He was rather short, and his face hung sadly, and his voice sounded antique, slow, and gloomy, as if it echoed up from some old dungeon where he was sitting, slumped in despair. "You are wondering how we came to this sorry state."

"Um, yeah," said Gregory. "This is nice and all, but the real Norumbega didn't smell like compost."

"The real Norumbega. Yes. The Old Norumbega. Ah! Ancient days, now faded." The old man shook his head, looking around the Court sadly. He explained, "Forgive me: I am a most gloomy wight. We are in this state, living in these decayed corridors, because we have been abandoned by our automatons."

"So we heard," Gregory said.

The old man shook his head. He said, "Came our sad and bedraggled horde through the portal, fleeing from the Thusser, and we assayed to build a new City of Gargoyles right in that place, in Three-Gut, and to live there in splendor and merry might. The automatons began to quarry walls and courtyards from the flesh, and had gone some way toward building another city of broad boulevards and fair turrets — when the Great Body swallowed. Alas." He shook his head. "Alas. 'Twas a fearsome epoch: the Season of Meals. The whole of what the machines had built was washed away. Many of our number were washed away, too, and we suspect that buried deep in the gut, there are still colonies of our people who have not, for untold ages, struggled up to find us.

"When the flood was passed, we demanded our automatons begin once more. Again they built, and again the Great Body swallowed, and our city was washed away. We now spake sharply to our servants and bade them shape up. They suggested we build in another place. We

68

would have none of it, and ordered them to follow the plans we had originally set forth.

"They went back to the tissue quarries and carved out more bricks and paving stones. But we could not help noticing that their numbers seemed to have dwindled. Many of them left us. They did not wish to be washed away. And yet, the brunch came again, roaring down the gullet like a spring freshet, and many mannequins were destroyed. Most of the others fled, too frightened of our wrath to speak out against us.

"One led us to this place. We carried everything with us. We demanded he and the remaining automatons build us a palace here. They had barely begun when they were gone. They, too, left us. Fled in the night." He took a sip of his wine and looked sharply left and right. "Ingrates. Varlets," he muttered. "We built them. We made them. We taught them." He noticed the two humans staring at him in wonder and dismay. He held out his hand. "I am the Earl of Munderplast, Munderplast being a verdant land out in the Throttling Pipes. I am the head of the Party of Melancholy."

Gregory asked, "Is that a good thing?" Brian shook the man's hand.

"Is anything a good thing?" asked the Earl of Munderplast in dreary tones. "Will anything come to anything? I think not. It is all dying."

The three of them — two boys flanking the old man — looked out over the glittering tin roofs of the shanty city, on the walls of which were painted advertisements for Norumbegan products: DOCTOR STYMSON'S MAGICAL PITUITARY PILLS ... HALOGEN RECEIVERS BY GALVO-BRITE ... AUTO-DRONES BY BEDWYR & CO. ... MADAME MABINANT'S FRIPPERY AND FROCKERY — WE FEATURE DRESSES FOR THE DARLINGEST DEBS. Shadows rolled over the city, cast by bubbles in the veins above.

"You can go back to Old Norumbega," said Brian. "That's what we're here to tell the Emperor. All you have to do is stop the Thusser. They've cheated."

"They're moving in," Gregory added. "It's awful. You have to go back. Have a big smack-down. Wham! They've messed up the Game. Completely. You've got to go back."

Brian urged, "Then it would be yours again. The old city under the mountain. All the caverns. You wouldn't have to live here anymore."

The Earl of Munderplast looked at them both through tired eyes. "Warms the heart, to hear young, energetic bairns such as yourself drivel on about how after night comes morning ... believing something can happen ... other than the ruin that shall eventually devour us whole ... taking you and your little smiling faces with us. Indeed. 'Twill be sad, to see your bright, shining cheer turn to horror as you're washed away in brunch or drowned in flux or cut apart by rogue mannequins." He shook his head. "Alas."

Brian said, "You can't just give up. I'm telling you that the Thusser have forfeited the Game! By the Rules, you can just go in and end the whole contest! You can take your old kingdom back!"

70

Munderplast smiled sadly. Somewhere in the hall, a phone was ringing insistently, ignored by all. "My boy," said Munderplast, "I can do nothing. The Party of Melancholy is currently in the minority in the Imperial Council. The ruling party there at the moment is the Norumbegan Social Club. A very different band of people. Jolly. Fond of giggling and swell pleasance. Our fine Regent is at their head. Duke Telliol-Bornwythe. He and the Norumbegan Social Club hold all the power. Unless he were to die — Great Liver forbid such a sad turning — and an election be held for a new regent, we of the Melancholy Party shall be sitting in the backseat of this dismal jalopy for some years."

The phone kept ringing.

"Of course," said Munderplast, "if the Regent were to die, then it might be possible for a statesman such as myself to suggest to the young Emperor that —"

"Does no one have hands?" shouted the Regent across the crowd. "Will someone get the phone?"

"Sorry, old thing," said someone wearily. "Can't reach it from here. Arm isn't long enough."

There was a general murmur of agreement. None of them had arms long enough. The phone was fifteen feet away. It kept ringing.

"You have to help us," Brian pressed the Earl of Munderplast. "Not just with that. Our friends have been locked up."

"Oh," said Munderplast. "Those automatons? You call them friends?"

71

"We brought one of them from Old Norumbega," said Gregory. "The troll. He's part of the Game."

"He's more than that," said Brian.

Behind them, the Regent was surging through the crowd, trying to get to the phone.

"I see. You sympathize with the metal help."

Another man standing nearby — a handsome, young-ish nobleman with black hair slicked back and a polka-dot bow tie — said, "Clockwork-lovers, hmm? I wouldn't get your hopes up, chaps, for a fond reunion, tears in every eye, embraces all round, picnic in the gills, tra la la. They're being reeducated. The two automatons."

"What do you mean?" Brian demanded.

"Scrubbed. Fixed. So they're no longer rebellious."

Brian felt his fingers grow cold. He and Gregory looked at each other in horror.

"No!" said Brian. "You've got to stop people from doing it! You can't let them!"

"Why ever not, old thing?"

"Because they're our friends. We won't — we won't tell you our message. We won't tell you anything, if you don't release them, if you don't —"

The young man said, "Afraid, chaps, you don't have much choice. You're rather over a barrel, being in our midst and surrounded by armed guards and all."

"See and behold," droned the Earl of Munderplast to the boys. "Only two and half minutes into our parley, and already sorrow has come to you. Verily, nothing shall turn out —"

"*HUSH!*" hissed the Regent from across the room.

The crowd had gathered around the door into the hall. Right outside the door, there was an old wooden phone box with a mouthy phone like the one in General Malark's headquarters. The Regent was speaking on it theatrically, loud enough so that everyone could hear.

"Ah. Mr. Malark. Yes, we were expecting your call. . . . I said, 'Mr. Malark'. . . . Mister . . . *Mister* . . . Because, sir, you are not a general. . . . Allow me to clarify: I am the Regent of the Empire of the Innards, which extends through the whole of the Great Body, explored and unexplored. I am therefore the only current head of the armed forces. There is but one army in the Empire, and it has no generals named Malark. I was explaining this to your lackey only an hour ago."

There was a general murmur of appreciation from the crowd, a rumble of approval. The Regent put his finger over his lips and silenced the Court with his hand.

"Yes, sir, he arrived here. . . . Yes. . . . Yes, indeed, we have the two little human cublings with us here in the Grand Hall. . . . They're a little greasy and they have no conversation, but no, they're no worse for wear. . . . Oh? . . . Oh? But surely you've heard all this from the excellent Mr. Dantsig. . . . No? . . . Really? You haven't heard from your submarine? . . . No? . . . Now, isn't that a bit rum? Very odd."

The crowd, finding this hilarious, started snickering and talking. The Regent, who now looked fit to bust with laughter, squeezed his eyes shut and waved them all back vigorously. He mimed a big, comic *Shhhh!*

Brian and Gregory exchanged a frantic look.

73

"Yes, well, I do have an explanation, Mr. Malark." He paused for dramatic effect, then said, delighted, "We do have some sense of what might have happened. Because we have imprisoned your envoy, your marines, and your troll, and they're all going to be reeducated. . . . Yes . . . Tutored . . . Sternly . . . What do you think of that? . . . Insofar as you can think . . . Oh, I'm so sorry. . . . So very sorry . . . Perhaps there is a can opener there into whose arms you can cry? . . ."

At this, the young nobleman in the polka-dot bow tie let loose a loud guffaw. "Classic," he muttered.

"You've got to stop this!" Brian hissed urgently.

"Hush," said the Earl of Munderplast. "Can't you see, the Regent is speaking on the telephone. There."

Brian, loud on purpose, mustering his courage, proclaimed, "We're not going to tell you our news if you don't release our friends right now!"

Dark eyes swiveled to glare at him. Mouths were sour. The end of his sentence was still loud, but it was awkward, weak, and uncertain.

He did not speak again as the Regent continued, "And what? And what will you do? . . . Ah? . . . Ah? . . . But you can't. . . . You can't even call me a name. . . . You aren't built for it. . . . Try. . . . Just try. . . . Oh, I say, that was actually rather good. . . . Hmm, yes, that will do. . . . Yes . . . Well, I think that perhaps this conversa — What? . . . What? . . . Oh, I'd like to see that. . . . That really would be rich. . . . Yes, of course I invite you to try. . . . Please, by all means . . . Yes. . . ." Then he snarled, "You

74

little hand-pump, you wouldn't dare," and hung up, slamming down the mouthpiece. The call was over.

With a gentle smile, the Regent turned to the Norumbegan Court.

"I am pleased to announce," he said, "that the Mannequin Resistance has just declared war. They say they're coming to besiege New Norumbega."

The room went wild with confusion, anger, and delight.

NINE

New Norumbega's Imperial Prison was not impressive: a messy ring of huts strung together around a circular courtyard that was paved with flagstones of ancient jerky ripped from the wall of the Dry Heart, striped with fats.

Dantsig and Kalgrash, handcuffed, were marched through the yard. They stumbled past pits where prisoners called up through wooden gratings for food, drink, and mercy. Guards goaded the two automatons on.

"All right, all right, all right," said Kalgrash irritably. "Stop shoving! I bite." He clacked his pointed teeth.

In lean-tos, soldiers played cards or snoozed.

"What's the big —" Kalgrash started, then stopped himself, nearly slamming into Dantsig.

Dantsig, mouth dropped open, was staring to the side.

One wall was lined with rough wooden shelves that had been sloppily painted blue. Kalgrash saw, lined up on those shelves, stretching for forty feet or more, rows and rows of mannequin heads, caught in expressions of fear and surprise. Necks that had been disconnected from bodies that still floated out there in the mire, in Three-Gut. Eyes that were blank. Brains that were shut down. The prisoners taken at the siege of Delge.

Then he grew truly terrified. The Norumbegans really did see him and his kind merely as machines. Not like Wee Sniggleping, who adored each of his creations and took pride in its successes and eccentricities.

A guard shoved Kalgrash in the back, and the troll stumbled forward.

They were led into a dark shed, pushed into the center of the room, and a plywood door was dragged across the uneven floor to shut them in. Kalgrash heard it latch.

A guard looked through slats of wood and said, "Promise you won't escape."

Dantsig looked shifty. He nodded.

"Say it. I command you to say it."

Dantsig flinched as if there was some inner battle. And then he growled, "Yeah, I promise."

"There's a good automaton. And you?"

Kalgrash looked at the guard like the man was crazy. "What do you want?"

"Promise you won't escape. Your word."

"I promise," said Kalgrash, crossing his fingers behind his back.

The guard walked away.

Kalgrash and Dantsig sat in the dust.

Dantsig looked defeated. His face was pale. His arms were limp.

77

"You saw them?" Kalgrash said.

Dantsig nodded grimly.

"There were so many," said Kalgrash.

The two mannequins didn't speak for a long while.

Their cell was made of uneven bits of wood and metal. Though it was gloomy, it wasn't entirely dark, since light fell in through cracks between the panels of fiberboard. Somewhere nearby, there was a hive of wasps. They came in and out on errands.

After a time, Dantsig stood and paced around the cell, his eyes narrowed.

"Damn them," he said. "We'll never get out of here."

Kalgrash thought this was odd. "We just need to wait until there aren't any guards around," he said, "and we can untie the twine that holds the door on."

"Are you tweaking my beard?" Dantsig said to him. "This place is tied up tight as a Christmas roast." He kicked at the wall. The whole hut shimmied. "These walls must be six feet thick. The door is banded with iron. The Norumbegan breathers are masters of construction."

Kalgrash stood and looked at Dantsig carefully. "Is that really what you see?" he said. "'Cause I see something a whole lot different."

"What do you see?"

"This place is built like a doghouse. For an old dog. Who doesn't lean too much on walls."

"Are you out of your tin can? The Norumbegans don't do anything half gut. It's all full-on with them. They build their cities to last a million years. This prison will keep us locked up until the blood runs out of the

Body's veins and the gorge rises and the Innards split with rot."

"Dantsig," said Kalgrash, "part of the wall is made out of old orange crates."

The troll walked over to the door. The bottom part of it was plywood, and the top was some slats of rough wood. Kalgrash surveyed the room beyond them. A couple of guards sat at a table, talking quietly in the language of the Norumbegans.

When he turned back to Dantsig, the man was staring at him moodily. Dantsig asked, "Are you serious?"

Kalgrash nodded. "Here," he said, "read the writing on the wall."

"What do you mean?"

Kalgrash pointed. "There's writing. There's the picture of an orange, and some writing. Read it."

Dantsig walked over and glared at the wall. "Stone," he said.

"Balsa wood," said Kalgrash. "Read it. See the words?"

Dantsig concentrated. He muttered, "They make us worship them. That's how we're built. For worship. They can do no wrong. We think every single one of them is beautiful. More beautiful than we can ever be. That's what they've done to us. They could have horns and yellow claws and we'd think they were the belles of the ball." He was getting angrier as he glared at the wall. "We just take a little look at them and we're chockablock with 'Yes, sir,' 'No, sir,' 'Very good, sir' . . . and bowing and scraping and 'By your leave.' Fresh Poictesme Navel Oranges." He stopped short. Then he crowed, "Fresh Poictesme Navel Oranges!" He looked toward the guards in the outer chamber and dropped his voice in hushed excitement. "I can read it. I can see something's there. Or if there was something there, it would say, in Norumbegan, 'Fresh Poictesme Navel Oranges,' and there would be a picture of an orange right next to it!" He grinned wolfishly. "Is that what you see?"

"I see a battered old box that's been tacked onto the wall with brads. You know, those little nails? And it says something in runes, and then there's pictures of oranges, and I know I don't need to eat, but I'd really like one right now. Oranges are great. The way they split into sections is like they're built to be eaten." Kalgrash got a sad, citrusy look on his spiky face.

Dantsig was squeezing his eyes shut and opening them again, staring hard at the wall. "I've lost it. I can't see it anymore. But you're right, I bet. I can tell. You're right." He looked around him carefully. "Let's sit in the middle of the floor," he said.

They sat back-to-back in the middle of the floor.

"So," whispered Dantsig, "tell me what you see. Can we break out?"

"Sure. There are guards."

"We wait for our moment."

"Got it."

"Then we move."

"Sure."

"Forget our promises."

"Mine's forgotten."

"You'll have to be my eyes. Tell me what things are made of."

"They're mostly made of junky stuff."

"Let's keep quiet now. Don't want to attract attention."

"Gotcha."

"We're going to do this."

"That's the spirit."

So they sat, facing opposite directions, their arms on their knees.

Through the afternoon, people came to examine them. Guards came, and a wizard, and a servant from the palace tasked with looking them over and providing a report for the Imperial Council. No one talked to them. Guards lifted up their arms and opened up panels in their backs and took notes, then swung the panels closed and left them alone.

At some point, the generators that lit the lux effluvium so bright shut off to bring night to the Dry Heart. The cracks in the walls faded. The shed got dark.

Finally, Dantsig got up and walked to the door. He looked out through the wooden slats. "The guards have left the table. Is that what you see?"

"That's what I see, Captain."

"So you think you can get this door open?"

"The only thing holding us in here is you thinking we have to stay," Kalgrash said.

"You lucky little dingus," said Dantsig. "You're not built like the rest of us. Do you see how they do this to us?"

"Sure, sure, sure." Kalgrash fiddled with the door. He

lifted it carefully out of its rut in the dirt. He fiddled with its catch. Then he reached over to the twine hinges and began to untie the knots.

When a few of the twine hinges were untied, he lifted the door from its setting. He and Dantsig scuttled out, glancing around watchfully for guards.

Kalgrash and Dantsig crouched behind the table.

"How are we going to deal with them?" Kalgrash asked, nodding out at figures in the courtyard.

Dantsig made a face and thought long and hard. He looked around.

Then he smiled.

He pointed at something on a chair.

"That's how," he said. "Right there."

TEN

Gregory had met a girl. She wore a gown of silk, but her shoulders were bare. Her skin was smooth as lotion. Her hair shone. The two were talking. They had been introduced by the Earl of Munderplast. ("Ah! Your eye, my boy, is upon that fine young creature.... Follow me thither.... Gregory Stoffle, may I present you to a true angel of delight, a very paragon of sweetness, and (as the young people say) a 'solid sender' yclept Gwynyfer Gwarnmore, daughter of the Duke and Duchess of the Globular Colon.... It warms an old heart to see you two smile at one another as if you were unaware that the flesh you so much admire will soon be dust and dry straps of muscle on a frame of rotting bone.... There we are. Enjoy!")

"Wow," said Gregory. "That was quite an intro."

Gwynyfer laughed. She didn't speak. She didn't have to.

They watched each other carefully, ready for flirtation.

"So," said Gregory. "I'm from Earth."

"I know. We all know."

"And you're from the Globular Colon." She nodded at that and Gregory nodded slowly with her. "That's awesome," he said. "Super neighborhood."

"Really." Her tone was ironic. "You like it?"

"Great schools. Really good hockey team."

She touched him on the nose. "You've never been."

"No. But I may pass that way." He winked. "Get it?"

She laughed again.

He told her, "We're trying to free our friend Kalgrash. He's an automaton."

"I thought you were here to warn us about the Thusser."

"That, too. We're very exciting. We've got a finger in every pie."

Gregory was starting to feel secure again. After days of nothing but weirdness, he felt like he was on firm ground. He knew how to deal with girls.

Except that Brian interrupted. "Gregory, we've got to go. We have to try to meet with the Emperor and the Regent. We've got to talk to someone, quick."

"The Emperor?" said Gwynyfer. "The Stub?"

Brian looked confused. Gregory made the introductions: "Brian Thatz, let me present you to Gwynyfer Gwarnmore, the daughter of the Duke and Duchess of the Globular Colon."

"It's good to meet you," said Brian without humor, "but we've got to go."

"We were just talking," said Gregory.

84

"Well, any minute, they're going to take us in to meet the Emperor."

Gwynyfer Gwarnmore smiled a secret smile.

"What's going on there?" prodded Gregory cutely, as if coaxing a baby to give up its sippy cup. "What's the widdle smile about?"

"I just don't think you're really going to get much help from the Emperor."

"He's a kid, right?" said Gregory.

She shrugged. Gregory couldn't help but notice that her shoulders were superb. "I guess," she said.

Brian hesitated. Gregory told him, "I'll be with you in a couple."

Brian nodded and walked away.

Gregory jabbed his thumb back at his friend. "Always on the job. It tires me out. Sometimes I want to just lie back, eat the buffet."

Gwynyfer smiled at him, and he felt the glow, as if the acoustic-tiled ceiling had just lifted and let butter in.

He felt his brain drenched in things she was not saying.

✳ ✳ ✳

Brian, meanwhile, was listening to the young noble-man with the polka-dot bow tie and the slicked-back hair, who old Munderplast had introduced as Lord Rafe "Chigger" Dainsplint, a prominent member of the Norumbegan Social Club.

"Outrageous," Lord Dainsplint was murmuring to

another young buck of the Norumbegan Social Club, this one a vaguely bucktoothed type with floppy blond hair. Dainsplint said beneath his breath, "The Regent's a fool. An absolute fool. Why did he let the bally mannequins declare war? Why right now?"

"You mean," said the floppy-haired gent, "with the Fest coming up."

"Exactly, Gugs. The Fest. Next week. And it will be one sorely drippy Fest if the city is surrounded by manns with cannon."

By *manns*, he apparently meant *mannequins*. Brian thought that even his abbreviations sounded snobby.

"It is not our way to invite trouble," said Lord "Chigger" Dainsplint. "Lolling, that's our way. Letting the bloody manns do whatever their little tin hearts desire, so long as it's far away and dull."

"What if the manns actually find a way around their prohibitions? And manage to attack us?"

"I *know*, Gugs. It's not impossible. And do you know, the thing which bothers me in that case — the little detail I find troubling — is the utter lack of walls. It's my understanding, Gugs, that an important part of resisting any besieging force that has catapults and mortars and howitzers and so forth is a bloody wall. And maybe a moat. What was the Regent *thinking*? Really. This is the end. He's crackers."

Suddenly, the floppy-haired man called Gugs caught sight of Brian listening. He said to Lord Dainsplint, "Ah, Chigger, old pal, it appears small apes have large ears."

86

Chigger Dainsplint turned. "Well, hello, little chimp! Still worried about those Thusser?"

Brian glared at the man. He didn't want to be rude to his elders, especially not his elders by several hundred years, but his elders were being rude to him. "You should be worried, too," Brian reprimanded. "Once they settle Old Norumbega, they might come through the portal to settle New Norumbega and the Innards."

"Not particularly likely," said Chigger. "I've never met a Thusser who'd asked specially to live in a spleen."

"The little thing is slightly peevish," said Gugs. "Is it right in the head, do you think?"

"It does seem to say the same things over and over," said Chigger. "Like a seal clapping in an empty big top."

Brian had never heard an adult be so mean to him. He was shocked.

"The Thusser," said Gugs, "are hardly anything now but an old wives' tale."

Chigger Dainsplint said, "Quite right, old fish. Nothing doing."

Suddenly, it was time to try to pitch the reconquest of Old Norumbega to the Emperor. Trumpets were blowing. Heralds were rolling back some fire-retardant folding doors on tracks, revealing an inner throne room.

A herald announced, "Now come forward the members of the Imperial Council, His Excellency the Regent, and the two human diplomats! With fear and adoration, bow before His Imperial Majesty, His Sublime Highness, the Emperor of Old Norumbega, New Norumbega, and the Whole Dominion of the Innards, Elector of the

87

Bladders, Prince of the Gastric Wastes, Sovereign of Ducts Superior and Inferior, Lord of All!"

Brian looked hastily toward Gregory, who was taking too long shaking Gwynyfer Gwarnmore's hand.

"This way, old bean," said Chigger Dainsplint to Brian, beckoning with a jerk of the head.

The rest of the crowd fell silent. They slid to the ground, touching their heads to the porous, pink floor.

Eleven remained standing, walking forward, stepping over the prone bodies: Eight members of the Imperial Council (including Lord Dainsplint, his pal Gugs, and the gloomy, medieval Earl of Munderplast), the Regent, Brian, and Gregory. They all worked their way across the Grand Hall to the throne room.

Passing through the great archway, between the fire-retardant panels into a new, lower, darker chamber, a room of cheap old wallboard scribbled with royal designs in flaking paint, a room of unmatched chairs and a brown hassock, the boys saw for the first time the young Emperor of Norumbega and, on either side of him, his father and mother.

Brian and Gregory both immediately recognized the parents: They were the bright young things who had, the year before, ridden ghostly palfreys through the Haunted Hunting Grounds. They had bickered with Brian and Gregory on the Imperial barge while the boys tried to grab their crown. They had ridden down the slope near the palace on lunch trays. They had once been the rulers of this eldritch tribe: a blond man, witty and urbane, and the love of his life, a playful woman with a knowing look.

Now they were middle-aged. In human years, they would have been fifty or sixty at least. They sat on either side of the throne, both gray, wearing simple circlets of gold on their heads. The man, who was introduced as Ex-Emperor Randall Elismoore Fendritch, wore an old crew-necked tennis sweater with pulls in it and dirty white flannel trousers. He was sunk deep in his chair, his head upright, but his back slumped, his legs sprawled out in front of him, his shoes scuffed. His wife, Ex-Empress Elspeth Fendritch, wore a flapper dress from the 1920s. The lace near the underarms was stained yellow with old sweat.

They had abdicated for their son, who presumably sat between them, on the throne. Gregory stared. Brian looked quizzical.

It was not a person enthroned between the Imperial couple. It was a Stub. A vaguely conical lump of white flesh, perhaps almost a foot tall. On one side, facing forward, was a single, wide eye. To mark the other side, there was a patch of acne.

The Regent bowed before the Stub, and, having announced the Stub's parents, announced the Stub itself: "Gregory Stoffle and Brian Thatz, I present you to His Imperial Majesty, the Stub. Long may he prosper."

The councillors looked at the boys expectantly.

Ex-Emperor Fendritch looked at them expectantly.

Ex-Empress Elspeth looked at them expectantly.

Brian and Gregory repeated raggedly, "Long may he prosper . . . ?"

"Excellent," said the Regent. "Close the panels. We'll converse."

✳ ✳ ✳

For the next hour, the boys told their story yet again.

The Ex-Empress and her husband recognized the boys immediately. "Hullo," said Elspeth, drinking some whitish water from a tumbler, "I believe it's those little human wags who sneaked your crown."

"Whisk me if you aren't right. So it is, Elsp. The same little blighters. I remember them wet."

The Ex-Empress asked, "You win your Game?"

"We did," said Brian. "We won it for you."

"Grand," said Elspeth without any enthusiasm whatsoever. "You make off with the ancient, sacred crown of the realm, never to be seen again, you send the Thusser into a diplomatic panic, and then there's a war, but yes, swell, congratters on the Game, I s'pose."

"Ah, time travel," said the Ex-Emperor wistfully. "Remember, dearest, the time travel? There is no company, chaps, like oneself in a few hours. Especially if one bets on the horses."

"So you were the future," said Elspeth, a little sharply. "You were the future, and now here you are. The future stands in front of us."

Brian nodded. "I guess."

The Ex-Emperor was taken up with a plate set on a

90

TV tray in front of him. "I need someone to cut my meat into smaller pieces," he said. "This is awful. Very tough. It's like trying to eat mah-jongg."

"His Ex- and Her Ex-Imperial Majesties are members of the Council," explained the Regent. "I am the head of that Council. We shall all be most interested in your story."

"Grippers," said Elspeth.

"Go ahead," said the Regent.

Brian and Gregory started to talk.

"Address the Stub," said the Regent. "He is the Emperor of us all."

Acutely uncomfortable, the two boys spoke to the Stub, which occasionally looked at them, but only as its maniac eye swept over the room, lingering one place, darting to another, the eye of a man trapped behind a wall.

Halting, hesitating, interrupting each other, the boys told the story of how they'd played the Game. The boys spoke on in that throne room in that ramshackle city buried somewhere in the guts of a pulpy world. The murals on the walls, Brian and Gregory could now see, were floral designs, perhaps drawn by the Emperor and Empress themselves some years before: wreaths, swags of flowers, ferns in vases, sketches of old Emperors wearing the crown Gregory had stolen, all painted with poster paints or drawn in thick pastels. They were darkened by the smudges where torches hung. The room smelled like burning oil.

As the boys told their story, the audience did not seem to be very interested in what they had to say. The six members of the Norumbegan Social Club kept exchanging looks — and neither Brian nor Gregory could tell what those looks meant.

The Ex-Empress and her husband were particularly entertained, at first. They liked very much the parts about themselves, and often asked questions.

"Were we very lovely to see, boys?"

"Did you think us the charmingest thing ever to ride before you in panoply? You may be honest. Deathly honest."

But then the story evidently went on too long. The Ex-Emperor and his consort grew bored and started to stare. The members of the Norumbegan Social Club were blowing smoke rings. One was arranging papers from his briefcase. The Earl of Munderplast was bent double in his chair, as if with gas pains, his arms crossed.

Only the Regent listened, and he listened closely. His eyes swiveled from Gregory to Brian, watching both faces. There was nothing of the practical joker about him now. He seemed deadly serious.

Eventually, on the other side of the fire-retardant panels, music started up. It sounded like jazz tunes, but taken apart and stuck back together again wrong. When it became clear that Chigger and Gugs were tapping time to the music, wishing they were elsewhere, Brian stopped mid-sentence. He said, "You know, we're trying to help you, too. We've come a long way."

Gregory agreed, "We came through that stupid portal for you."

"You could at least listen," said Brian. "What we're telling you is important. It's about your own kingdom."

"It's just," said Chigger, "you've spoken for so very *long*."

"Hear, hear," said Gugs, raising his pipe.

"Because we need *your* help and you need *our* help," Brian protested.

Chigger fixed him with a gaze. "We," he said deliberately, "don't need any help. From anyone. We are a sublime species."

Brian gaped. He didn't know what to say. He was tired and hungry. Fleetingly, he thought of his home, how much he wanted to be there — and then remembered that Boston itself and his parents and their apartment were all threatened by the spread of the Thusser settlement — and that if he and Gregory didn't get this elfin court to intervene, if he didn't convince these snobby, drawling men in their bow ties and vests to observe the Game again, the Thusser would gradually blot out everything in North America — so he didn't know whether there would even be a home when he got back to Earth. He wondered what else he could say. These courtiers were so sure of themselves, so quick with their words, and everything about the way they spoke and thought was strange to him. He tried to come up with more arguments.

Suddenly, the Regent rose. "The worthy gentlemen, the worthy lady will be pleased to hear that I have a recommendation to make to His Imperial Highness, the Stub. Having listened intently to these boys' story, I have hit upon a plan of action that I intend to pursue."

Brian and Gregory shuffled away from the center of the room. The Regent, Duke Telliol-Bornwythe, walked before the Imperial Council. The jazz music played in the background, sounding like fragments of broken night-club mirrors reflecting dancers in white silk gowns and kid gloves. "We have," said the Regent, "not always been happy here. Some say this city is not the equal of that fine metropolis in which we lived centuries ago, beneath the mountain. Therefore, I propose that we shall abandon this place."

"What's this?" protested the Ex-Emperor Fendritch.

The Earl of Munderplast had sat up abruptly, and finally was listening.

The Regent nodded. "Indeed. Abandon it. That's my plan. Leave it to the mannequins, see? They arrive, surround the place. Prepare to take the city by storm.

"We, meanwhile, have all left — except maybe a skeleton crew of soldiers and drones who'll stay behind to carry out the gag.

"The mannequins can sit waiting for us to engage them in battle for as long as they want. Nobody will resist them. I'm sure that, finally, they'll move in on the city. But it will be an empty victory. Nothing but a shanty city. Empty. No one here.

"We will be back in Old Norumbega, beneath the mountain. The city which we built with our own labor and which we should, by rights, rule."

"Lord Regent," said Chigger Dainsplint, "this is the absolute end."

But Brian was overjoyed at this suggestion. "You mean, sir, you'll stop the Thusser?"

"No speech by the chimplings," said the Regent sharply. "This is a meeting of the Imperial Council, and I demand all simians quiet their hoots." He smiled. "But yes, my lad, I do indeed intend that we will retake the City of Gargoyles. We'll enforce the Rules, give the Thusser the boot, and move back into our old haunts. What?"

Chigger Dainsplint said, "This is absolute idiocy."

"If necessary, we'll exile the Thusser to this place," said the Regent. "They prefer things a little drippy. All the mucus will be congenial. No one will be here, once we've gone. No one but the machines, of course, who the Thusser can keep or dismantle as they see fit."

Brian did not feel so good about that — the idea of the automatons facing a Thusser invasion — and he started to say something, but the Regent glared at him and shut him up.

Already the rest of the Council was protesting.

"This is our *home*, Regent," Ex-Emperor Fendritch complained. "You're asking us to flee? Without a fight?"

"New Norumbega *is* our home," Chigger Dainsplint agreed, slicking back his hair with a thumb.

"So say you," said the Regent, "because you own a third of the city, Dainsplint. But our citizens may feel differently."

Lord Dainsplint argued. "We can't even slap down the ruddy mannequins — we don't have a chance against the Thusser Horde."

"You're sending us to our deaths," Gugs proclaimed. "And at a deuced inconvenient time, too."

"It's the Fest next week," one of the other councillors pointed out.

"That's right. We still haven't discussed the Fest," said Lord Dainsplint.

The quietest of the councillors raised his hand timidly. "I have my report on floats."

No one listened to him. Lord Dainsplint said, "We are not a people made for warfare. We're made for commerce and delight and whatnot. And you are dragging us —"

"My mind is made up," said the Regent. "I have spoken."

"You must listen to the Council," Dainsplint said.

"I do not need to listen to anyone but the current reigning Emperor," said the Regent. He turned to the Stub. "Your Majesty?" He bowed.

The Stub sat on its throne. Its eye swiveled back and forth. It showed no sign it knew anyone was calling it by name.

"Clearly the old plug's not in agreement," said Lord Dainsplint.

"His acne," said the Regent, "burns a particular red at the moment. I call that heated with excitement."

The Ex-Empress suggested, "He may need to be rubbed down with lard. It soothes the skin."

"So it is decided," the Regent pronounced.

"It would be terrible," said Lord Dainsplint dangerously, "if the current Regent and the head of my party were to think himself a hero, but act the fool, and be

96

martyred for his silly ideas. Cut down in the prime of his power. It would look poorly in the history books."

"It would be equally unfortunate," the Regent responded, "for one of the most prominent men in my party to be convicted of treason and spend the rest of his days in a dungeon. Or, even worse, to be used as bait for the mannequins." He smiled. "You are all dismissed."

"We shall not go," the old Earl of Munderplast growled, "until we have held further parley upon this matter."

"Chaps," said Gugs, "we're missing the tea dance."

"There is that," Lord Dainsplint complained.

"At least send the humans out," said Ex-Empress Elspeth. "You never know where there might be spies."

"You are excused," said the Regent.

The two boys backed out of the room, facing the Emperor, as they had been told to do by Dantsig.

The panels slid shut behind them. In the Grand Hall, there was a dance going on. Couples swayed lightly to the music.

Gwynyfer Gwarnmore was at their side. "And how did your audience go?"

Gregory looked to Brian. "I dunno. How *did* that go?"

"Well, I think. The Regent is on our side. I really think he's going to do something."

"If the others don't stop him," said Gregory.

"Spiffers," said Gwynyfer, and smiled.

"The, uh, the Emperor," said Gregory, "he isn't really like we expected him."

Gwynyfer nodded. "He *is* a bit disappointing. The whole Court was quite surprised when he was born. It happened to the old Emperor, too — the Ex-Emperor's uncle: His heirs were all just spirals or dolls or piles of dust. People thought it was a Thusser curse."

"Isn't anyone worried?" Brian asked. "That he's your Emperor?"

"He doesn't seem like he'll ever be a great dancer," said Gregory with a smirk, and Gwynyfer laughed and shook her head.

The Council meeting went on while Gwynyfer and the boys stood at the side of the dancing throng. The heralds played their weird jazz on their trumpets and trombones and krummhorns; the lords and ladies danced, smiling, in their faded finery; a crooner sang of love — and in the blood vessels and lower guts, transport subs full of mannequin soldiers swarmed toward the Empire's capital as their onetime overlords debated the decorations for the coming Fest.

✳ ✳ ✳

In two hours, night fell. The electrical generators that caused the lux effluvium in the veins above the city to burn so brightly were gradually shut off, and the sky faded to a faint blue glow.

All over the city, little parties in dirty courtyards lit up their grills and poured out drinks into chipped old cups. For some hours more, the Court continued to dance in the Grand Hall and to promenade on the piazza, watching the carrion bats descend into the huge garbage heap that piled up next to the palace's Great Keep.

And some time after that, the lights in the palace went out. A few guards patrolled the hallways. They did not notice a fellow soldier passing them, as if on the way to some duty.

The Regent sat in his bedroom, his hand and face dissected by light that fell through the remains of some old stained-glass window. The lines of the lead that held the panes in place fell across his skin, wrote their way along his robes and down his sleeves. He considered how clever he had been, and relished his forthcoming glory. He worried about how difficult it was sometimes to *control* them all, those piffling dukes and braying duchesses — how tough it was to pull the strings without others seeing. He figured he would have to look into the history of that old Game, rediscover its Rules, find the wretch Archbishop Darlmore. No one had talked about that yet. . . . And he'd have to watch carefully. There were so many who thought he ruled too absolutely, for a Regent. They wanted him to —

There was a soft knock at his door.

He opened it. A soldier stood before him. Without invitation, the soldier stepped in.

The Regent caught the scent of thought and recognized its imprint before he saw the face in shadow beneath the helmet. "Ah," he said. "It's you."

"I'm sorry, Your Excellency."

"You think you are going to kill me."

The soldier said, "Yes."

"You know," said the Regent in a joking tone, "the thing about plots on one's life is —"

"The time for witty banter is over," said the intruder, stabbing the Regent in the gut and dragging the knife upward.

The Regent fell. The soldier leaned down and, with another stroke of the blade, made sure the Regent was dead. He left the knife in the body. It wasn't his knife anyway.

Then he stepped back out into the corridor.

Over the next hours, the black lines from the lead in the stained-glass windows moved across the corpse, reading it carefully.

In the morning, when the light was strong again, when the galvanic engines were switched on and the veins bubbled and shone bright, a servant came in to serve breakfast — screamed — and the body was found.

Across the Empire, the Regent was declared dead.

ELEVEN

It was still night when Brian first noticed something wrong in their chamber. They had been given a tiny room with two bunks, a little round window, and almost no floor. He was on the bottom bunk. He lay awake on his pallet. He was anxious.

The walls were decorated with magic marker. The designs were alien: long, parallel lines, diagrams that must have had some mystical meaning, curlicues that looked like heads of lettuce. They were brightly colored, and Brian could make them out, even in the dark.

He tried to close his eyes. He couldn't sleep. He couldn't shake the feeling that time was passing, and the Thusser were spreading, and the only beings equipped to stop them were completely incompetent. He had never imagined the Norumbegans were this irresponsible, this frivolous. It did not —

He opened his eyes. He thought he'd felt something on his face.

Nothing.

It was nothing but a breeze. It must have come in through the open window.

He closed his eyes and turned over. He folded his pillow over his head. He tried to think positive thoughts. The Regent, Duke Telliol-Bornwythe, was convinced, for one thing. He clearly wanted to at least try to claim back the City of Gargoyles. And —

The window had been closed when Brian went to bed.

Brian's eyes snapped wide.

The round window was open. It had somehow been pried.

Something could have slipped into the room.

"Gregory," Brian whispered.

He heard his friend move in the upper bunk, and fall back asleep.

He whispered again, "Gregory," and then he fell silent.

He'd seen the claw.

A huge hand was carefully feeling its way into the room, as if something was about to shove itself through the open window.

Brian sat up. He crawled out of bed. He stood and watched as —

"Kalgrash!" he cried.

At this, Gregory sat up. "Wha —?"

"Shhh!" said Kalgrash. "Shhh, shhh, shhh!" His head popped in through the window. "What do you think this is? Hush the band and stop the ticker-tape parade."

"How did you get out?"

102

"Long story."

"Why am I not surprised?" said Gregory.

"How are things going here?"

"Fine," said Brian. "Have they reprogrammed you?"

Kalgrash pawed at his own skull. "Uh . . . naw. Don't think so." He knocked briefly on his head. "They don't realize that I'm not set up to serve them like the rest of the mannequins are. As usual, intelligence is my secret weapon."

"Good job," said Gregory. "You hide it really, really well."

"Someone's cranky about being woken up," said Kalgrash.

"So now you're out, where are you hiding?" Brian asked.

"That's a tough one." He admitted, "The real problem is me. Dantsig might be able to get away with walking around looking Norumbegan. But, eh, yeah, some of us have knifelike teeth used to rend the hide of the mastodon. And full Renaissance body armor. And claws made to swipe at the flanks of scaly wyrms. We find it hard to get nannying jobs."

Brian said, "You need to tell Dantsig that the Mannequin Resistance is coming to lay siege to the city. On his account, too — because the Regent broke his word and took you guys prisoner."

"Hey," said Gregory. "How are you outside our window, anyway?"

"There's a balcony," said Kalgrash. "We used rope. Dantsig found out which room you were in."

"How?" Gregory asked.

"Ask him yourself," said Kalgrash, jerking his thumb upward.

A pair of black leather shoes swung past the window.

Dantsig dropped down beside Kalgrash.

He was wearing a soldier's uniform and helm.

"Hiya, kids," he said. "Just taking care of some business."

"How'd you find out where we were?"

"In this getup?" said Dantsig. "I just asked inside. Hey, Kal, we got to go."

"Wait!" said Brian. "Where do we find you?"

"In prison," said Dantsig.

"You can't go back to prison!" Brian protested.

Dantsig looked cagey. There was an awkward silence.

"He promised," Kalgrash said. "It's expected he'll be there in the morning."

Brian realized that the automaton could not go against a promise made to one of his Norumbegan masters.

"But hey," said Dantsig, "did you see how I did this? Slipping out at night? Full charge, huh? Bright red danger?" He made a weird sign with his hand that might have been a Norumbegan thumbs-up.

"You still have to obey the Norumbegans?" Gregory said. "They've imprisoned you! And now you're out! So run away!"

"Look, kid. It's easy enough for you to say, there in your pj's. It's not so easy for those of us hanging out here, from a rope. For us, we have to find ways to get around orders."

"What were you doing?" Brian asked.

"I don't know," said Kalgrash. "I was lying on a dome, counting veins in the sky."

"There was something I had to take care of," said Dantsig. "Let's go, Kal."

"Don't go back," said Brian. "They're going to reprogram you. That's their plan."

Dantsig hesitated. He looked sour. "Maybe they won't," he said.

"You've got to stop them if they try," Brian urged. "You can't let them."

"Just run away!" Gregory exclaimed. "Go out into the desert or the snot-field or whatever that is out there! You don't need to eat! You don't need to drink! Hide out until General Malark arrives to —"

Someone knocked on the wall. "Hey," said a muffled voice through the plasterboard. "Can you two stop arguing?"

Brian and Gregory looked, astounded, at each other. Then at the window.

The window was empty of trolls.

✳ ✳ ✳

There was only one newspaper boy in Norumbega Nova. Most Norumbegans thought they were too good for jobs, for work, for hawking tabloids, so they were still in bed, heaped up with covers, in tiny rooms blackened by smoke and built out of old wooden doors and dried clippings of flesh, staring at their ceilings when the news broke.

"Historic edition!" cried the paperboy. "Historic edition! Regent murdered in his sleep! Mannequin Resistance threatens attack! All of New Norumbega thrown into confusion! Collectible edition!"

All over town, the Norumbegans were slow to rise.

"Are we, darling, thrown into confusion?" asked the Duke of the Globular Colon.

His wife blew on her coffee. "I don't feel so terribly confused, Chev, dear. . . . Tousled. . . . The pillow has not been kind to my coiffure. But not confused."

Their daughter, Gwynyfer Gwarnmore, watched them with electrified eyes. She was excited. Something was happening. The Court of Norumbega would never be the same. She bowed her head. "Your daughter requests permission to step outside and buy the paper."

"Your father assents." He raised his hand negligently.

She raced outside to stop the paperboy from bawling his news.

✳ ✳ ✳

Gregory and Brian awoke to the sound of screaming in the corridors. Assuming the Mannequin Resistance had already arrived, they quickly got dressed and rushed out to see what was happening.

Out in the halls, members of the nobility were shouting to each other. Drones paced by obliviously.

106

The robots carried loads wrapped in burlap on their back.

When the boys heard that the Regent was dead, even Gregory, usually so jokey, was shocked. "There he was . . . he was right there," Gregory kept saying. "I can't believe it."

Brian was biting on his lip. "You realize what this might mean?" he said. "The Regent was the one who wanted everyone to fight the Thusser. Now who knows . . ."

"This sucks," said Gregory.

"I wonder," said Brian. "Who did it?"

"This is such a mess, I can't even imagine," said Gregory. "We've got to get the Council focused. On Earth. Going back."

"Yeah," Brian agreed.

"They have to get the Thusser out of our houses."

Brian looked concerned. Gregory noticed Brian had looked concerned whenever he mentioned the Thusser being in the cities. Despite what Brian said, Gregory distinctly remembered them being everywhere. Walking along streets by telephone poles. Sitting in Laundromats. Crouched in airplanes. And sitting at the kitchen table, watching Gregory's mother cook.

He remembered.

"Gregory," said Brian. "I know it's bad. But I'm telling you, the Thusser have made you have memories that aren't real. They're making us forget what the world was like without them."

"I remember them being at my soccer games since I was a kid," said Gregory, pouting.

Brian shook his head grimly.

A magician strode along the corridor, wearing a double-breasted suit. Trumpets were blasting warnings from the balconies.

The city, now, was full of confusion.

✳ ✳ ✳

Slick Chigger Dainsplint and the bucktoothed Gugs ran across the Grand Hall, whispering to each other.

"Poor old blighter," said Gugs. "I rather told him to watch his neck."

"It's my understanding that his neck was just fine. The problem was really in the chest region." Chigger smiled tightly at some baronets who bowed deeply to him.

Gugs looked very carefully at his friend, almost inspecting him. He asked, "I say, Chigger. When did it happen?"

Chigger looked back, equally careful. "The death?"

"Yes. When did it happen, I wonder?"

Chigger said, "I believe it happened right after he was stabbed, old thing." With that, he strode off to conduct preparations for the burial ceremony.

Heralds were blowing lamentation tunes in the piazza.

✳ ✳ ✳

Though the Norumbegans did not like unrest, they did like gossip, and the alleys were full of it. Elfin women and men sat on overturned oil drums, arguing about the Court. The little, low-ceilinged eateries were full of babble, talk of knives and midnight and a soldier seen who had not been a soldier for real. The murder just proved what they had all suspected: No one up there in the palace could be trusted.

Street artists spray-painted stenciled images of the Regent in his skullcap on pebbled walls. Poverty-stricken lords hung black sheets out of the windows of their huts in mourning. Everyone turned their pots and pans upside down to keep luck in their houses.

Through the main square, a Court magician walked, surrounded by guards. He was headed for the prison to begin an interrogation.

✳ ✳ ✳

The Earl of Munderplast sat on his bed, half dressed. He looked down at his bare knees, knobby and ancient.

"My love," said his wife. "My love, won't you simply tell me where you were last night?"

✳ ✳ ✳

Kalgrash and Dantsig were crouched on the floor, playing marbles with balls of dried earth, when the magician in pinstripes kicked open the door.

"Where did you get the uniform?" he demanded.

Dantsig crossed his arms. "I don't know what you're talking about."

"You were seen. Up at the palace. Walking through the halls in a uniform. Where'd you get it?"

"I found it." Dantsig said no more. The sorcerer in the suit waited. Dantsig stared right at him, determined to say nothing.

The magician reached into his coat and pulled out a large red magnet. He walked gradually toward the automaton.

Dantsig slid backward on the floor. Guards came forward and grabbed his arms.

"I don't want to scramble you. Tell me where you got the uniform."

Dantsig looked from face to face. "The outer room. It was lying on the bench. So I borrowed it," he said. "But what's —"

"That's as good as a confession," said the magician. "I charge you with the death of His Excellency the Imperial Regent of Norumbega, Duke Telliol-Bornwythe. The offense is treasonous. It carries a sentence of non-death. Torture. Continual collapse and reactivation." The wizard gestured flatly to the two mannequins who crouched on the floor. "For the moment, take them out and shut them down," he said. "Until the conviction is official."

Kalgrash screamed. He tried to fight. The guards clustered close about him.

He threw them. He took three bulky steps toward the door.

Then he looked back.

Dantsig was not following. The automaton was shivering. Pallid. The magician stood by the man's side, holding the magnet near his heart.

"Another step, troll," said the wizard, "and your friend will be magnetized. His engine'll be wrecked. His memory blanked."

Kalgrash hesitated.

"That's right," said the magician.

And to the guards near the troll, he barked, "Now."

They brought up some kind of electrified wand — slapped the troll on the shoulders.

Kalgrash gave a strangled cry, his eyes wheeled, and he fell to the ground, senseless.

TWELVE

Later that day, funeral rites were held for Duke Telliol-Bornwythe.

The Norumbegans always knew how to make the most of a celebration, and burials were no exception. The Court had mourning costumes and ornaments stored away like some family's prized Christmas decorations, and all day, the drones and their overseers labored to carry boxes of black sashes and banners out of the vaults. They prepared the city for a gala interment.

By four o'clock, crowds had gathered on the streets, awaiting the Court's huge parade, in which the body of the dead Regent would be carried from the palace to the field of tombs outside the city and buried deep in the muscle of the Great Body's Dry Heart. Citizens thronged in the alleys and on metal rooftops and wicker porches to watch the procession pass.

In the great plaza just below the palace, the Court gathered to watch the parade start on its route. They themselves would have to join at the end and walk in step behind the corpse's carriage. They wore black top hats, veils, black dresses, dark swallowtailed coats, and their faces were marked with face paint in signs of mourning (two blue stripes streaking from the eyes to symbolize tears; a line of white dots across the forehead to suggest vision into another world; or a fat red bar across the neck to indicate death). Drones in black robes passed through the crowd, passing out deep glasses of the Wine of Weeping and little sandwiches made of the Bread of Suffering, ham, cheese, and Dijon mustard.

There, among chattering nobles, stood two human boys — one, stouter, with glasses, looking extremely uncomfortable. The other looked like he had recovered from all shock, and he was ready for a good show. They both wore black satin sashes, despite the fact that they were otherwise much less formal than the crowd around them: Gregory in cargo pants and a polo shirt, Brian in jeans and sneakers.

The boys jumped when someone put an arm around them both. Lord Chigger Dainsplint stood between them, smiling as if he knew something they didn't.

"Terribly solid of you to show up and mourn our Regent," he said.

"We were told to come," said Brian. "We . . . we don't have to, if you think it's not right. . . ."

"I'm not sure how truly, deeply cut up your friend here is about the passing of our dear duke into the other world."

"I'm plenty cut up," said Gregory, through a full mouth.

113

"You've had seven sandwich halves," said Dainsplint.

"Grief makes me hungry."

"Then you'll be ravenous to hear that your mechanical friends have been shut off. They're both being held as suspects in the murder. One of them was seen by palace staff wearing a guard's uniform and sneaking around the corridors right around midnight, the witching hour. Which was when Duke Telliol-Bornwythe took the old iron to the gut."

"What?" said Brian. He turned pale. "Kalgrash and Dantsig? They're dead?"

"No, no, no, no. They never were alive. And at the moment, they're just shut off. Until after their trial."

"*After* their trial?" asked Brian. "But then how will they defend themselves?"

"Well, see, that's why the blighters have been shut off. This way there won't be any confusion. People so often say awkward things when they're tried for murder."

"Dantsig and Kalgrash *didn't do this*," Brian insisted.

"Right around midnight, one of the servants saw a guard he didn't recognize walk toward the Regent's bedroom. A man with a goatee. A few minutes later, the intruder comes out and walks the other way. We know your pal Dantsig was in possession of a uniform. He had it on last night. And he was in possession of a goatee. So it does not look good for your chums. Oh, look, the sadness is starting."

The palace band had issued forth from the gates, and now crossed the square playing solemn music. Drummers

114

played low, growling beats. Ranks of palace servants in Imperial tunics walked in stately rows carrying wands and staves of power. Behind them came a troupe of girls in plain linen doing death dances in elaborate face paint.

"There's Gwynyfer!" exclaimed Gregory, waving.

She did not notice him, but moved smoothly in the motions of her troupe. They spun and skipped in ancient steps, a remnant of some forgotten religion that the Norumbegans had practiced when man had still lived in caves.

"Gwynyfer!"

"Gregory," said Brian, recalling him to their conversation.

"Yeah, there she is!" Gregory said, waving even harder.

She danced past through the crowd, moving lightly over the dirty road littered with crushed malt-ball boxes and wrappers for bat jerky. She was followed by a troupe of noble boys, near naked, painted a thick blue. Their hair stuck up straight with lime. They kicked a wooden head between them as the crowd cheered and screamed.

Gregory grinned and watched the ritual soccer.

Brian turned back to Dainsplint and protested, "You can't just condemn Kalgrash and Dantsig without a fair trial! There must be other suspects!"

"We're holding the two manns shut off until the wizard in charge of the investigation has unspooled their memories and read through them."

"When is that going to happen?"

"We hope, never."

115

"Then what evidence do you have?!" Brian screamed over the oboes' mourning dance. "You've got to look at their memories! That'll prove that they're not guilty!"

"That's precisely it, old duck. Why would we want to prove that? It would be extremely inconvenient for all of us. If it wasn't one of the mannequins, then it was one of us — and really, it could have been any of the great and noble in this palace. Then the whole rotten Court would be thrown into disrepute. This way, with your Dantsig fingered as the perp, the people can gather around a common enemy — the Mannequin Resistance. Boo, hiss. Otherwise — look around at these faces. Look at those chaps in the toppers and the ladies in the weeping weeds. Any one of them could be guilty. We all hated Telliol-Bornwythe. We'll all hate whoever takes over for him. (And may I express, incidentally, my own fond wish it might be me who next carries the uranium baton of the Regent. Let the world hate me. I don't give two bits about hate. It improves the complexion, like wind.)"

"So you're saying you don't believe in a fair trial?"

"What I'm saying, my boys, is that it would be a deuced mess if your clockwork friends woke up or if we plumbed their memories and they turned out to be innocent. So the Imperial Council will keep on delaying the Wizard Thoth-Chumley from investigating properly until *after* the trial. By then, the manns will be convicted and thrown in the clink, to be tortured, killed, reassembled, and tortured again until we're all tired of the game, at which point they'll be scrapped for parts. And the real

116

murderer — if it wasn't your tough nut Dantsig — will sleep in peace. Such is the way of the world."

Even Gregory looked horrified at this speech. He stared, agape, at the grinning man who lounged between them.

"It must have been someone *else* in a guard uniform!" said Brian. "Let me talk to them! To Dantsig and Kalgrash! They'll tell me the truth."

"That's the problem, little man."

A clumsy, ancient automaton, brought out only for funerals by the look of it, staggered past, decorated to symbolize the Norumbegan Empire Herself, Grieving. Her face was a painted mask of sorrow. Two fountains squirted from her eyes. Her hand reached mechanically into a hole in her chest. She pulled out red flower petals and threw them to the crowds.

Brian suddenly turned to Chigger Dainsplint. "Where were *you*, then?" he said. "You could be guilty. Where were you at midnight?"

"Why, if my little human friend isn't a detective as well as a weeping advocate for the rights of manns. As it happens, I have an alibi. Gugs and I were down in the basements, playing cards until the hours went wee. Here, turn away. *Turn away.*" He swiveled the two boys away from the parade. A great, squawking fanfare went up — more like a klaxon than a trumpet. Everyone in the crowd swiveled, covered their eyes, ducked.

"It's Death," said Lord Dainsplint.

"What do you mean?" Gregory asked, trying to turn and look. Dainsplint grabbed the boy's head roughly and kept it facing toward the wall.

117

"It's someone dressed as Death," Lord Dainsplint explained. "He walks in the parade. If you catch a glimpse, you're the next person to die."

"Death?" said Gregory, still trying to look. "What's he look like? What's the costume?"

"No one knows, you imbecile. If they looked at it, they'd die. So no one's ever seen the blasted thing."

"So how do you know there's anything there?" Gregory asked. "There might be nothing. There might not be anyone."

"You've touched the matter with a needle. Now stop trying to turn your soupy little eyes on the unknown and wait for the all clear."

The yodeling of the warning cry on some primitive horn was awful to hear. Brian shut his eyes.

Another trumpet blast announced that Death had passed.

Now came the corpse itself, led by another troupe of dancers. They wore long peacock feathers and pheasant plumes and golden ornaments all over their bodies. The throng threw red flower petals at them, and the dancers threw white petals back.

Right behind them was the dead Regent, held aloft by courtiers dressed as the Old Gods of Norumbega. He sat on a chair made entirely of flowers and basketry. He was sitting up, facing forward, his eyes studded with two glowing gems. He bobbed as he moved along the dirt in flurries of white and red. His dead hands clutched the arms of this final throne, tied in place with satin bows and twine.

"A last word to you, Brian, old lump. This is what I came to say to you: Watch yourself. Both of you, listen. No one wants to hear about the old days. No one wants to hear about Earth, or the City of Gargoyles. No one at all wants to remember the Thusser. We don't want to hear about the Mannequin Resistance. We want to forget it all. That's doubtless why someone killed the Regent — if it wasn't your friend Mr. Dantsig. You're disturbing people. There are already whispers around the Court that you need to disappear. Yet you insist on talking about things that aren't good for you or good for any of us. So: Shut up, my friend, and live to whine another day. Keep up your clack, and find yourself poisoned or stabbed in the gut. See?"

With that, Lord Rafe "Chigger" Dainsplint tipped his top hat, bowed, and joined the crowd of courtiers that was following the funeral cart.

Brian and Gregory were pushed along. They were part of the procession, too, now. They followed along the main avenue, rose petals falling all around them. They could feel people point at them from windows and doorways, gawking at the human cubs. They felt thoughts of the citizens skitter across their minds, the psychic prefixes and suffixes of the throngs who watched the parade.

"You don't know Dantsig didn't do it," said Gregory.

"No." Brian looked miserable. "But I bet he didn't."

"He threatened the Regent. I heard him. He said he'd finish him."

"If we could only talk to Kalgrash. I bet he could explain."

119

"You saw Dantsig last night. Come on! He could have done it!"

"Do you really think so?"

"I don't know."

Brian thought about it. "Would he have agreed to go back to the prison if he'd just killed the Regent? No, I don't think he would have. He would have found some way around his programming. He would have worked out an excuse to escape."

"Maybe he couldn't."

"Maybe," said Brian, "Dantsig was framed. Maybe he was set up. I think that's what Lord Dainsplint believes."

"You mean, the real murderer arranged for Dantsig to get out of prison for the night wearing a uniform, just so he'd look guilty?"

"That's exactly what I mean," Brian said. "So right after this, we're going down to the prison. We're going to try to find out where Dantsig got that uniform. Because I bet that he didn't have to go far to find it. And I bet that whoever left it out for him to find was the real murderer."

The dancers in front of Gregory and Brian spun around and flung out their arms. The funeral throne with its corpse bobbed through muddy streets strewn with crushed flower petals and trampled snack wrappers. The procession passed between great hillocks of garbage, out into the white plains burning with heat, and at last to the tombs, where a choir stood ready to sing the Regent's requiem.

Brian and Gregory were no longer among them.

120

THIRTEEN

The captain of the guard at the prison spoke in a torrent. When Brian and Gregory presented themselves at the gate and said they wanted to see Kalgrash and Dantsig, the captain, lying on a bench, said, "You can see them, and I do mean *see* them, sure, but not talk to them, no, because they're all shut off and I shouldn't even be letting you in anyway, but, you know, I don't see it's no harm. I been letting people in all day for small change." He opened the gate and let the boys in. "Now listen, you can't go into the cell, because that's illegal, but I'll take you to the guardroom outside the cell and you can look in at them, but remember, these guys is, they're killers. You should've seen what they made of this place last night escaping, and now, whoo-boy, I tell you, now we know they're assassins sent by the Mannequin Resistance, whoo-boy, I look at them and I think, we are lucky they didn't do more mayhem when they were scraping their way out of the clink. They could've done a number on us — I mean, this one of them, he has teeth like something you'd gore a buffalo with — big number in fancy old armor — never seen a piece like him. The toffs up the palace, they told us keep a lid on the Mannequin Resistance angle, but that's an angle everybody's talking about, so we got crowds coming here before the funeral just to take in the bodies of these manns. I'll tell you, these guys're something else. Cold, hard killers. Come on this way. That's the cell in there."

Gregory looked around the round courtyard, the open guardrooms, the pits in the dirt. He couldn't believe it. The place was a dump.

He felt bad for Brian. Bri was clearly freaking, but trying to pretend he was in control.

Brian said, "So ... Did anyone come visit them yesterday? Did anyone come before the murder?"

"No, I mean, they wasn't news then, except it was kind of funny, they were expecting we'd release some of the other manns we got in captivity here in some kind of trade, but really, they're all turned off and their heads stacked up over in the shed. No way we were going to activate them again just so they could take up the banner again and rob people down in the Entrails or whatnot. The Regent handled that pretty good except that windup general declaring war against us, which we heard they done, and now who knows, because there aren't many of us willing to be guards and soldiers, though it's a calling and an honor, and we really do not want to have those manns surrounding the city because, for one thing, we don't got no moat or no towers or nothing like in the old days, when we had them things, and I don't

122

want to be standing there in this getup with a blunder-buss and all the manns who been living out in the Lower Extent of Pipes, fighting off antibodies with their bombs and pistols and crossbows and shurikens and suchlike."

They had reached the guardroom. Behind wooden slats, the marines who'd accompanied the boys in the sub were slowing down, not having been wound. They stumbled gradually about in their cell.

Behind another door, tied shut with rope, lay Dantsig and Kalgrash.

Gregory saw Brian look sharply away. Brian made a show of walking around the guard nook, examining the heating coil and its frayed wire, the table with its deck of cards and burnt saucepans and spoons and cheese-crumbled knives.

Brian said, "I heard that one of them — the one with the goatee — he wore a guard's uniform last night when he got into the palace."

"Yeah," said the captain of the guard. "Big, big stink there, I'll tell you. Big, big stink because, see, where'd the uniform come from, see? I mean, what I'm asking is, if it was one of us who didn't have on our uniform, then, you might ask, what were we wearing? For example, Talbot, who wasn't on duty yesterday, but who sometimes, he wants to stand in front of Nature in his altogether and let the wind play over him and remember simpler times. If it had been him standing stark naked with his arms spread under the dying light of the veins and dreaming of hunting antelope and spearing aurochs, wearing nothing but

123

the skin the gods painted him with back when mammoths roamed the Earth, if he'd been doing that while meanwhile these characters over here sneaked his uniform and it fit just right and then they went up the palace and offed the Regent, you can see there would be some difficult questions that would come to me as captain of the guard about who I hire and whether they ain't too nostalgic for days of savagery and yore." The captain sorted through some potato chips on the table and ate several. "But Talbot wasn't on duty and none of the rest of us, we don't go in much for stripping at work, so the palace is yelling, 'How did this joker get a uniform at your establishment?' and I'm, 'Didn't get one here — no way,' but, see, that one, his name's Dantsig, he told the Court magician who's investigating, Thoth-Chumley, that he just picked up the uniform off that bench there and it fit perfect, and chippy, choppy, la la la. So I gotta wonder, how did it get there?"

"Are you *sure*," asked Brian, "that there's no one who came yesterday who might have left it there?"

The captain of the guard thought about it hard. He ate some chips. He looked carefully at the bench and then at the deactivated prisoners lying on the floor of their cell. "Well," he said finally, "there was some guy down from the palace. He come down yesterday evening during the tea dance, says he has a message from the Imperial Council for the prisoners. We let him in and he came in here, and he could've left the uniform, folded it up on the bench, I guess. Say, yeah. He could've. But why? That's what I'm asking. Why?"

Brian pressed on. "Who sent him exactly?"

The captain shook his head. "No one exactly. He just says the Imperial Council. I mean, we would've needed a signed piece of paper if he wanted to go into the cell, but he just says he wants to talk to the prisoners, and there ain't no law against that. But I know he's on the straight and narrow. I know that. He's been up at the palace for years. I know him."

Gregory saw that Brian was distracted by something in the cell. He jumped in and asked the guard, "Do you remember the guy's name? The servant? Because he could tell us who sent him down. And what his message was."

The captain closed one eye. He squinched it up. He ate more potato chips. "Gwestin," he said, after chewing. "Lambert Gwestin. Nice guy, friendly, serves up at the palace. Been up there for years. Used to be a plantation owner out in the Sixth or Seventh Lung, but his estate deflated. Since then, he's been working at the Court and hoping for the big chance."

Gregory looked over at Brian. His friend was transfixed, as if it were Brian, and not Kalgrash, who'd been shut off. Brian stood at the slat door, looking into the dingy room.

Gregory went to his side.

Kalgrash lay there on the hard-packed dirt. He looked dead. In a sense, he was dead. His claws were half uncurled. His mouth sagged open, revealing his jagged, nail-like teeth, which usually stuck out when he gave his big, goofy grins.

By his side were scrapes where he and Dantsig had dug their fingers into the dry flesh of the floor to make

125

marbles. The marbles themselves lay near Kalgrash, a game disturbed.

Gregory saw that Brian's eyes were full of tears, and, staring at Brian's pale face, he hoped that there wouldn't be enough water to actually have the eyes overflow and make tracks down the cheeks, because then Brian would actually, literally be crying, and even though Gregory wanted to comfort his friend, crying weirded him out. As long as the tears just welled, Brian was still not crying, and Gregory didn't have to say anything.

Brian looked at the marbles. "He's so playful," said Brian. "Life's a big joke to him." Gregory watched the water tremble. He anxiously calculated: tears or no tears? No tears? Tears?

Trying to head off the crying, Gregory said, "Don't worry."

He couldn't say more, with the captain of the guards looking on.

But he lost his own bet, and as Brian rested his hand on the rough wood of the slats, the tears fell, just a few, into the muck at their feet.

✳ ✳ ✳

They could not find Lambert Gwestin in the palace. Almost no one was there — everyone was out enjoying the parade and the requiem mass.

Having walked the empty chambers and corridors for fifteen minutes or so, they came back out into the harsh light of the piazza. Courtiers were starting to return, chatting comfortably, hailing their neighbors. Three of the blue-painted boys still played soccer with the wooden head, though the parade was over.

Gregory looked around the square. "What do we do now? Since we can't find Lambert Gwestin?"

"I've been thinking . . . we should find out where the guards' uniforms are stored. And see if anyone from Court asked for one yesterday."

"Good idea," said Gregory, touching his nose.

The boys talked to the soldiers who stood by the giant front gate, and they were directed toward a guardhouse on the side of the square. As they crossed over to the door, the boys ran into the Earl of Munderplast. He walked arm in arm with his wife, who wore a long lace veil. The earl himself was dressed in black satin robes.

"Hello, sir," said Gregory.

"Ah! The humans," said the earl. "You have missed a most edifying burial. I do so love a sung requiem. It always calls to mind the sorrowful fact that one day, it shall be I who am laid in the tomb under the stone, when I have reached the end of my years, or when this dear one," he said, raising his wife's thin hand to his lips, "succeeds in poisoning my salad."

"Nonsense, Mundy," said his wife. "I won't hear such talk." She gazed away at the rooftops, and murmured, "You never eat salad."

Gregory said, "Sir, we're looking for a palace servant named Lambert Gwestin. Do you happen to know where he is?"

The earl looked at Gregory, astonished. "I certainly do not," he said. "I don't keep track of the to-ings and fro-ings of palace servants and housecarls. How do you expect me to know them by name?"

"Especially," said his wife, "when they all insist on being called by different ones."

"Precisely, my darling. Your Gwestin is doubtless out enjoying some robust and merry fest or funeral barbecue."

Gregory was surprised when Brian suddenly asked, "Sir, where were you when the murder happened? At midnight?"

The earl fixed him with a look. "That," he said, "is an impertinent question. I was with my darling wife, tucked away in our bed, clipped close in her arms as we slept the sleep *of the innocent*."

"Were you?" mused Lady Munderplast. "Yes, I suppose you must have been."

"I didn't mean . . ." said Brian awkwardly. "I just meant, where were you when you heard the news?"

"The news? I heard it not until this morning. Because the tragical corpse was not discovered until dawn. I would dearly love to dally, parleying with you about the high deeds and noble doings of the servant class and standing by while you accuse me of treason in a high, piping voice, but I am afraid we must progress to the funeral dinner and darts."

He and Lady Munderplast bowed and walked on.

As soon as they were out of earshot, Gregory said, "He wasn't home. You could tell it. She wanted us to know."

"I wonder if she really hates him," said Brian. "Maybe she was just trying to make us suspicious." Brian wrapped his thumb absently in the hem of his sweatshirt, then unwrapped it. "He talked about the Regent dying last night, when we met him. He could have known about a plot."

"Or he might just have hated the Regent like everyone else. Who knows?" Gregory jerked his head in the direction of the guardhouse. "Let's go check out the uniforms."

The assistant quartermaster of the palace guards sat behind a tall desk, reading a copy of the *Norumbega Vassal-Tribune*.

Gregory snapped on a winning smile and leaned across the desk. "We're on a mission. The Imperial Council — someone up there — they've asked us to make a few discreet inquiries. Would you mind answering a couple of questions?"

The man looked up. He did not speak. He was thin, and his pointed ears were tremendous.

"Great," said Gregory. "Thanks. Number one: Did anyone requisition a guard's uniform yesterday?"

The man shook his head.

"Okay. Thanks. You're golden. . . . Steal?"

"Steal?"

"Did anyone? Steal a uniform?"

The man shook his head. "No," he answered.

"Counted?"

"We've counted."

"And?"

The assistant quartermaster shrugged.

"Thanks," said Gregory. "You're —"

"Two. Not one. They stole two." He held up two spidery, thick-joined fingers.

"When?"

"Yesterday."

"When yesterday?"

The assistant quartermaster shrugged.

"Morning? Afternoon? Evening?"

"Afternoon."

"How do you know?"

"We counted."

"When?"

"This morning. When we heard."

"Heard what?"

"About the mannequin."

"Yesterday, did anyone come by?"

"Anyone?"

"Courtiers. Did any courtier come by?"

"No."

"No noblemen?"

"No."

"Servants?"

"Servants?"

"For example, a servant named Lambert Gwestin."

"I know Lambert."

"Huzzah."

"Lambert Gwestin didn't come by."

"Other servants?"

"None. Or nobles."

"Hmm."

". . . I think."

"You think?"

"We were betting on a bear race."

"All of you?"

"Out back."

Brian said, "There are bears?"

The assistant quartermaster pointed back into the dark recesses behind him. There was a huge, stuffed grizzly there, its fur falling off with age. It had, presumably, been hauled all the way from Earth.

"It's stuffed," said Gregory.

The assistant quartermaster nodded.

"You were all betting on a stuffed bear."

"Pulled with rope."

"Ah."

"Two."

"Two stuffed bears."

"Correct."

"So no one was really watching the guardhouse, at that point."

"No."

"You were all . . ."

"Out back."

"For how long?"

The assistant quartermaster shrugged. "No one really wants to be a guard," he said. "No glamour. Low pay."

"I see."

"I want to be on the radio."

"That's a beautiful dream."

"So anyone," said Brian, "could have come in and taken two uniforms yesterday afternoon?"

"Yes."

"Anyone," said Gregory.

"Yes."

"Lambert Gwestin could have been here?"

The assistant quartermaster shrugged. "We like to play games and have fun. It lightens up the day."

"Thank you for telling us," said Gregory.

"You're going to tell the Council, aren't you?" said the assistant quartermaster. "And then I'll be executed."

"We won't," Brian rushed to reassure him. "We won't tell anyone."

"Why don't people just do their jobs?" said Gregory. "Then everyone around here wouldn't be worried about whether they were out back betting on stuffed bears or standing with their arms spread in the prison courtyard, buck naked."

"Oh, Talbot."

"Talbot?"

"Buck naked. He dreams of the veldt."

"Sure," said Gregory. "The veldt."

He and Brian thanked the assistant quartermaster and left. They didn't think he would have anything else very useful to tell them.

✳ ✳ ✳

"So there were *two* uniforms stolen," said Brian. "That proves what I was saying."

132

"What were you saying?" asked Gregory.

They were sitting in the Grand Hall at a long trestle table. Courtiers sat all around them, talking and laughing. Servants brought small, parched roasts and straggly grilled vegetables on platters.

"Why would someone steal two?" Brian asked. "Because they want to leave one where Dantsig will find it. They know he'll put it on so he can slip out of the prison. And then they can bet that someone will see Dantsig and remember him in that uniform. And that he'll be blamed for the assassination. Meanwhile, the assassin wears the other uniform."

"But wouldn't he or she be recognizable?"

Brian thought about this. "I guess. Unless somehow the assassin was disguised. With a fake goatee or something."

"A fake goatee?" Gregory raised an eyebrow.

At this point, a servant arrived with two sorry-looking hamburgers on a platter. The buns were huge and there was ketchup everywhere. "Compliments of the Imperial Council," said the servant. "The cooks have whipped up some delicacies from your homeland."

"Thank you!" said Gregory. The servant bowed and walked away.

"All the killer needs is just enough evidence to raise strong suspicions about Dantsig," said Brian. "They know that Dantsig won't get a fair trial, because he's a mannequin. No one will ever stop to ask if there was someone *else* sneaking around in a guard's uniform yesterday at midnight."

133

"How did they know Dantsig would willingly go back to the prison after breaking out?"

"Maybe they didn't," said Brian. "They probably thought he wouldn't. Maybe they thought he'd escape into the desert. Then it would look even *more* like he was guilty." Brian brought his hamburger up to his mouth. He didn't see the glint of metal or the hint of motion twitching the bun.

"So both Lord Dainsplint and the Earl of Munderplast threatened the Regent with death last night, or talked about how he was going to die."

"But so did Dantsig, when he was captured."

Brian nodded, about to bite. He paused, thoughtfully. Something in the burger crawled closer to his mouth.

"Hey," said Gregory. "There's Gwynyfer!" He waved. "Come on over!" he called. "Sit with us!"

She smiled and waved back. She came over, slipping her purse down from her shoulder into her hand. "Hi ho."

"Gregory and Brian," said Gregory, pointing. "Remember?"

She laughed. "Of course I remember. You're celebrities."

"We're humble, though. Movingly humble. Hey, great dance today."

"Oh!" exclaimed Gwynyfer, rolling her eyes. "Too exhausting. My feet . . ."

Brian went to take a bite.

And his hamburger attacked.

There was meat — a small disc of meat — but also

134

a kind of a spinning top with blades — a tiny metal octopus — flailing at his lips, trying to hack at his face.

He screamed and flung the burger.

It hit the floor, and the razor puck skittered toward him.

He raised a leg. The puck hacked at the other. It began to crawl up his pants, slicing.

He screamed. The blades dug deep.

Gwynyfer made a guttural grunt of disgust and whacked at the device with a ladle. The iron octopus tumbled. Landed on the ground. Slid. Skittered back toward Brian, slicing at the air.

Brian leaped up onto the bench.

People were screaming all around.

The thing bobbed and tried to jump to attack.

Brian wobbled where he stood. His leg was bleeding through his pants.

He fell heavily. He had the air knocked out of him. He couldn't breathe. He struggled to move his arms. He fought to regain his breath.

The thing was all over him, running toward his face, his head, his ears, his eyes, his screaming mouth.

And then someone kicked it off his chest — stepped on it.

The servant who'd served the burger. He ground the deadly toy with his heel until bladed tentacles and springs popped free. Its engines squealed. The servant kept squashing.

Finally, it was still.

The servant reached his hand down to help Brian up.

"The staff extends its apologies, sir," he said.

"What . . . what was that?"

"It was not on the menu, sir. I have no idea."

Brian couldn't stand on the one leg. It was red with slashes. He held it suspended.

"Thank you," he said. "You saved me."

The servant nodded. "At your service, sir." He bowed.

Brian sat heavily. "Thanks," he said again. "I'm Brian."

"I'm Mr. Gwestin," the servant said. "Lambert Gwestin."

FOURTEEN

The Norumbega Vassal-Tribune

SERVING THE INNARDS SINCE 1282

IMPERIAL COUNCIL SEEKS NEW REGENT
WHILE NATION MOURNS

NEW NORUMBEGA — Even while the citizens of the capital gather in the streets to watch the funeral procession for the late Duke Telliol-Bornwythe, the Imperial Council has met to discuss who shall take his place as Regent to His Imperial Majesty, the Stub.

The new Regent will rule the nation in the Emperor's name until the Stub, now almost a year and a half old, is of an age to take up the scepter himself. All Norumbegans of noble birth and noble creation are eligible to vote for one of the nominees.

There are, at present, two leading candidates for the position of Regent. The late Regent's own party, the Norumbegan Social

Club, has put forward Lord Rafe "Chigger" Dainsplint as their representative.

"It would be a great honor to serve," says Dainsplint, "and all that." His lordship, in a conversation this morning, pledged to return his party to the values that it has held as sacred for centuries: "Frequent galas, some heels-ups, chortling. We all need to worry about *less*, not more. It's your duty to celebrate. Put on your red slippers, get into waltz position, and think of the Empire."

Lord Dainsplint's call to celebration is in stark contrast to the announcement of the late Regent last night that the Empire was considering war on two fronts: a war of defense against the Mannequin Resistance and an invasion of Thusser territory on Earth. It appears Lord Dainsplint would reverse this policy and shelve the assault on Thusser positions. "Old Norumbega?" says Dainsplint. "People can hardly remember what the place was like. I wasn't born yet. Wasn't it dark? I seem to remember my mother saying it was dark."

The Norumbegan Social Club is currently the favored party in the Imperial Council. If Lord Dainsplint is elected, it is expected that the Social Club will hold a seven to four majority in the council chamber.

The other leading candidate for the Regency will be the Earl of Munderplast, president of the opposition Melancholy Party. In an interview this morning, he pledged to continue his party's commitment to mourning all that is lost and shattered, to weeping among the ruins. "There is plenty in this terrible time to lament about," says the earl. "Plenty ghastly and full fell. At our height, in the days of the first Empress Qui, no automaton would have dared raise his hand against his master. In those years, we had never even heard of the Thusser Horde. Doleful, doleful days these are."

The election of one of the candidates will be held on Tuesday the 36th, the day before the annual Fest of St. Diancecht.

The Court has already begun planning the Inauguration Ball. Speaking recently at a press conference, the Dancemaster General has proclaimed

MANNEQUIN RESISTANCE ADVANCES ON CAPITAL, CAPTURES OUTPOSTS IN UPPER GUT

OUTER THROATS — Word has reached the capital that the Mannequin Resistance may be making significant gains in their march on New Norumbega. Emergency telegrams received this morning reveal that several fortresses, estates, and townships in the Upper Gut have been taken by automaton forces.

The first telegram arrived shortly after 6:00 A.M. this morning from the parish of Windham-on-Gag, located low in one of the Outer Throats. "OVERWHELMED BY FORCE OF MANNS," reads the telegram. "ALL HANDS IMPRISONED. GENERAL MALARK SENDS GREETINGS."

It appears that the automaton army must have originated in Three-Gut, most likely at the mannequin fortress of Pflundt. Late last night they apparently forced their way from Three-Gut into Bronson's Gullet by way of a hiatal hernia, pausing there to fight and defeat a small force of knights in the region before continuing toward St. Eustace and the Duchy of Burnborough. It is estimated that they could reach New Norumbega within two or three days.

In the absence of a regent, no precautions are being taken to repel the invaders.

FIFTEEN

Lambert Gwestin," said Brian. "We've been looking everywhere for you."

"I express the deepest regret that I wasn't available when you sought me, sir," said Mr. Gwestin. "I was at a mourning barbecue down in the city."

The courtiers in the room were aghast. Many had risen in horror as the gadget attacked. They were whispering in small groups, expressing sympathy for the Earth child. Gugs was expressing his disappointment that he hadn't known about the attempt to assassinate the child beforehand, since by all rights, someone should have taken bets as to whether the little machine or the boy would survive.

Lambert Gwestin ordered one of the other servants to fetch Brian water.

Gregory said to him, "We have about a thousand questions for you."

"I will be most delighted to prove of service, sir, once your friend has been fully revived."

Brian took a deep gulp of water. He sat himself carefully on the bench. With the toe of his sneaker, he prodded the wreckage of the little infernal device.

Gwynyfer said, "You're bleeding badly."

"I know," said Brian.

"All over the floor." She made a face. She was exchanging glances with some girls across the dining hall.

Others by the long tables were sitting again. Many, however, didn't seem to have much appetite.

Lambert Gwestin asked Brian, "Now, sir, that you have caught your breath: How may I be of use?"

"First of all," said Brian, "who gave you these hamburgers?"

"A drone. They bring the platters up from the kitchen."

"Did you notice anything strange about my burger?"

"No, sir. I am sorry, but I didn't inspect them. I simply read the note from the cook and delivered them."

Gregory said, "So we have to figure out who gave the order to the cooks."

"I doubt, sir, if I may be so bold, that you will find any record of a request to insert a bladed engine in your food. None of our cooks would have included such an item in your dinner without question, unless it were specifically called for in the recipe. Am I right to understand that the hamburger does not, in its native land, come with a small, murderous machine?"

"No," said Brian.

"Except when you buy a Happy Meal," said Gregory.

Brian speculated, "Could someone have stopped the

141

drone on the way from the kitchen to the Grand Hall and slipped that thing into the burger then?"

Lambert Gwestin thought this over. "That would be possible, sir. The machine may have been introduced into your dinner at that point."

"Can we check with the drones?"

"I regret that is an impossibility, sir. The drones are equipped neither with memory nor with the power of communication. Furthermore, they do not distinguish between people. Even if we could identify which drone carried the supper, it would not be able to recognize who stopped it to deliver the device."

"So all we can say is that someone tried to kill me, and probably was between the kitchen and this room about four or five minutes ago."

"That is correct, sir. On behalf of the palace staff, may I express my utmost mortification at the incident. It is our most ardent wish that this incident should not reflect poorly upon the generosity and magnanimity of our noble leader" — here Gwestin bowed reverently — "the Emperor, the divine Stub, may the saints protect him always; may he taper ever longer." Gwestin folded his hands in front of him. "The oversight was ours, and it is we who should be flogged, if flogging is required."

"Thanks," said Gregory, "but we'll pass on flogging. But there's something else you can help us with."

"Whatever way I may be of assistance, sir."

"Yesterday," said Brian, "you received orders to take a uniform down to the prison and —"

"Hello, chaps," said Chigger Dainsplint, appearing at

142

their side. "Heard you had a bit of a row with your supper, Bri-Bri. None the worse for wear, I hope? I say, you do look a little perforated."

"There was something in my food," said Brian. "It cut me."

"Well, man versus supper. I suppose the tables had to turn sometime." Dainsplint snapped his fingers and another servant ran over. "Take young Master Thatz up to the chirurgeon. See that his leg is fixed up. And you," he said to Lambert Gwestin, "I want to hear everything that happened."

"Could we," said Brian, who was being pried away from the bench, "could we ask Mr. Gwestin one more question?"

"Certainly not. You've been carved up like a Christmas roast. Hobble on, Earth boy. Go see the apothecary."

"It's quick," said Brian.

"Away with you."

"I can ask the question," said Gregory. "Mr. Gwestin, we were wondering —"

Lord Dainsplint said, "The children can speak to you later, Mr. Gwestin. For the moment, the Imperial Council will want a full report. These children have ambassadorial status in the capital, and we need to find out who is responsible for this outrage. Come, come. Walk."

With that, Brian, Gregory, and Gwynyfer watched the servant and the lord walk off together.

Gwestin was saying, "I am most heartily sorry, my lord, and I trust that this will not reflect poorly on his

143

Imperial Majesty, the Stub, our hope and hero, long may he —"

Then a door slammed behind them.

"Too bad," said Gregory. "Just when we were all getting along so well."

✳ ✳ ✳

The "chirurgeon," as it turned out, was a doctor. His name was Dr. Brundish. He lived up in a wooden turret, surrounded by gadgetry and jars of leeches in different sizes and colors. He himself was a large, lumpy sort of man in goggles and a skullcap. It was a little hard to figure out his body, which seemed, beneath its robes, to have foothills and ranges leading back from his shoulders and down from his neck.

"A scrape," he said, looking at Brian's leg. "A scrape, a scrape. You were in a scrape. With a miserable little device."

Gregory and Gwynyfer hung back, smirking at each other.

"The leeches," said Dr. Brundish, "will clean the wounds." He pulled some out of a pickling jar and applied them to Brian's ankle. "They'll suck out poisons."

Brian looked away from the leg as he felt the creatures hunch along toward his cuts, seeking gore.

"Then we'll put on some bandages and you will be right as rain." Dr. Brundish smiled with huge, yellow teeth. "Please," he said to Gregory, "do not play with that. It is not a toy."

Gregory had on a stethoscope, and was snaking it toward Gwynyfer. "I can't hear you," he said to the doctor. And to her: "So do Norumbegans have hearts?"

"Put that down," said the doctor.

Gregory protested, "I'm asking a scientific question."

Gwynyfer thwacked the chest piece with her finger. Gregory jumped — she laughed.

Gregory pulled the ear tips out and put the stethoscope down on the desk. Rubbing his ears, he concluded, "Ouch. Heartless."

"Oh?" said Gwynyfer. "Better than brainless."

There was a knock on the door. Dr. Brundish grunted, "In," and the door opened. Lady Munderplast, wife of the earl, stood there. She still wore her black suit, but she'd pulled her veil back and settled it around her shoulders.

When she saw who was there, she first inclined her head to Gwynyfer. "Miss Gwarnmore," she said. "Lady Munderplast extends her greetings."

Gwynyfer made a formal curtsy back. "The daughter of Duke Gwarnmore greets Lady Munderplast and wishes her many dawns."

"Mr. Thatz. Mr. Stoffle. We met before dinner. I am Lady Munderplast." To Brian, she said without any hint of compassion, pity, or interest, "I was so sorry to see you attacked just now. Impudent, impudent supper."

"Thank you, ma'am," said Brian.

"You needn't take it personally. Better men have eaten worse." She looked around the dark, yellowish chamber, at its syringes and devices. "I have no wish to delay you, but a word . . ."

145

The doctor rose from his stool. "Do you wish, milady, for me to absent myself from the chamber so you may speak to the little ape?"

"It is but three sentences. If you would stand outside the door, I would be gratified."

The doctor shambled out of the room, bowing. Lady Munderplast waited by the open door, staring at Gwynyfer.

Eventually, the girl said, "The daughter of Duke Gwarnmore inquires if it is Lady Munderplast's wish that I also should remain in the chamber for this communication, so that I may assist the noble Lady Munderplast, who is dear to my heart and a constant model for a young lady just entering the vexing labyrinth of the Court."

Lady Munderplast fixed Gwynyfer with a glare. "Lady Munderplast thanks the daughter of Duke Gwarnmore for her solicitous care for our aged person, but we do not require that Miss Gwarnmore should stay behind and listen in. Nonetheless, we thank her for her kind offer to drink in our gossip and spew it right back out to her gaggle of knock-kneed, stick-legged debutantes."

Gwynyfer, looking irritated, bowed and stepped out.

Lady Munderplast closed the door behind her, waited a moment, and in a move not unlike Gwynyfer's of a few minutes before, thumped hard enough on the door-panel that the girl and the doctor, who were both listening on the other side, dimly apologized and stepped away.

Lady Munderplast faced Brian. "What I have to say is this: My husband, the earl, lied to you. He was not at home last night. I left him at the dance at around ten, when I

146

could no longer abide his dismal pronouncements on the calisthenics and gyrations of the young. My maids undressed me and laid me in my tube shortly thereafter. I was awakened at about one o'clock by the return of my dear spouse from locations unknown. That is roughly three hours unaccounted for. I clarify that because I have no idea whether you creatures are capable of doing sums."

"Where do you think he went?" Brian asked.

"I do not know. It is not the first time he has lurked abroad in the night. Perhaps he wishes to frequent cheap saloons or shoot skeet in the dark. The ways of my husband are mysterious, yet dull. Never has the unknown provoked so little interest."

Brian asked, "Do you know whether the earl was angry at what the Regent announced last night he was going to do? Going to war against the Thusser and reclaiming Norumbega? And starting a war with the Mannequin Resistance by arresting Dantsig and the rest?"

"My husband thought all of it was foolishness. But he also told me he did not know whether the Regent meant what he said in the throne room. Munderplast suspects that the Regent was simply announcing those things because he knew they'd be passed on to others unknown. Perhaps the Regent merely wished the mannequins or the Thusser to *believe* he had determined to return to Earth and seize Old Norumbega. Do you see? He spoke of warfare because he knew such a threat would reach the ears of his enemies. Both the late Regent and my husband have long presumed that there is a spy on the Imperial Council, and, of course, most people suspect that the two of you are spies as well."

"Us?" said Brian, shocked.

"You, indeed."

Gregory said, "Do you think I'd be standing here, ma'am, if I had a submarine car?"

"Well, the rumor at the Court is that you are spies for the Mannequin Resistance. One simply can't know. One would read your thoughts, but as one attempts it, one cannot penetrate particularly deeply. I wonder why. Have you thrown up some kind of impenetrable mind-shield? No, I suspect not. It is (probably) like trying to dive for pearls in a mud puddle." She frowned. "At all events, I thought you would wish to know that Munderplast was not accounted for last night. And if my husband is involved in any skulduggery, I have no objection to you making it public. It will enliven our domestic life."

She swung the infirmary door open.

Dr. Brundish was sitting in a chair on his landing — which he used as a waiting room — reading a Norumbegan magazine called *Glamour* (UNHAPPY WITH YOUR SKIN? GET RID OF IT! BELINDY DRUNCHFYST SPILLS THE BEANS ON LIFE, LOVE, AND HER NEW INVISIBLE BEAU! 25 PLACES IN THE GLANDS YOU'VE NEVER BEEN — BUT NEED TO GO!). Gwynyfer Gwarnmore was leaning against the far wall with her arms crossed, frowning. The doctor closed his magazine.

"Milady Munderplast has finished with her revelations?" he snarfled, bobbing his head low.

"Your Lady Munderplast," said Lady Munderplast, "will not finish with her revelations until long after she is laid in the tomb." She pulled her veil back over her face, nodded to Gwynyfer — who curtsied back — and strode off.

The doctor bustled back into his office, followed by Gwynyfer, who walked in with an air of gorgeous fury. Dr. Brundish closed the door behind them. "What a fine lady, Lady Munderplast," he said. "A fine, fine figure of a woman." He paused and looked romantically at the eaves.

It took him some time before he recalled that Brian was being sucked dry by leeches.

SIXTEEN

That evening, Brian lay in bed, miserable and scared.

As he had hobbled back to his room, supported on one side by Gregory and on the other by Gwynyfer, they had wandered through a vague kind of game in the Grand Hall: The members of the Norumbegan Social Club, dressed in black tie, were squealing with pleasure and rolling an old truck tire across the room, trying to not hit two ranks of robotic drones, which had been instructed to trudge slowly back and forth in opposite directions, holding out their arms like Egyptians.

The tire came soaring toward the three kids, and Gregory had chuckled, whooped, and jumped out of the way. But Brian, of course, couldn't jump. It had hit him and he'd fallen down.

He was not hurt. His glasses had fallen off. He could tell the men of the Social Club were laughing secretly.

"All clear, old thing?" said Lord Dainsplint. "Terribly sorry."

"No problem," said Gregory. "Good shot."

Gwynyfer helped Brian to his feet. Brian carefully replaced his glasses on his nose. He was ashamed. He winced as he stood.

They began to roll the tire between the drones again.

A farmer in a tunic was standing at the end of the room, pleading, "Can I have my tire back now, your lordships? Yes, very funny. Very funny, my lord. Now can I have my tire back? Please?"

"I don't have it, old thing," said Lord Dainsplint, rolling it to the next man. "The Chancellor of the Exchequer has it."

The Chancellor of the Exchequer rolled it to the next man. "I don't have it, either, my good sir," he said. "I believe it's in the possession of His Excellency the Lord High Castellan."

"My cart," said the man, "can't go with only the one wheel."

Brian felt a rush of hatred for them all — the whole Court of New Norumbega — all of them playing their stupid games that decided the fates of families and nations.

"You okay?" Gregory asked.

Brian nodded. "Just — let's go back to our room. You can leave me there. I don't want to walk around any more tonight."

"If that's okay," said Gregory. "I mean, me just leaving you."

And Brian had been even more upset to notice how eager Gregory was to get rid of him. He could tell that

151

Gregory was embarrassed for Brian, that Gregory wanted to get Brian out of the way so that he, too, could try to be as witty and as playful as these men in their tuxedos, with servants at their command.

And so Brian lay in bed in their room, exhausted almost to the point of tears, thinking of Kalgrash — kind, friendly Kalgrash — lying there inert, shut off, in the prison down the hill, his claws half unfurled. Brian thought of all the times people had insulted him that day, called him stupid or ape, and it just made him tired. He didn't want to have to make deals with these people and beg for information. He thought of his parents, round and cracking jokes, sitting down at dinner (spaghetti), how horrified they would be to hear what was said about him, how they'd put an arm around him and tell him he was wonderful, not to give up. They'd tell him how much they loved him.

It meant nothing, Brian felt with a hollow ache. What did it matter what his parents thought of him or said? They were in another world, and he was stranded here. He couldn't see them. He couldn't protect them. They wouldn't know what hit them when the Thusser appeared. Who knew how much time had passed back in Boston? Months, maybe. They could already be part of a Thusser settlement. They might be protruding out of their walls, eyes empty, while Thusser men planned further horrors at their table, or some young Thusser couple, back from the kill, kissed on their bed in front of them.

Brian could not believe that the fate of his parents, of Gregory's, of everyone he knew lay in the manicured hands of these elfin idiots, these ditsy pranksters giggling in their ruins beyond the end of time.

He curled up in his bed. In an hour or so, he'd have to get up and put some kind of magic unguent on his leg. The pain sprang through him.

He crushed his head down into his pillow. Outside, he heard the cheers as some vapid game was won.

He tried to sleep.

✳ ✳ ✳

The night was warm. The veins had gone dark an hour before, but heat still rose off the granules of the desert.

Gregory and Gwynyfer strolled on a balcony that ran most of the way around the palace. They looked out over the huts and alleys of the city. Smoke rose from bonfires. Far, far out in the dark plains of the Dry Heart, the lights of small villages shone, and perhaps a caravan traveling into the capital with goods from some distant ventricle or aorta.

"There is a cluster of hearts," said Gwynyfer. "Like a bouquet."

Gregory asked, "Where's the blood?"

"There's some growth — it's weedy; the Wildwood, we call it — that blocks up the valves. That's one of the reasons some people think that the Great Body is dead." She leaned on the railing. She looked up at the ceiling of muscle far up in the darkness. She said, "Maybe it's been dead since before I was born. The last time there was a pulse in the veins of flux was years and years ago. But who knows?

153

We just call these organs hearts because they seem like hearts to us. Maybe they aren't at all. Maybe the Wildwood is actually part of them. I don't know."

Gregory stood by her side and looked up with her at the unmoving heart. The soft night air blew past them. He couldn't help notice how close her arm was. It was an incredible arm. It had a dimple at the elbow. Gregory found himself wishing that he could take Gwynyfer to school with him, show the others how they laughed together.

"It's sweet," she said, "that you and your friend want to find out who really killed the Regent. It's not very Norumbegan to care."

"You know, we do what we can to help."

She smiled. "How ducky for us."

He wagged his finger. "You don't believe we can figure it out, do you?"

"It would be fun if you did."

"Fun?"

"Nifty."

"Well, Brian's pretty smart. And I happen to be pretty charming."

"Are you?"

"Sure."

"Let's see proof."

"I can burp 'Do Your Ears Hang Low.'"

She rolled her eyes and murmured, "You and the Minister of the Interior."

Gregory pointed out, "You must care about the murder. You're helping us solve it."

Gwynyfer shrugged. "It's a lark. You can't know how dull the Court often is. Curtsying. Walking in processions. Waiting on the Stub. Who sweats, by the by. It's a bit thrilling to have two humans here who actually *care* about a thing. And the murder, of course — the delicious, chill-making murder."

She smiled at Gregory, and he could see pleasure in her smile.

"You're not like other girls," he said. He figured women always liked flattery, and in this case, what he said was true, anyway. Other girls didn't have pointed ears. "I wish I could introduce you to people at school. They'd be amazed."

"That would be lovely. Would they ask me what songs I can burp?"

Gregory countered with polite sarcasm: "Oh, sorry, madame. Please, tell me, what's the Globular Colon like?"

She laughed. "Actually, it's lovely in the spring, when it's green."

"Do you have a castle there? On your estate?"

She looked at him quite carefully. From inside, there came a crash as the radial tire knocked down a drone.

Gwynyfer said, "My parents describe it to people as a castle, but it's a shack of four rooms. That's how most of the Court lives when they're away from the palace." She gave him a look of defiant shyness and said, "Everyone boasts about their estates and hopes no one else ever visits. We all have shameful secrets to hide." She crossed her arms. "But who wants to take the time to *build* something? Who will *do* it for us? Too, too weary-making.

155

"That," she said, "is why it's so outrageous that the mannequins have left us, all but a very few. We need them."

"You deserve a castle," said Gregory. "Someone should build one for you. You look like a princess."

She turned and smiled at him.

They were very close to each other.

Gregory was suddenly aware that their arms were touching. He really wanted to kiss her.

But he didn't dare.

So they stood there, side by side, almost kissing, feeling warmth trickle from arm to arm, drunk on the balmy night, the hot, bracing scent of burning plastic, and the sweet, enfolding darkness of the Dry Heart.

❋ ❋ ❋

And down below them, at the base of the palace's keep, a servant's door opened and Lord Rafe "Chigger" Dainsplint slipped out, wearing a cloak with a hood. He scurried down the steps and skirted the edge of the square.

Through the night city he walked, while boys ran past with torches and striped beasts rifled through garbage heaps. Through windows, old boom boxes played the fragmented dance tunes of Norumbega, blaring through tinny speakers to courtyards filled with shrieking families.

Toward the edge of the city, things were quieter. The silence of the granular desert hung heavy in the air.

The night was cooler. Occasionally, someone stirred in a shack. Dainsplint picked his way along narrow passages between houses. He stepped over sleeping men.

Finally, he reached a turquoise hut. He looked one way and then the other. He opened the door and slipped in.

He closed the door behind him.

"I fear," he said to the person he found there, "that I've made rather a mistake."

The person he met blew out the single candle.

Then everything was dark.

SEVENTEEN

In the streets of the Thusser suburb at the foot of Norumbega Mountain, time ran quickly, and houses billowed and wobbled as they became less like human dwellings and more like the pulpy nests of Thusser settlers with dark-ringed eyes who arrived every day with their suitcases filled with devices that resembled broken glass.

Beneath that suburb, in the City of Gargoyles, the old stone houses and domes and obelisks and arches sprouted luxury pods, more like plant bladders than anything built by human hands. These were the condominiums of the Thusser Horde.

Through the dim streets, lit by the bellies of the fungus-like condos, the Thusser shuffled, whispering and passing blackly in crowds through the avenues.

In a vault beneath that city, beneath the cathedral that overlooked those flinty streets, in the midst of the Thusser settlement, a human woman and an old Norumbegan man sat trapped and weakened.

Prudence was slumped near the blank portal. Around her were scattered plastic bags once filled with lunch meats. She and Wee Sniggleping had been sitting in this chamber for weeks. They could no longer leave to fetch food. The Thusser were too thick on the streets up above them. Days passed with nothing to do but read the old issues of *People* and *Teen Vogue* they'd bought back when they'd been slipping out regularly to the Halt'N'Buy.

They were out of food. Prudence had been suffering from a headache for several days. They were out of water. They'd had to use the mausoleum of former emperors for a toilet. The stench crept in over the stone sill.

For the past day, neither Prudence nor Sniggleping had moved much.

For two weeks, they had not seen any light but the light of the lantern. Its magical charge grew weak. Staring directly at its twist of burning wire, Prudence could almost imagine that it was not light that came from it, but just another kind of shadow. Spots clotted the room. When she held her breath, they pulsed.

It had been some hours since she and Sniggleping had spoken. He was doing better than her, still sitting upright, watching her with concern.

She rolled her head toward him and said, "They're not coming, are they? They've gotten lost or killed."

"Or time," said Sniggleping, "is moving so slowly on the other side of the portal that only a few seconds have passed for them since they went through." He shook his head. "We don't know."

"We have to go through. We can't stay here."

"Remember," said Sniggleping, "that we don't know that we can get back without someone here to receive us. To open the gate from this end."

"We can't stay here," Prudence repeated. "The Thusser are going to find us." She put her hands on her head. Her hair was a scraggly mess. "I can hear them," she said. "They're up in the cathedral. They must be using it for something."

"You may hear them," said Sniggleping. "Or that may be your panic clanking. It may be your fear murmuring, my darling."

They fell silent, then, for a long time. They stared into the darkness of the chamber, at the plastic bags of trash, all that remained of their supply runs earlier in the month.

After an hour, Prudence became convinced she saw faces watching her from the darkness. They were glowering and pale. She wondered offhand, half dreaming, if they would leave if she sang. They did not move, however. The lamp grew dimmer. Prudence stared at the faces and they stared frankly back.

For a while, Prudence closed her eyes. When she opened them, the shadows were deeper, and the faces were more present than ever.

Sniggleping saw them, too, but he did not want to speak. He thought that by acknowledging them, he'd invite them to become solid sooner.

The faces watched the two who sat in the circle of light. They ringed them.

Gradually, Prudence saw bodies also. They wore black wool overcoats. Their hands were very white. The faces still glared at her.

Sniggleping remained silent. He did not want the final catastrophe to begin. He wanted a few last minutes before the awful things happened.

But Prudence did speak. "They've arrived," she said, and she meant the Thusser. Sniggleping dared to look at her. To nod.

"Yes," one of them agreed. "We are here."

Sniggleping waved his hand vaguely in the air. "I didn't hear you come in," he said.

"You were thinking of something else."

The figures walked forward, and they were solid, gathered around Prudence and Snig, thin and dangerous as knives.

One of the Thusser said, "You sent agents through the portal."

"Did we?" said Sniggleping.

"You did. We have ears in the Court of New Norumbega. We have kept ourselves informed."

Prudence concluded triumphantly, "So the boys've reached the Court. They're not dead."

"Yet," agreed a Thusser.

"You are, of course, under arrest," said another. "You destroyed our operative in this world, the vehicle Deatley. You have attempted to invoke the Rules."

"It's only fair," said Prudence. "You're breaking the Rules."

"Fair," said the Thusser, "is what the powerful do, and the story they tell about it afterward."

With that, the Thusser closed in on the two who sagged by lamplight.

Prudence coughed and gagged, feeling the wet hands clamped over her mouth, fastened on her wrist, dragging at her legs. She kicked and bucked. She screamed Sniggleping's name. He called for her. The Thusser lifted her and carried her toward the archway into the crypt. She twisted and managed to hang free long enough to bump up steps. She was half heaved, her hand sputtering along in the dust, scraping grit.

Then the cluster of Thusser was gone.

Only one was left. A single Thusser man with a mouth full of teeth and a glare in his eye.

He began, slowly, to run his hands over the lintel of the portal. He began to read what was written there. He began to activate the gateway to the other world.

EIGHTEEN

At breakfast, the boys kept their eye out for Lambert Gwestin, but he was nowhere to be seen.

"Maybe he doesn't work breakfast," said Gregory. He watched without pleasure as the servants brought another platter of steamed eels on the table. He complained, "How is it you people have figured out magic, but you still haven't figured out the cheese Danish?"

"We're the Court," said Gwynyfer. "We get delicacies at every meal."

Brian and Gregory found the delicacies hard to take. Though few of the Court actually made it to breakfast in the dining hall of the palace, the servants brought out course after course of meats in heavy sauces: hard little birds, eels wound into knots, the heads of some horned animal decorated with marzipan lace. The gravy on the heads was thin and watery with lumps of flour. The grease on the birds was starting to turn white.

Gwynyfer took a silver spatula and eagerly heaped a five-winged roast onto her plate. After she'd taken a few bites, she told the boys, "Last night some refugees arrived from down in the digestive tract. They escaped from the Mannequin Resistance. Later, they're going to have an Imperial audience with the Stub. You really should see it. It will be a lark."

Brian considered, "Maybe it would be a good time to bring up the Thusser again, and the idea of going back to Old Norumbega."

Gwynyfer looked a little impatient. "That would be quite dull. You've talked about that before. You should make up something different."

"But," Brian said, "Earth needs you to enforce the Rules of the Game."

"And we need you to entertain us," said Gwynyfer. "Things aren't easy in the Innards. We don't want to think about the awful things and the boring things." She put her hand on Brian's wrist. She told him, "It would be so much better for you *and* for us if you worked out a trick with fiery batons."

Brian stared dejectedly at her hand. Gregory glared jealously at it.

"Let's go," Brian said to Gregory. "We have to find Mr. Gwestin."

Gregory didn't want to leave Gwynyfer. He said to her, "Do you want to come along?"

She shrugged and nodded.

They asked the head butler where Mr. Gwestin was. He informed them Mr. Gwestin had been transferred and no longer worked in the dining hall. No, he did not know where Mr. Gwestin had been sent. The Seneschal might know. It was the Seneschal's business to oversee the running of the palace.

"It's very suspicious that he's been reassigned," said Brian as they wandered off to find the Seneschal. "Yesterday it seemed like Lord Dainsplint didn't want us to talk to Mr. Gwestin."

"Lord Dainsplint doesn't want you to investigate the murder at all," said Gwynyfer. "He wants to win the election for the new regent. If it turns out that the assassin is from his party — the Norumbegan Social Club — and you prove it beyond a reasonable doubt, he'll never win. He must suspect that members of his party are involved."

"Suspect," said Gregory, "or *know*?"

Gwynyfer agreed, "Or know."

"It could even be him," said Brian. "Except he was playing cards with Gugs. That's his alibi." Brian looked thoughtful.

Gwynyfer said, "The Earl of Munderplast is worried about the same thing, I'm sure. If it was someone in the Party of Melancholy who murdered the Regent, no one will trust them anymore. All the baronets and dukes from, I don't know, the pancreas and the eight kidneys will drop the party like a hot ingot. The earl will lose the election."

Brian mused, "I wonder where he really was that night."

Gwynyfer said, "For a long time, there have been rumors that the earl was part of a conspiracy to overthrow the Regent. Cloak-and-dagger stuff. No one's ever proved it. It's very spine-tingly."

165

"And a nice spine it is," said Gregory, gesturing at the slow curve of her shoulders and her back.

She smiled. "This? It's just something I threw together."

They found the Seneschal marching in the opposite direction. He had on a large, lumpy hat and carried a huge account book under his arm. Men in robes scurried alongside of him, offering inkstones and quills.

Gwynyfer stood directly in his path. She curtsied. "The daughter of the Duke of the Globular Colon greets the Lord High Seneschal of New Norumbega."

Irritated, he stopped in his tracks and inclined his head. He made some ritual sign of welcome with his hand. In a voice scratchy and exasperated he said, "The Lord High Seneschal greets the daughter of the Duke of the Globular Colon and wishes her a thousand years of youth. Is there something that the Lord High Seneschal can do for Miss Gwarnmore, in the hopes that she will move out of his way so that he can pursue his business without being hampered by debutantes and monkey-born brats?"

Gwynyfer said, "It is the wish of Miss Gwarnmore that she be informed as to the reappointment of one servant named Lambert Gwestin."

The Seneschal nodded, perched his great book on one hand, and drew it open. He scanned a list. He said to a scribe, "Turn." The scribe turned the page. "Turn." Another page flipped. "Two fifty-seven," he said, and another scribe leafed through to that page.

The Seneschal ran his finger down the page and

looked up. "Mr. Gwestin was reassigned at Lord Dainsplint's command to shoveling duty in the generator room."

"One thanks the Seneschal for his timely and accurate information."

"The Seneschal wishes Miss Gwarnmore a thousand glittering pleasures and requests she go play roll-a-hoop outside rather than blockading the august progress of the Imperial bureaucracy."

Gwynyfer got a mean look on her face. "Miss Gwarnmore hopes that the Seneschal remains as well as can be expected, at his advanced age."

Frowning, the Seneschal slammed his book shut. "The Seneschal expresses the hope that Miss Gwarnmore will in the next years make fewer of the stupid mistakes commonly associated with people of her extreme youth." He bowed to the three kids and swept past them, his scribes jogging to keep up.

The generator was in the basement of the Keep, buried deep in the tissue of the Dry Heart. The door read No Admittance.

Gwynyfer threw it open, and they walked in.

Gwestin and another servant, dressed in grubby overalls, shoveled dry manure from carts into a huge furnace. The heat was unbearable.

"Mr. Gwestin!" Brian yelled over the roaring. "Mr. Gwestin, it's Brian Thatz."

Gwestin turned from his work. He said something to his partner, jammed his shovel in the heap, and walked over, wiping his hands on a handkerchief.

"No admittance, sirs and madam," he said, pointing to the door.

"We've just got to ask you one question," said Gregory.

The man frowned.

Brian rushed to add, "We're really sorry you're down here. We think it might be on our account."

"Yes, sir," he said. "I am sorry I am down here, too. What have you come to ask me? You need to leave. If Lord Dainsplint discovers I've talked to you, it could mean . . ." He rumpled his mouth and shrugged.

Brian and Gregory looked at each other. Then Brian explained, "It's about two days ago. Were you asked to take a uniform down to the prison and leave it on a bench there?"

"Yes."

"We were wondering," said Gregory, "by who?"

"By who?"

". . . were you asked?"

"By note," said Gwestin. "The uniform and a note were tucked in my mail slot. They had the seal of the Imperial Council on them. The note asked me, on behalf of the Council, to go down to the prison and ask to see the automaton Dantsig. I was told to leave the uniform folded on a bench without any of the guards observing."

Gregory said, "And you didn't ask any questions?"

"The note had the Imperial Council's wax seal on it."

"You didn't think it was at all suspicious?"

Gwestin looked a little annoyed. "I have learned, sir, in my capacity as a servant to a court of pranksters, that

I should not ask questions when told to fill a bed with herrings, or burn off another servant's hair, or apply glue to certain gargoyles. We do not have much choice in what we do, sirs, madam. We are in debt to the Court and we serve them. They are our rightful rulers, whatever we may think. Though we may fear they make a mockery of our Imperial Highness's wishes, it is not our place to question."

"Can we see the note?" Brian asked.

Gwestin shook his head. "I destroyed it, sir, when I was done. It specified destruction."

"Because the handwriting..." Brian began, but Gwestin interrupted him.

"And now I am here in the basement shoveling dung, when I wished only to serve our gracious monarch, the Stub — may he long prosper, and may his eye never shut. I wished only to wait upon the proud Imperial throne that my family has bowed before for millennia. But Lord Dainsplint, seeing you speak with me, felt this service would prove to be a better channel for my enthusiasms."

There was an awkward silence.

Brian, Gregory, and Gwynyfer thanked him. He stood looking at them accusingly. He still had to go back to shoveling manure. Brian felt awful. He didn't know what to say. He apologized again. Gwestin nodded and walked away, back to his shovel. He dug it into the mound, and began heaving.

The furnace roared.

169

✳ ✳ ✳

They had not gone far when they ran into a Court sorcerer striding through a door from the huge hillock of trash outside. The stench of garbage blowing in was overwhelming. The wizard was an old, thin-nosed man with a short, clipped, salt-and-pepper beard. His double-breasted suit was too wide for him, and slumped at the shoulders. He was followed by a troop of guards. The door slammed shut behind him with the clatter of a crash-bar.

They knew he was a wizard because he introduced himself. He bowed to Gwynyfer and said, "The Wizard Thoth-Chumley presents himself to the daughter of Duke Gwarnmore of the Globular Colon and expresses his wish that the entrails of this Great Body shall align to bring the young woman great luck and happiness." She curtsied and flattered him in reply.

When he bowed to the boys, the suitcoat drooped and his necktie almost slithered out. Catching it, Thoth-Chumley said, "To the human ambassadors, Brian Thatz and Gregory Stoffle, I present my greetings. I have been charged with the investigation of the murder of our late Regent, Lord Telliol-Bornwythe. I think you know the mannequins who are under suspicion. Is that right?"

Keeping an eye on the guards, Brian nodded cautiously.

Thoth-Chumley looked unhappy. He fished in his suit pocket and pulled out a plastic sandwich bag. In it was what looked like a furry, brown bug.

170

"All morning, men have been sifting the hill of trash. And we found this." He shook the bag.

"What *is* it?" said Gregory.

"Can't you guess?"

"Yeah. Shouldn't you flush it?"

Thoth-Chumley shook the bag again. "Mr. Stoffle, it is a goatee. We found a false goatee in the garbage." He smeared its tendrils through the plastic. "See the glue? It has been attached to someone's chin." He waved his hand vaguely, and a guard stepped forward with an extra helmet. "The goatee was found concealed in litter, rolled in a tunic, and crammed in this helm. We assume these disguised the killer. He or she took some trouble to bury them in the trash heap." Thoth-Chumley stuffed the bag of beard back in his suit pocket. He crossed his arms. "Perhaps the young people understand what this means?"

Gregory shook his head, confused, but Brian exclaimed, "It means Dantsig didn't do it, and you know it."

Thoth-Chumley nodded, a grim look in his eye. "For your machine Dantsig, there would be no faux goatee. You'd only need a faux goatee if you wanted to look like him and you didn't have anything on your chin. And there's also the helm and uniform we found. The automaton Dantsig left his on the bench in the prison, right back where he got them. He didn't want there to be any suspicion the next morning. So it appears, boys, Miss Gwarnmore, there were *two* false guards wandering through the palace that night. And one of them was trying to frame your mechanical friend for the Regent's

171

murder." The Wizard Thoth-Chumley frowned. "The Court will not be pleased with this news. I wish we hadn't found this. No one wants to hear the murderer is one of us. I don't think things will go well for me." He shook his head. "I don't like my chances of outliving the week."

Brian, however, was excited. "But now you know it's not Dantsig!"

"I don't *know*."

"But you believe he's innocent!"

"It could be anyone. The whole Court had their motives. The whole Imperial Council. Lord Dainsplint, his friend Count Gugs Ffines-Whelter, all of them . . . These people own New Norumbega. The Dry Heart belongs to them. They own huge estates in other organs. They would have been ruined if the Regent's plan had gone through, and the Court had abandoned this city for our old kingdom on Earth. They all probably wanted to kill him." He looked like he had a headache. "So many people to question." He scraped his shoe on the floor and a wad of wet cling wrap dragged behind it. He said, "At least we're out of the garbage for a while."

He waved to the men behind him. "Come on," he said. "We need to arrange interviews." He bowed to Gwynyfer and spoke politely of her future fortune.

As he walked off down the corridor, they heard him issuing orders: "We have a lot to do, gents. Eochaid, find me the Lord High Seneschal. Edward, take the evidence to the office. Aillil, find a sandwich for me somewhere. I need to stop by my chamber and grab a protective amulet.

172

It's a cinch there's going to be a formal curse on me by dinnertime."

He left behind him the clot of cling wrap sticking to the floor.

✳   ✳   ✳

Upstairs in the Grand Hall, the Court gathered to hear the refugees from distant Throats tell tales of the Mannequin Resistance. Gregory, Brian, and Gwynyfer squeezed in, peering over shoulders.

The noblemen and women, the counts and countesses and duchesses and lordlings, were dressed as if for some weird underground medieval banquet. They wore spreading hats and long sleeves and tunics and gemmed stockings, and they waited on either side of an aisle that led directly to the foldaway panels that hid the Stub. The refugees stood humbly in a line, waiting for their turn to approach the throne. Their clothes were blackened with smoke.

With a flourish of buzzing instruments played by boys in peaked caps, the panels were drawn aside, revealing the dark, crayoned interior of the throne room. There sat the Imperial Council in unmatched chairs painted gold. The largest chair — the Regent's — was empty.

The Stub rested upon its cushion. Someone had placed a collar of white ermine around it and laid a crown on its lump. The single eye darted about fearfully, wincing at the honking fanfare of fairy trumpets. The crown was starting to slip.

Gregory, Brian, and Gwynyfer were at the back of the crowd of courtiers. Brian had to keep bobbing up on his toes to see.

Lord Dainsplint came forward and announced, "His Sublime Highness the Stub, Emperor of Old Norumbega, New Norumbega, and the Whole Dominion of the Innards, Elector of the Bladders, Prince of the Gastric Wastes, Sovereign of Ducts Superior and Inferior, Lord of All, is prepared to hear the supplications of his people. Come forward and prostrate yourself before his mercy!" He bowed and retreated to his seat.

One of the refugees — an old man — tottered forward. He stopped a few feet from the Stub and, with a show of joint pain, slowly got down on his knees, then his belly. He lay facedown, arms spread.

His muffled voice floated faintly over the silent crowd. ". . . of Dellwich . . . His Imperial . . . wishes to present his complaint to . . ."

"Louder!" yelled courtiers. "Louder!"

"Speak up!"

The old man on the floor cleared his throat, and, louder, said, ". . . presents his compliments to the Court of New Norumbega. May Your Imperial Highness never see sorrow. May Your Highness never see tears."

"Story!" someone shouted.

"Yes, story!"

The man lying spread on the floor said, "The Mannequin Resistance surrounded our town, Your Highness."

"Quite impossible," said Lord Dainsplint. "They can't raise a hand against a Norumbegan."

"They have worked out *excuses*, your lordship," said the man. "Lies to themselves that allow them to act against us. They took most of our townspeople prisoner. They called it picnicking. Most of the population of the town is still picnicking behind a barbed-wire fence."

At this, the Court stirred uneasily.

"And, sir," said the Earl of Munderplast, "how did you and your family escape?"

"Hopping in sacks, your lordship. The mannequins could not fire upon us, seeing as we were merely entering into the spirit of the picnic. They had no excuse. The sheriff of Dellwich and his deputies almost made it out by simulating a three-legged race. Until they tore their handkerchiefs and neckties off their ankles and began to sprint in earnest, firing their guns. They destroyed three or four of the mannequins. Then the mannequins . . . they raised their muskets and killed them all." The man shook his head. "All dead," he whispered into the floor. "The sheriff, the deputies."

At this, there was a mutter of horror. Men growled: "They should allow us to kill them." — "The impudence!" — "They are ours to kill." — "They die when we say, 'Die!'"

"What are . . . what do the blighters want?" Gugs asked anxiously.

"They claim that we have no right over them or their land. They want the guts for themselves. They want the

Regent to declare them independent of the Empire. They say that if they are not given their independence, then they will depose the Regent . . . for the good, they say, of the Norumbegan people. They claim they fight for us, Your Highness, not against us. This is their excuse. And at the same time, they threaten us."

More refugees were asked to come forward. They all had stories of terrible politeness, unutterable courtesy: a heavy knock on their doors at midnight, followed by a beautifully engraved invitation to be arrested . . . robot captors shaking hands before shackling their prisoners . . . clockwork men kicking in windows and grabbing screaming kids, all the while apologizing profusely for the mess and promising to clean up if madam would simply direct them to a dustpan and broom.

Hearing these tales, Brian didn't know what to think. Up until this point, he had, he realized, kind of been on the side of the mannequins. He could completely understand why they would want to rebel against the Norumbegans, who strode into their villages and shut them all down, who killed them without even believing that they could feel pain or sadness or horror.

But now he didn't know. In spite of their politeness, the mannequins sounded brutal. They imprisoned whole villages. They shot people who tried to escape. He couldn't figure out who was right.

And the anxiety of not knowing struck him as awful, like not knowing which way was up after stumbling off a fairground ride. He put his feet down as if the ground was solid, but discovered instead he'd been spun around too much, and the pavement retreated and the grass got closer and he thought he'd throw up his cotton candy.

He took a deep breath and got into line behind the last refugee.

He had something to say.

✳ ✳ ✳

Brian stood in front of the Stub. "Your Highness," he said, and he bowed.

"Get on the floor," said Lord Dainsplint.

Brian would not get down on the floor in front of this Court. He was no servant of theirs.

"I'm not..." he said uncertainly, "I'm not getting down on the floor. I'm a, you know, an ambassador. I can stand." He didn't wait for anyone to argue against him. Feeling himself blush, he simply launched into what he had planned to say. "I just want to say to the Court that you have got to think about your ancient rights. Um, my lord the Earl of Munderplast, you're always talking about how things were better in the olden days, and you, Lord Dainsplint, you're always talking about how you want to have great parties. Well, I need to remind you that everything you used to have could be yours again. It's all just sitting there — a whole kingdom from the good old days — and all you have to do is go kick out the Thusser. The Earth is...well, the Thusser Horde is spreading over the face of the Earth, and human cities will fall. And then they'll start to look for new places to conquer, and who knows, maybe they'll look here? So, I

177

suggest that you think about what the Regent said before he was killed, and —"

"Didn't the runt try this once before?" Gugs asked. He tapped his head. "Unless my old wiring's on the fritz."

"No, we've heard it before," said Lord Dainsplint.

"I know it might be hard to fight the Thusser," said Brian, "but you're the only ones who can enforce the Rules and —"

"We can't enforce the Rules of your Game," said Dainsplint.

"It's not *my* Game," said Brian. "It's yours."

"But," said the Ex-Empress Elspeth, "*we* wouldn't enforce the Rules. What, with a whistle and a pair of grubby shorts? No, I recall — do you remember, Randall? The sorcerers at the time engaged some Rules Keepers. Referees. They would enforce the Rules. We'd just have to activate them. Then they would take care of the whole ruddy mess."

Brian was wild-eyed with hope. "So why don't you do that? You could just *do* that?"

"*Because,*" Lord Dainsplint insisted, "we have better things to do with our afternoons."

"That's crazy!" said Brian. "All you have to do is claim what's rightfully yours! You could so easily save the Earth!"

"Not quite so eazers, Mr. Thatz," said the Ex-Empress Elspeth. "Do you know how to activate Rules Keepers?"

"Where are they?" Brian demanded hysterically. Wildly, he pictured a big on-off switch.

178

"In another *world*, darling," said the Ex-Empress. "And don't forget, we've lost all of our *paperwork* over the last several hundred years. No one remembers the Rules of the Game. The Thusser wizards set it up with us and no one wants to ask *them* for advice, the old cows."

"And the rest of us," said Lord Dainsplint, "are too, too bored. Let us move on."

Brian got the distinct and irritating feeling that the elfin councillors were being so stubborn precisely *because* it would be so easy for them to help.

Then the Earl of Munderplast rose. He wore a scarlet velvet shift and a skullcap. "Beausires," he said, bowing to the Court, "I argue for our ancient hunting grounds and palaces. I do not think that the human cubling is necessarily wrong. Imagine, I ask you, the glories that were once Norumbega. If we could walk again among those ruins, would it not be a grand thing?"

Brian looked at the earl, full suddenly of hope.

The earl continued, "The Melancholy Party would like to consider investigating the method by which we might call forth the Rules Keepers to enforce the Rules. And I, as a candidate for the Regency of the Stub, proclaim that if I am elected, I will reclaim the sunken kingdom of Norumbega for our use, *not* so that I may lead us to a brighter future, of course — out of the question, I'm afraid; there's naught to come but doom and bale — but to a more deliciously gloomy appreciation of everything we shall never again be, all the tears wept which shall never —"

179

He stopped speaking. He was looking out over the crowd, his eyes focused peculiarly on the sliding glass doors that led from the Grand Hall out onto the balcony.

Everyone turned.

Something flashed, out in the desert.

A marquis slid one of the doors open and stepped out on the balcony, his hand over his eyes.

The city below was in turmoil. The sound of horns and cries drifted up to the palace.

"What's that?" said Lord Dainsplint. "Sounds like unrest. I suppose one of us should swan out on the terrace and throw down pieces of eight."

"My lord," said the marquis on the balcony. "It's the valves. Into the flux."

People rushed to peer out the doors. Brian found himself crushed against the wall, barely able to see.

There were gasps and exclamations of surprise. He ducked. He peered through the crook of a baronet's elbow.

Far out past the outskirts of the city — out where he had first entered the Dry Heart with Dantsig and the marines — valves had popped open, and rank after rank of soldier was crawling out.

The veins far above shone down on metal muskets and cannons raised on winches from holes in the ground.

The Mannequin Resistance had arrived, and its soldiers were surrounding the capital city.

NINETEEN

The Rebellion Courteous, as later historians called it, culminated in a siege of New Norumbega.

Mannequins had set out from Pflundt and other fortresses carved into the phlegm floes of the gut — some in subs, others on foot. The submarines could navigate through the flux all the way to the Dry Heart. There were far too many mechanized warriors gathering from around the Great Body to all fit into subs, however. The rest had a long, gastrointestinal march up from stomachs to throats, where they now waited until someone could shuttle them through blood to the hearts and to the capital city in its desert aorta.

The aristocrats of Norumbega, as they stood on their palace's balcony, staring sullenly out across the salty plains, had no idea of how many more mannequins still waited to be shipped to the siege. They saw only that the numbers of the invaders were great.

With spyglasses, they made out butlers and chambermaids, nurses and ladies-in-waiting, all of them armed to defy those who had built them, those whose hair they had once adorned with jewels. Soldiers from ancient wars stood next to cannons. All the clockwork mannequins who had once served the Norumbegans now demanded to be left alone.

"Well," said Ex-Emperor Fendritch, looking down sadly at his pointy medieval slippers and waggling them, "I suppose if it's really and truly war, I should put on some sensible shoes."

The Earl of Munderplast spoke from the back of the crowd. "It is not war," he said. "Because they are incapable of attacking us. We are their government. They have been built, they have been shapen to bloody well obey." He explained, "They have to twist the truth to convince themselves that the good of the Norumbegan people is served by attacking its government. But we, my friends, have a wonderful surprise, an ace in the hole." He bobbed his eyebrows, and said, "They've come here to oppose the Regent. But the Regent is dead. When we tell them this, they won't be able to attack us. They'll have no excuse."

He swept toward the hallway. "Your Graces," he explained, "I wish to speak upon the telephone."

As a few days before, the Court had gathered around the door and the phone while the Regent had spoken to mannequins, they crammed themselves into the hallway again. "Do you admire the vigor and bravery and gentilesse with which I assume command?" asked the earl loudly, as he dialed a number on the phone's rotary dial. "Then you might consider voting for me, O vox populi, in a few scant days. I still propose that we reconquer our old territories, so that we may better weep for — Ah, yes, hello. Goodly maiden, may I speak to Mr. Malark of the Mannequin Resistance? . . . No, not 'general,' 'mister.' . . . Yes, I shall wait."

He stood, slightly stooped, with the phone held to his ear. With the other hand, he played with the cord that attached it to the box on the wall. Then he flipped through a phone book idly. The crowd stirred uneasily.

"Ah, hail and fair welcome," said the earl. "The Earl of Munderplast greets his servant Mr. Malark. . . . I call on behalf of the Imperial Court of Norumbega. . . . Yes, there appears to be an expeditionary force of soldiers and warriors doughty and brave surrounding our capital city, and we wish you to remove them. Or order them to submit, and we shall allow them to return to service posthaste. By this evening, they may be laying out our nightshirts upon our beds, building us roads, sewing us zoot suits, arranging fondant roses in our bakeries. . . . Listen, varlet, you have no choice. No excuse . . ." The earl smiled in triumph. "You came to confront the Regent — and he is dead. Verily, dead! No enemy of yours any longer! Enemy only of the crocodile spirits who haunt the next world, the shadow land of Tuat. Gone."

Everyone smiled in satisfaction.

The earl repeated, "No excuse, thou lowbred gizmo! If you stand up now against us, you stand up against your own government. And that, you may recall, you are incapable of doing. You've hied yourself all this way for nothing."

And then his face fell.

"You *knew*?" he said. "Of his death? Ah, I suppose you did, since your servant killed him. . . . Your servant, Mr. Dantsig." He listened intently. Then the earl covered the mouthpiece and told the crowd, "Mr. Malark claims that Mr. Dantsig is innocent of the assassination. . . . And how do you know, then, that our Regent was killed, if you did not order it yourself?"

There was, apparently, no response on the other end of the line.

"Thing," said the earl, "I demand a response, thing."

He looked at the earpiece. He tapped at the mouthpiece. "Hello?" he said.

And then the blast hit the palace.

The sliding glass doors in the Grand Hall blew in, blasting shards against the wall. Shutters and wallboard clattered across the floor. Gregory collapsed, dragging Gwynyfer with him, and they crouched together in the silence afterward. Their ears rang.

Smoke and plaster dust filled the air.

He looked around to find Brian. The Court was on its knees, hiding behind walls, knocked flat. Many were cut. In its recess, on its throne, the Stub bled.

Finally, Gregory saw Brian untangling himself from a society dame who was slapping at him with her lorgnette. Brian helped an old couple to their feet.

The mannequins had lobbed a bomb into the square at the base of the palace. The smoke still rose, still blew in through the shattered windows. Dukes tottered in from the porch, holding themselves up unsteadily.

The Earl of Munderplast still stood by the phone, holding the mouthpiece, dazed.

"I suppose we should all change before dinner," said the Ex-Emperor.

"What we need . . ." said Gugs, coughing plaster out of his lungs, "what one could really *do* with right now is a person named Sir Something the Brave."

Far out at the rim of the city, loud voices were speaking.

The mannequins were addressing the population through megaphones. The words were indistinct.

"It appears," said Lord Dainsplint, looking directly at Brian, "that there was a better spy in our midst than we had previously thought. Well, isn't it an infernal mystery who that might have been?"

Gugs suggested, "Anyone fancy a little bet on the outcome of the war? Anyone?"

The Court looked around the broken room. There was a silence, save for the distant squalling of voices through bullhorns.

"What are the clockworkers saying?" asked the Ex-Empress.

Gregory said hastily, "We'll run down and listen, then come back and report. Come on!" He gestured to Brian and Gwynyfer.

He led the two of them quickly out of the Grand Hall. They ran down the great staircase and toward the gates of the palace.

Behind them, the Court of Norumbega prepared for war.

✳ ✳ ✳

Down the hill through the shantytown the three kids ran, Gwynyfer leading Gregory by the wrist. The square was a crater. The guardhouse was a crumpled shell. Guards were shoving beams off piles of wall. They were digging through muddy mounds, looking for their brethren. Because they were Norumbegans, several had already given up, and were watching their bloodstained officers scramble through the rubble. They were taking wagers as to how many had lived and how many had died.

The streets were chaotic. People ran up and down the main boulevard, shouting to one another. Several had already stacked their things in wagons, and were ready to flee.

But as the kids got down toward the edge of the city, people were quieter. They were listening to the voices broadcast from bullhorns in the desert.

It took a while before they could make out the words.

"Hey," said Gregory, pointing. "Isn't that the doctor? From the palace?"

Dr. Brundish hobbled along in front of them, looking anxiously around him, his goggles reflecting the light of the veins.

"Where's he headed?" Gwynyfer wondered.

The doctor held a carpetbag in his hand, filled with clanking objects.

Instinctively, Gregory felt like Brundish didn't want

to be seen. He pulled his two friends behind one of the shacks for a minute. He watched Brundish disappear around a corner.

"Okay," he said, and motioned for the other two to follow him.

"You're very dashing," said Gwynyfer.

Gregory didn't take time to make a joke back.

Dr. Brundish, hopping as if his legs weren't fully human, made his way down an alley. The others followed him. The houses were painted pastel.

Now they could make out the individual words echoing from the salty desert. "Citizens of New Norumbega — citizens of New Norumbega — we are here to serve you. If you will please be so good as to step aside, we will painlessly rid you of your leaders. We are delighted to announce that the long tyranny is over. Please evacuate the city through the western gate."

Gwynyfer whispered, "There is no 'western gate.' Idiots. There's no actual *wall*."

Dr. Brundish hobbled along, his carpetbag now dragging in the dirt. He looked carefully behind him, adjusting his goggles.

The voice in the desert continued, "We have a few humble suggestions for the reorganization of the state. If they are ignored, we are thrilled to announce that we will provide complimentary bombing and detonation services beginning tomorrow at noon."

Gregory slid around a corner.

And felt a hand around his throat.

187

The doctor shoved him against the wall. The jowly face grimaced. Brundish's claw tightened around Gregory's neck.

Gregory grabbed the hairy wrist. Brian and Gwynyfer came around the corner, saw what was happening, and ran to tug on the chirurgeon's arm.

"Following in my tracks?" he growled. "These shoes fit me alone." With his free hand, he reached into his pocket. The doctor pulled out a little pistol inlaid with pearl-and-ivory designs. Brian scampered backward — ducked — and a bullet burst in the adobe behind the boy.

Gregory had torn free. He lunged for the doctor to knock the man's shooting arm. The doctor fired again at Brian. Brian staggered to the side. Gwynyfer darted behind him.

The doctor moved like a fat spider, swiveling to block their retreat. He raised his gun again. Gregory jumped on his back and head-butted him from behind. The thick body reared and flailed.

The gun dropped.

Brian scrambled forward and grabbed it.

The doctor shook Gregory off. "Don't cling," he grated. "You're all going to fall. All of you!" He scuttled backward. "I am vanished!" he said. "Before the general doom. The palace will fall. Better to be far away when the bombing starts." He backed up.

Then he looked down and saw that Gwynyfer was holding his bag.

"Give me the bag," he said.

"Why do you want it?" she said. "It's an awkward size. Too bulky for a clutch. Too small for luggage."

He scrambled toward her, claw outstretched.

"And the colors," she said, swaying it out of his reach, "could not be uglier."

"Give me my things, Miss Gwarnmore."

"Why are you fleeing?"

"We all should be."

"Why'd you try to kill Brian then? He's dull, but not criminally dull."

The doctor grabbed at the bag, snagged it. He pulled. She pulled.

It tipped. Came open.

Out spilled clothes — socks, boxers, sleeveless tees — and devices.

What looked like a walkie-talkie. And five of what looked like bladed octopi. Little things that might be slipped into a boy's burger.

The doctor gasped. He snarled. And he began to run.

The three kids watched him go.

"I wonder what frightened him?" Gregory said.

And then heard the scissory sounds at his feet.

The octopi had come to life.

TWENTY

Running down an alley in a city surrounded by robots, being chased by small clockwork monsters with razor blades on stalks, hurtling along toward a palace filled with cruel elvish aristocrats, Gregory felt that perhaps he needed to make some changes in how he spent his free time.

He thought, as he hopped over some fallen masonry, that maybe he should waste more time in front of the television, more time playing video games, less time embarking on quests to save North America from interdimensional invasion. Why were people always telling you to go out and play? This — *this* is what happened when you went to hang out in the woods.

Brian had fallen behind, and Gregory turned to see how his friend was doing. Brian was still keeping well ahead of the little cluster of metal insects.

"I wish," Brian puffed, "sneakers were made of something better. Harder."

His rubber soles were sliced and scored.

Gregory paused to pick up a roof tile in two hands. "Yeah," he agreed sarcastically. "I don't know why iron sneaks never took off." He hurled the tile at the fleet of bugs. It smashed between them. Two spidery units quivered and stopped flailing. The others kept swarming forward.

It took another several blocks before the kids had outrun them.

They did not feel safe until they had made it most of the way back up to the palace.

Behind them, the voices still rang out in the desert air. "Citizens of Norumbega! We are here to serve you. . . ." People hung out of windows, listening.

The kids walked up the muddy avenue.

Gregory said, "So the doctor was probably the one who tried to kill you last night at dinner. Some bedside manner."

Brian was silent. For one thing, he was still waiting for Gwynyfer to apologize for calling him "dull." He suspected she wasn't going to take it back.

Gregory wondered, "Why would he try to kill you?"

"I don't know," Brian admitted. He looked pointedly at Gwynyfer.

"Are you waiting for something from me?"

Brian said, "I'm a little tired of people talking about how boring and stupid I am."

"Then," Gwynyfer suggested, "why not try being clever and charming? Start now: Say something witty."

Brian gave her a dirty look and didn't respond.

191

Gregory wished Gwynyfer wouldn't be so snippy with his friend, but he had to admit that Brian had been kind of sulky ever since they'd arrived in the Dry Heart. He thought Brian could at least make an effort, seeing as everyone in this whole Empire was so sharp, so funny — exactly the kind of people who Gregory wanted to hang out with when he grew up, exactly what he'd always dreamed of being: sly, knowing about things, cool in a crisis.

"Could the doctor have been the assassin?" Brian asked.

"I doubt it," said Gwynyfer. "Your friend, the servant in the dung heap, said that the note he was given was sealed with the official wax mark of the Imperial Council. Whoever wrote that letter must have had one of the eleven signet rings that make the Imperial mark. That means the Regent or the ten councillors. The doctor isn't a member. He's not even an aristo."

"An aristo?" Brian asked.

"An aristocrat. A nobleman. He's not of the first blood. The Children of the Goddess Danaan."

"And he wouldn't have fit into a guard's uniform," said Gregory.

"What do you think this is?" Gwynyfer asked, holding up the old walkie-talkie.

"Wow," said Gregory. "Where'd you get that?"

"It fell out of his bag."

They stepped to the side of the road, and Gregory switched it on.

Nothing came out of the speakers. Gregory turned it

192

over. He rattled it. He opened a compartment on the back. "No batteries," he said. "Is this a standard size?"

"Double A," said Gwynyfer.

"You have double A batteries here?" Gregory asked. "In the Great Body?"

She looked at him appraisingly. "You expected something more exotic?"

"Sure. It's a world of magic. So maybe rechargeable triple A's."

Brian was looking at the device in Gregory's hand. "It has a place to talk as well as to listen," he pointed out. "It's a two-way radio of some kind."

"Funny," Gregory said. "I wonder who he's communicating with?"

"We could search his room," Brian suggested. "Before anyone knows he's gone."

Gwynyfer looked appalled at the suggestion. "That's an excruciatingly low idea," she said.

Gregory handed her the walkie-talkie. "Still, let's check it out," he said. "You're the one who wanted to break out of your whole tea-at-three, kneeling-on-your-face-in-front-of-a-flesh-blob-at-four Court rigamarole."

She shrugged, looking a little miffed that Gregory would support his friend.

Gregory looked down.

"Oh," he said.

And stepped on one of the metal bugs, which had finally caught up to them again.

193

General Malark sat in his command sub, frowning at the telephone.

The fate of his clockwork people, he knew, was in his hands. The rulers of the various fortresses and outposts and castles of the mechanicals — spread throughout the hollows and corky glands of this infinite body — had all reposed their trust in him. He had at his command a vast force of servants-turned-soldier. He loved them each. He was proud of all. They had eked out their living from nothing once they'd fled, embarrassed, one by one, from their masters. They had built a civilization for themselves in these dripping channels and snotty caverns. Their fortresses were carved into the living phlegm. Their guns, their subs were made of brass and bronze and iron that they'd refined from minerals in the flux and lux effluvium. They deserved victory.

He climbed up the gangway and emerged, saluting his soldiers, on the plains on the Dry Heart.

He raised his binoculars and surveyed the citadel of his one-time masters.

He saw great walls with mighty turrets rising above the glistening saline desert. He saw wide, tree-lined avenues and brightly hung marketplaces. He saw, above it all, on a hilltop, rising from the steep roofs and spires and domes, the palace itself, shining like alabaster, its towers sparkling in the light from the veins of lux effluvium.

He was programmed to see this. He was designed to be awed by his masters.

And so he and his fellow soldiers did not see the rubble of shanties. They didn't see the citizens in old, torn clothing

194

faded with light and browned with dirt, running in confusion through tangles of faulty electrical wiring and sloppily painted billboards. He couldn't recognize the palace as a slumped mound of dried flesh rinds and mud walls and stubby towers built of plywood and old two-by-fours, less like a fairy-tale castle than a thicket of tree houses.

And because he could not see that the city could be his whenever he bothered to march into its streets — which lay open to all invasions — he decided grimly that it was going to be a long siege. He thought of all the bombs they'd have to lob, all the catapults they'd need, all the fiery weaponry they'd have to blast this impregnable fortress with.

He did not realize that if he even deployed a tenth of his power on the city, he wouldn't just conquer it — everyone alive within it would die in rubble and flames before he even noticed he'd won.

✳ ✳ ✳

Within the palace, everyone was scurrying to and fro, engaged in frenzied preparations. The Court of New Norumbega, in response to the gathering troops on the horizon, had decided to hold a special tea dance. It was important, in this time of trial, to admit no fear. They were not going to let rude mechanicals intrude on their fun. But in all the frenzy of invasion, it was difficult to get shirts ironed and to find stockings without runs.

"We've got to report on the mannequins' message," said Gregory. "That's why we were sent down there."

195

"The Imperial Council has to send a delegation down to hear their demands," said Brian.

"I don't like the odds if the mannequins start firing those cannons," said Gregory.

"No?" said a voice behind him. It was Gugs. "Would you bet, say, thirty Imperial kroner that we don't survive a siege? Forty? I know you're nothing but raw kiddies — but surely your mamas give you pocket money, what?"

Gwynyfer bowed to him, making a sign with her hands. "Gwynyfer Gwarnmore, daughter of the Duke of the Globular Colon, greets Count Galahad Ffines-Whelter of Nettleton and Garje, and expresses her wish that his lands be ever fertile and his . . ." at which point Brian and Gregory stopped listening because they were very tired of Imperial etiquette.

Gwynyfer passed on the message that they had heard broadcast at the city limits by the mechanicals.

"They said," she concluded, "that the people of the city should evacuate through the west gate."

"West gate?" said Gugs. "What are the dazed manns on about? There is no west gate. No gate at all, that I can reckon."

"I imagine," said Gwynyfer, "that they can't see the city as it is. Because they've been built for humility and worship."

Gugs tapped his nose. "'Spect you're right, old girl. Well, if that doesn't raise the odds of us surviving the old heave-ho by their catapults and the boom-boom of cannons, I don't know what does. Good news for us all." He said to Gregory, "Sure I can't interest you in that wager?"

"My mom cut off my allowance," Gregory said. "I was mean to the cat."

"Unless," said Brian loudly, "we made a bet for something else."

"Oh yes?"

"If they flatten the palace," Brian said, "you have to demand that the Council votes to find those old spells to activate the Rules Keepers and kick the Thusser out of Old Norumbega."

"And if the manns can't knock the old place down?"

"Then we'll give you a . . . a hundred kroner."

"Hundred kroner? Not exactly equal, old chimp."

"And a foot massage," said Gwynyfer.

"That's the ticket," said Gugs. "'Specially after a dance, I cramp. It's all that step-ball-change."

"You people really don't have any sense of proportion whatsoever, do you?" Gregory asked Gwynyfer.

"There's nothing more important than trivia," said Gwynyfer. "You only touch your change purse twice a day, but your feet you wear forever."

Brian and Gugs shook on the bet. Gugs went off to get the terms of the wager down in writing.

As the three kids continued up to the chirurgeon's office, Gregory said, "What do you think the odds are he'll actually remember to pass on the message about the mannequins' demands?"

"He's forgotten it already," said Gwynyfer, shrugging. "But don't put odds on it. You know he'll take the bet."

197

They reached the door of the doctor's office. Gwynyfer said, "You really do wish to break in and slither about his rooms without him? It's not too skulk-making?"

"He tried to kill me," Brian pointed out.

Gregory gestured to the chirurgeon's door. "Go ahead," he said. "Make me a skulk."

He had no idea what "skulk" meant, but she and Gregory laughed together. She put her back against the door and swung it open, still clinging to it, her head back, her eyes facing Gregory, her mouth tilted forward and lined up with his.

Brian followed them into the chirurgeon's quarters. He felt a little like a third wheel.

He said, "If it could only have been someone on the Imperial Council who sent that note to Mr. Gwestin, we need to know everyone who's on the Council. One of them must be the murderer."

"It was probably Chigger," said Gregory. "Chigger Dainsplint. He always seems like he's up to something."

"Everyone's up to something," said Gwynyfer. "Otherwise, the nights get long and there's nothing to talk about next day at lunch."

"Later," Brian asked, "can you point out all of the members of the Council and tell us about them?"

"At the tea dance," she said, already starting to shuffle through papers on a desk. "They'll all be there."

Gregory looked around the room. "Wow," he said. "Dr. Brundish clearly did not expect he'd be coming back."

The room was torn apart in a frenzy of packing and preparation. Drawers were still open. Grubby clothing was balled up all over the bunk, as if he'd pulled it out of his bureau, tore his way through it to find what he needed, and left the rest.

The leeches, faintly glowing, still made their slow way around their jars, morosely hunting for blood.

Brian rattled through the desk drawers. He scrabbled through quills and bottles of colored ink. "Hey," he said. "Batteries."

Gregory fitted them into the radio device. He turned a knob.

Nothing.

He pressed some buttons.

Now the thing started to receive. The three leaned close to it.

"Can you turn it up?" Gwynyfer asked.

Gregory fiddled with the knobs. A huge burst of static. Then voices.

Many voices.

They were all distant. They spoke as if giving orders, but all at once. They were too muted to be understood.

Gregory put it down. He fiddled with some knobs. Static. Then voices again. The same ones. Still distant.

Irritated, he shut it off. "I thought we had a real lead there," he said. He kept fiddling with it. Gwynyfer patted him on the back.

Brian and Gwynyfer kept on searching the room. They found all kinds of compounds in bottles. They found sprays and pills and salves. They didn't know anything about any of them. There were lots of books of medicine and sorcery.

"Do you think Dr. Brundish works for the automatons?" Brian asked. "Or if he even is an automaton?"

Gwynyfer shrugged. "It's possible," she said. "Do you two never get bored with sleuthing? What say we go up to the belvedere and hit golf balls into the trash heap?"

Brian looked at her steadily. "You're in the middle of a siege."

"No," she said irritably, "we're at the beginning of one. You aren't our conscience."

"Well, maybe you need one," said Brian, who was tired of being insulted.

"Hey, hey," said Gregory, holding up his hands.

"I don't see why," said Gwynyfer, "I, a descendant of goddesses, need to listen to cheap advice about when I should or shouldn't putt."

"Brian just means," Gregory explained, "that —"

"Hey!" said Brian, lifting something out of Dr. Brundish's sock drawer. "Look at this!"

It was a dirty plastic bag filled with cosmetics. Brian unzipped it and laid the products on the desk. "A tube of . . . 'cover-up' . . . and 'eye definer.'"

"Whoa," said Gregory. "The dude was a lady."

"Dr. Brundish," said Gwynyfer, slitting her eyes, "was no lady." She picked up the tube of cover-up and read the brand name with a sneer.

"No," said Brian. "The dude wasn't a lady."

"Thank goodness," said Gregory. "Because he would have made the ugliest lady ever."

"And what's wrong with ugly ladies?" Gwynyfer asked

200

him. "Don't you think men should take their turn dating back hair, nail fungus, and weak chins?"

"Dr. Brundish," Brian announced, "was a Thusser."

The other two looked at him, astounded.

"What do you mean?" Gregory said, and Gwynyfer protested, "That's rot."

"How can you tell the difference between the Thusser and Norumbegans?"

"They both have pointy ears," said Gregory.

"Everyone has pointy ears," said Gwynyfer, "except you. Your race wasn't invited."

"What? To the ear-off?"

"The *Thusser*," said Brian, "have dark rings around their eyes. So if Dr. Brundish wanted to look like the Norumbegans, he would have to hide the dark rings with the cover-up makeup, and then redefine his eyes."

"Whoa," said Gregory. He looked at the eye definer and asked, "So what's most women's excuse?"

Gwynyfer answered sweetly, "Looking swell for idiots like you." She batted her lashes.

Brian could not believe they were flirting at a time like this. He said, "Dr. Brundish is a Thusser. He has probably been reporting everything back to the Horde for however long he's been here. How long has he been here?"

Gwynyfer shrugged. "Since I was a little girl. But that's outrageous. Everyone knows him. He's chirurgeon to the Ex-Empress and the Ex-Emperor."

Brian said, "I'll bet that walkie-talkie is how he keeps in touch with the Magister of the Thusser Horde."

201

"This?" said Gregory, pointing at the thing.

"Try it again," Brian urged.

They were almost afraid to listen in now, knowing that the radio might be broadcasting the sound of their breath to some alien world, some shuddering, webby home of evil, where Thusser, crouched in pods, whispered through mouths of thick teeth to their operatives in many worlds.

Slowly, Gregory reached out for the on-off toggle. He switched it. The set came on.

And a voice was singing a love song — a dapper little number clearly from the top of some otherworldly pop chart.

"It's a radio station," said Gregory. "Just a radio station."

They listened, perplexed. It sounded like some kind of old-time jazz from a nightclub in one of the black-and-white detective movies Brian loved, but played on weird buzzing instruments and all broken up, so that the melody glinted and reflected through a fugitive spray of alien harmonies. The singer had glue in his voice as he sang of hands and a pretty face and a moth around the street-lamp flitting.

The three kids listened in silence. Then they shut off the radio and sat thinking about the Thusser, about spies, about something far worse than a mannequin army that might soon surround the city.

TWENTY-ONE

The Norumbega Vassal-Tribune

SERVING THE INNARDS SINCE 1282

IMPERIAL CAPITAL NOT UNDER SIEGE,
SAYS CANDIDATE FOR REGENCY

NEW NORUMBEGA — Following the explosion of a lobbed missile in the Imperial Square, rumors circulated throughout the city that New Norumbega was under siege.

"Nonsense," said Lord Rafe "Chigger" Dainsplint, Norumbegan Social Club candidate for the post of Imperial Regent, speaking with reporters over the sounds of screaming and flames. "The very idea of a Mannequin Resistance is entirely beneath our dignity. What we have here is nothing more than an under-stairs servants' party that's got a little out of hand. Anyone who even speaks of this is clearly no friend of New Norumbega. This is nothing."

Fourteen died today in the blast, including Sir Pleckory Dither, Cupbearer to the Stub, who was crossing the square with his chalice when the missile hit.

When asked about the deaths, Dainsplint replied, "You know, we in the Imperial Council would hate to gag the Press. We rather prefer choking, with our thumbs pressed deep into your windpipes as your goggling eyes gape out at us. Any more questions, lads?"

There were none.

EARL OF MUNDERPLAST DISRESPECTFUL, PERHAPS TREASONOUS, SAYS RIVAL FOR REGENCY

NEW NORUMBEGA — Lord Rafe "Chigger" Dainsplint, Norumbegan Social Club candidate for Imperial Regent, accused his rival candidate late today of being "disrespectful of Norumbega's past and perhaps even treasonous."

Lord Dainsplint made the comments in a public discussion of possible policy in the wake of an alleged attack on the palace by the Mannequin Resistance (see page 26, "Imperial Capital May Be Under Siege, Says Man Under Rubble").

Following arguments made by human ambassador Brian Thatz, the Earl of Munderplast promised voters that if he were elected as Regent, he would invoke the Rules that would expel the Thusser from Old Norumbega and would restore "at least the memory of Norumbega's ancient glory."

While Lord Dainsplint publicly praised the earl, referring to him as "a spry old article," he immediately expressed discomfort for the earl's plan of action. "Seems to me," he said, "that Munderplast doesn't think much of the people of New Norumbega. His lordship wants to abandon our Empire's capital for some blasted old ruin. Apparently, the old boy doesn't believe that we're good enough for him anymore — or that New Norumbega is good enough for him. The dear old thing complains about the trash heaps and the stink of our clothes. He forgets that Norumbegans have always been the greatest nation among the sublime races and that we shall always be the greatest nation among the sublime races. He seems to care more about the human animal than his fellow sprites. That just makes me sad for him, chaps, because I hate to hear a man who's disrespectful of Norumbega's past and perhaps even treasonous. Quite angry-making, really."

The Earl of Munderplast replied, saying, "How can his lordship accuse me — me, of all people — of disrespecting our Empire's past when my whole party is founded upon sadness that —"

At this point, Lord Dainsplint interrupted to announce that he and the Norumbegan Social Club would hold public celebrations every afternoon and evening until the day of the election. His announcement was met with cheers and rejoicing by the assembled Court. Lord Dainsplint's "knees-ups" will began this afternoon with a tea dance for the Court at three, and will be followed by a lavish funeral tomorrow for Sir Pleckory Dither, who died in an unfortunate accident while crossing the Imperial Square around noon today. The rites for the dead will include funeral dining and dancing.

In a featureless plain of digestive jelly, blown by sour winds from distant bellows, in a ruin unbuilt, lay a portal to another world. It stood at the top of a grand staircase to nowhere.

In previous ages, the citizens of Old Norumbega had marched through it, bringing their birdcages, their bicycles, the portraits of their ancestors standing in gloom.

Now the plain was empty of motion. The veins above glowed a faint blue. Wind blew through columns and past foundations. Blocks of dead, pink tissue lay where they'd fallen when swept along centuries before by brunch in the Season of Meals.

The stairs near the black portal to Earth were stained from a campfire. A piece of a chair lay charred among old coals. Most of the ashes had already blown away.

There was nothing to mark day and night. No light but the somber blue.

At some time, the portal wobbled in its frame. The cavity shuddered. Its surface rippled.

A man came through. His ears were pointed. There were dark circles around his eyes.

He stood, surveying the sticky plains. He held up lightbulbs in his hand. He turned gears. He wrote symbols on a clipboard.

He disappeared back into the portal.

Time passed. Far out in the muck, some toothed and haunched antibodies paddling on round fins closed in on a school of spotted, long-legged trout and there was, for a time, a distant plashing. A quick, spasmodic frenzy, and then the gut was silent once again.

The wind blew. Hours passed.

And then the portal rippled again, and this time, the Thusser came in numbers. They glowered as they stepped through, all wearing long, dark overcoats with wide lapels. They stood upon the stairs, twenty of them, thirty, forty, moving down to make way for more. They looked out at the world they would soon conquer.

And more came through. And more. And more.

TWENTY-TWO

While the Thusser spread their dominion across the Earth and into the Great Body, and the Mannequin Resistance waited to firebomb the helpless population of the capital city, the Norumbegan Social Club held another tea dance for the Court.

The Grand Hall was lit with candles that streaked the walls black. A gentle, warm breeze blew in through the smashed windows, stirring the wide leaves of several plastic palms that had been brought in specially for the occasion. The curtains had been pulled aside so the Stub, wild-eyed, could observe from his throne. And the Court, dressed in their grubby finery, danced.

Gregory wondered if maybe he could ask Gwynyfer to take a turn with him around the ballroom. He imagined the weight of her arms on his. He didn't really know how to do ballroom dancing, but he guessed it had to do with holding on and swaying.

"So," Brian said to Gwynyfer, "you were going to point out all the members of the Imperial Council to us — everyone who could have used the Imperial seal."

She patted her forehead in despair. "Are you really — really — going to ask me about that? In the middle of a lovely party?"

"Fourteen people died this morning in an attack," said Brian. "Gregory's and my world is under siege. This is no time —"

She wailed, "How could you have come so *far* and still be so *uninteresting*?"

"Here's an idea," said Gregory. "I was thinking — Bri — Gwynyfer — I was thinking that the best way for you to point out the members of the Council without anyone noticing would be, Gwynyfer, if you and me were to dance, the two of us. As we went around the room, you know, in circles, you could say, 'Hey, there's Lord Honeybunny.'"

Gwynyfer smiled. "Is that an invitation?"

Gregory bowed. "Gregory Stoffle of the Grand Duchy of Brookline greets Miss Gwarnmore, daughter of the Duke of the Globular Colon, and extends his wish that tulips will spell out her name and the air around her hair will smell like candy canes. He respectfully requests that she joins him so that together, they might demonstrate to the ancient Court of Norumbega how to get down and shake up a jive panic."

Gwynyfer laughed. "Miss Gwarnmore reservedly accepts Mr. Stoffle's offer. May the brunch never flood his basement."

Gregory said, "That was beautiful, sister." He winked at Brian, put his arm around Gwynyfer, and danced into the crowd with her.

With his small, white face, Brian watched them go.

Gregory couldn't believe he had one arm kind of around Gwynyfer. His other hand held hers. It was like static electricity along his skin.

He couldn't believe how complicated her face was. It looked beautiful, every angle he saw it from. When she turned to the side, there was her profile — perfect and poised. When she looked right at him, her eyes were so clever, her eyebrows were so symmetrical, he felt like he had to say something.

He said, "Your dress is a smart little number."

It was plaid silk.

"Thank you. It's the perfect frock for murder investigation."

"Obviously."

"So there," she said, bobbing her head, "are the Ex-Empress and the Ex-Emperor. As the Stub's parents, they're the two most important members of the Imperial Council."

"How many members are there in all?"

"Eleven, with the Regent. But he'd dead. So that makes ten. There's Lord Dainsplint."

"Of course. Who had two motives to kill the Regent: both because he could try to become Regent himself, and because he wants to make sure that the Court stays in New Norumbega and the Great Body. Because like the wizard says, he owns a lot of land here."

"And you know the Earl of Munderplast."

"Who also has a motive: He was from the opposing party, and he also wants to become Regent."

"And Count Galahad Ffines-Whelter."

"Gesundheit."

"Gugs."

"Do you want to wipe your nose on my sleeve?"

"You know Gugs."

"Yup. Does he have a motive for killing the Regent?"

She thought about it. Her thinking face, Gregory noticed, was adorable. Finally, she answered, "I don't think either he or Lord Dainsplint thought that the Regent was acting in the best interests of the Norumbegan Social Club. They thought he'd lost his way. Maybe Chigger and Gugs were in cahoots."

"What's cahoots?"

"Chums. Plotting together."

"So that's five. There's five more left."

"Over there is Lord Attleborough-Stoughton. The financier. He has bags of money." With a wag of her head, she indicated a man in a fur coat with a bristly mustache. "He made millions on trains. He built the Esophagus Line."

"Reason for killing the Regent?"

"He hated the Regent. And I bet he would be very angry about any suggestion that we abandon the Great Body and go back to Old Norumbega. His financial empire is here. All his railroads. If the Court ever left the Great Body, he would lose everything."

"So we should figure out where he was at midnight two nights ago."

"Sure. Spiffing. Enjoy asking him. He'll adore that."

"Next?"

"Next," she said. "See that stiff with the monocle over there?"

"Monocle," Gregory said. "I didn't think anyone still wore monocles."

"It's not prescription," she said. "He just likes the way it looks."

It was an older gentleman, balding, with a fringe of white hair and a white mustache with ends that pointed straight up. His monocle flashed in the candlelight, runes running continuously across its rim where he could read them. He was dressed in white tie and tails. Looking around the gathering, he pouted, as if he approved of nothing.

"Wow," said Gregory. "He looks like he has the runs and he's trying to keep it in."

Gwynyfer laughed and nodded. "Yes," she said. "That's my father. Cheveral Gwarnmore, Duke of the Globular Colon."

Gregory looked at her, astonished. "Your father is on the Imperial Council?"

Gwynyfer furrowed her brow. "Of course," she said. "We're from one of the most ancient Norumbegan families."

And as Gregory was about to ask a surprised question, a crooner standing in front of the band began singing.

At the sound, across the room, Brian's eyes grew wide. It was the voice they'd heard over the Thusser radio.

He rushed, pushing and leaping, through the dancing crowd. Noblemen glared. Brian got to Gregory and Gwynyfer's side.

"Gregory!" he said. "Gregory! Do you hear that voice? That's the guy we heard through the radio!"

Gregory looked annoyed. "So go get his autograph," he said.

"No!" said Brian. "We heard him on the walkie-talkie! All gluey-voiced like that! Right after we heard a bunch of people talking, like the people in this room were all talking, I bet, before the band started playing. That radio — it's a spying device! There must be a bug in here — a hidden microphone that picks up everything happening in the Grand Hall and the throne room. The radio isn't just how Dr. Brundish talked to the Thusser — it's also how he listened in on the Council's secret business. That must be how the Thusser keep an eye on what's happening in New Norumbega."

Gregory stopped dancing. He was shocked, but what Brian said made a lot of sense.

"So much for tripping the light fantastic," said Gwynyfer. She stepped away from Gregory.

"Somewhere in this room," Brian insisted, "there's a microphone that's broadcasting everything to the Thusser." He began looking carefully around at the potted palms and the tables and the drones.

Brian was starting to attract the notice of the Court. They were glaring at him.

Gwynyfer's mother, bedecked with peacock feathers, swept up to them. "The Duchess of the Globular Colon inquires of her daughter what she is doing fraternizing with that human creature." She pointed at Brian.

"Mother, he says that the Grand Hall has been tapped by the Thusser."

The woman stared at Brian. Other couples were starting to gather around them now.

"You realize, Gwynyfer, that he's an unknown. It is he who has been trying to get us to abandon the city." Her aigrette trembled with disgust.

"Ma'am," said Brian, "I'm not —"

The man in the beaver fur coat — Lord Attleborough-Stoughton — glowered at Brian's side. "What's your angle, kid?" he asked. "Who are you tangled up with? You with the manns?"

"That's not what I heard," said Gwynyfer's mother, the duchess. "I heard the Thusser. He has the pallid, morally exhausted look of a spy for the Horde."

"Is it the Thusser?" asked Lord Attleborough-Stoughton. "Huh? Fess up, kid. You're in deep with someone."

Now Brian was surrounded by frowns. People were drifting over. "I read something in the paper about him." — "Thusser spy." — "Thusser." — "Really? Too, too sad. So young in years, so old in vice." — "That's the one? The one people are talking about?" They surrounded him. He looked at their faces. They hated him.

"That's ridiculous!" he said, but no one was listening. "It's ridiculous! I specifically said I want you to *defeat* the

214

Thusser! *Defeat* them! Because North America, where I'm from, is in danger! Why would I want to —"

"If anyone cares to shake on a small wager," said Gugs, "I'd bet a magnum of champagne it's the Thusser he's from."

The Duchess said, "The boy tried to convince the Regent to abandon our city."

"I did not!"

"What sort of game are you playing?" asked Lord Attleborough-Stoughton.

Duke Gwarnmore, Gwynyfer's father, just peered at the boy through his monocle.

Lord Dainsplint appeared at the edge of the crowd. "What's the ruckus, chaps? Oh, that miserable little blighter."

Brian protested to him, "You know I'm not in league with the Thusser! I'm the one who tried to convince you to stop them!"

"I know you're probably dangerous, and you're certainly no fun," said Dainsplint. "You're always piddling in our campfire."

Brian was about to reply, but Dainsplint held up his hand. "No! No! You're uninvited. No tea dance for you. Out! Out, I tell you!"

Brian retreated in shame.

Gregory watched him go. He shrank back into the crowd. He felt bad for Brian, but he didn't want anyone to notice him and throw him out, too.

The dancing had been so much fun.

Now the music had stopped.

Lord Dainsplint looked around. "Ho, ho, ho," he said without pleasure. "Back to the drollery." He waved a hand.

The band started up again, and the crooner began to sing.

And far away, through hundreds of miles of tubing and corky organ, in a camp by a ruined city, a Thusser radio operator with a headset leaned close to a console, nudging dials, smiling, hearing — faintly — Norumbega's song.

✳ ✳ ✳

Brian walked through the empty palace. Everyone else was up at the dance.

That was fine with him. He was so angry, he didn't want to run into anyone.

They weren't wrong, he reflected. He did want them to lose, at this point. He wanted the mannequins to march into the city and demand their independence and get it. The Norumbegans deserved to lose. They were lazy. They couldn't keep a thought in their heads for more than three minutes. They didn't care about anything or anyone. They were selfish.

Yes, but not just selfish. They were too giddy and bored to even be good at being selfish.

Part of the palace had apparently not yet been built. The staircase he moped down hung outside the palace, with only badly nailed two-by-fours where a wall should be, like a stitch in the keep's side.

And Gregory — Brian was angry at Gregory, too. Retreating like that into the crowd so he could keep dancing once Brian was gone. It seemed like Gregory cared more about flirting with Gwynyfer than stopping the Thusser.

Or, Brian admitted, than being friends with him.

Brian had reached a wooden hoarding that led around the curved belly of the palace. He walked along it, peering out the windows at the city and the siege.

The Mannequin Resistance was drawn up into lines, unmoving, in the desert. They were, he figured, waiting for someone from the Imperial Council to go out and hear their terms. Little did they know, no one was being sent.

As Brian leaned out of one of the windows, the plank flooring underneath him began to shake. Someone else was walking along the hoarding.

It didn't feel very solid. He scurried along to the next arched door that led back through the thick palace wall and stepped through it. Inside was an old reception hall with a black-and-white marble floor. As Brian walked across it, he realized it wasn't marble, but linoleum.

He heard someone fumbling with the metal latch. He didn't want to see anyone. He didn't want to be accused again, so he stepped back and lingered behind a wing-back chair.

It was the Earl of Munderplast, looking nervous. He shut the door and peered around suspiciously in the gloom — failed to see Brian — and rushed past.

217

Brian watched the old man go. He remembered Lady Munderplast's hint — that the earl had not been home the night of the murder.

And he decided to follow.

Carefully, he rose up and slipped along the corridor after the retreating nobleman.

TWENTY-THREE

As soon as the dancing resumed, Gregory whispered to Gwynyfer, "Let's try to find the bug."

"What bug?" she asked.

"The microphone that's picking up everything you say in here," he explained. He made his way toward the throne room. "It's probably in here," he said. "When we turned on the radio at first, the talking was kind of muffled. That's probably because people were standing out in the Grand Hall, a little ways from the transmitter."

The heavy curtains into the throne room were open, and people stood by the Stub, drinking tea and eating biscuits. A beautiful nanny knelt by the throne, holding up a series of plastic letters and whispering their names to the one-eyed plug.

Gregory and Gwynyfer stood near the Stub's chair, inspecting it for suspicious hardware. It was a wooden armchair, painted gold.

"Whoops," said Gregory, and dropped a Triscuit on the floor. He stooped to pick it up and stow it in his napkin. While he was down on his knees, he looked under the seat.

Nothing.

He stood, glancing around at the pastel drawings Randall and Elspeth Fendritch had done on the walls.

"Are you going to eat that?" said Gwynyfer, pointing to the Triscuit.

"What do you mean?"

"Five-second rule. You can still eat it."

"I was checking under the throne."

"Ahhhh."

"Let's look at the walls."

They moved along the walls, scanning them for irregularities.

Behind them, the Court danced and gossiped, talking of the awful Thusser and the chubby human kid and the boring manns.

And then, Gregory found it. High up on the wall, in the center of a huge, painted sunflower, there was a disc.

"Right there," he said. "See?"

Gwynyfer squinted. "It's raised."

"Something's attached to the middle of that flower."

"You're right."

"How are we going to get it? It's too high. You think I can drag the throne over here and climb up?"

"A better idea: dance."

"Come on. Don't you want to see if that's the Thusser's bug?"

"I said I have a plan. Let's dance."

220

Gregory and Gwynyfer spun around a few times. Then she said, "Now you're going to lift me up as part of the dance and spin me. Sit me on your shoulder. Spin around. I'll put my arms out and grab the disc."

Now this was a plan Gregory liked. Bold, flirty, and stupid. He was liking Gwynyfer more every minute.

He lifted her up, swayed around. She screamed laughter like she was having a great time — maybe she was — and held her arms up in the air. He spun them in a circle, staggering with her weight. He ran into the wall, and she slid down.

Adults were glaring.

But as Gregory and Gwynyfer resumed their fox-trot position, Gwynyfer slipped the disc from her hand into his.

Their fingers clasped around it.

❋　❋　❋

Brian crept along through dark, deep places in the palace, following the Earl of Munderplast. At this depth, the walls were uneven — huge hunks of dried muscle larger than courthouses, stacked and slanted above Brian's head. Torches were lit along the walls. Great, angular shadows sputtered. Brian followed the old man through chasms and defiles.

He did not see the earl look backward and notice him. He did not see the earl draw a knife.

The Thusser listening device was a disc with a hole in the middle and something like an earlobe.

Gregory said, "I have an idea. Let's go up to Dr. Brundish's lair and get the radio. Then we can show everyone how it works."

Quietly, they removed themselves from the dance.

＊　＊　＊

Now Brian saw that others were arriving through passages in the huge slabs of tissue. They were wearing black robes. They walked through the broken cavern-scape, all congregating on one point: a ramshackle amphitheater of jutting rock and uneven slope. The earl beckoned for them to pass him, whispering to each of them as they walked toward the rough-hewn stage. The earl himself hung back, surveying the meeting of this society in gloom.

Brian hid behind a boulder, twitching with excitement.

＊　＊　＊

Gregory and Gwynyfer stood in the chirurgeon's office.

"Now," said Gregory. "For the demonstration. I bet this gadget is broadcasting to the radio. So . . ."

He flicked a switch on the radio. He held the disc near his mouth.

The sound of talking and music came out of the speakers.

Gregory and Gwynyfer exchanged confused looks.

Gregory tapped the disc. "Testing," he said. "Testing, one two three."

No trace of his voice reached the radio.

"I don't get it," he said. Into the disc, he said, "This is a test. Broadcast. Hey. Yoo-hoo. YOO-HOO!"

Nothing. The radio picked up the band, the mutter of people socializing.

"It's still picking up the throne room," Gwynyfer said.

"Which means," Gregory concluded, "that we've made a stupid mistake."

"Hmm?"

"This isn't the Thusser's listening device. This is someone else's listening device. Two people had the throne room bugged. We picked off the wrong bug. And the Thusser can still hear everything that's going on down there."

✳   ✳   ✳

Brian crouched, watching six robed figures meet below. The Earl of Munderplast stood quite near him, looking down toward the others, arms crossed. He now wore a robe of black satin, too, and a hood.

Below, the six figures talked quietly amongst themselves. Brian could make out no words. Syllables thwapped like bats around the broken chamber. Echoes muttered in all the dead, muscled corridors.

And suddenly, the Earl of Munderplast and one

223

other moved back toward Brian. The boy instinctively cowered, trying to push himself into a crevice. But they weren't just walking past him — they were walking right at him.

He panicked. He didn't know if he should run or keep hidden.

They were looking directly at him. Time to run. He got up. He scampered.

They ran after him. The earl had a knife.

Brian hurtled down the uneven hallway, hands out, pushing off against the fallen walls.

The two figures rushed after him.

He didn't know the way back. He skipped over a crevasse. He looked behind him. They were gaining. Their hoods had fallen off: the earl and a young knight Brian had seen but did not know.

He turned a corner, hoped for stairs. No such luck.

He hurled himself along over an obsidian expanse of dried heart that felt like stone.

The hands grabbed him.

He was hauled backward.

The knight gripped him. The Earl of Munderplast put his knife to Brian's throat.

They pulled him back toward the amphitheater.

The others were waiting.

"Brethren!" the earl announced. "We have a spy in our midst." He and the knight gestured that Brian should walk down the ragged slope to the others. He stumbled and tripped, barely caught himself. The hands on his arms were firm. They bruised him.

He was thrust into the middle of the ring.

They stared at him.

"Brian Thatz," hissed the Earl of Munderplast. "Welcome to the final meeting of the Guild of Regicide Assassins."

TWENTY-FOUR

I didn't . . . I . . ." Brian couldn't speak. The men glared down at him.

"We gathered together some months ago," said the earl, "for the express purpose of killing the Regent in a way no one could ever detect."

Brian looked around wildly for a way out. They had surrounded him. The earl still held up his knife. Brian needed delay. "Why?" he said. At least, if they were going to kill him, he wanted to understand.

"We have, each of us, our own reasons," said the earl. "I wished, of course, to unseat him so that I could run for the office. I wished power for the Party of Melancholy. It is time for the Court, the flower of Norumbegan chivalry, to lay aside their *tea dances*," he said with disgust, "their *games nights*, their cheap frivolity. It is time for weeping, for lamentation, for *planctus*. We should lie listless upon couches. Recognize what we have lost."

Another figure pulled back its hood.

It was Gugs.

"I joined just the other day," he said, swinging his arm. "When the Regent announced we might abandon New Norumbega. Can't do that. Can't abandon the old family hoard. All those streets we own. The fam built this city. Not about to give it up, see?"

"So one of you . . ." Brian hesitated. "One of you, the other night . . . one of you dressed up like a guard? And . . . snuck into the Regent's . . . the Regent's room? And . . . ?"

The conspirators looked at each other. They did not look happy.

The earl dropped the knife to his side and turned away. His voice echoing in the amphitheater, he said, "The murder was committed at midnight. Some wily gome slipped into the Regent's room dressed, as you say, as a guard, and slit him open."

Brian looked between them. He didn't even know some of them. "Which one of you, um, did it? Actually did it?"

The earl said, full of despair, "At the hour of midnight, Brian Thatz, this parliament of conspirators was meeting. We wished nothing more than the Regent's death."

"So, which of you —"

"You misunderstand me, human," said the earl. "We were here. At midnight. Hearken?" He turned to face Brian again. His eyes were full of shame. He walked his fingers up and down the knife's blade. "Do you see what I am saying? We were *all* here. Together. Plotting. Look around at our sorry faces. We all wished to kill him. Any one of us would have raised our daggers anent his treacherous throat. But none of us — *none of us* committed the murder." He concluded bitterly, "The fact that we are

227

conspirators, plotting against the life of the Regent — that is the very proof that we had nothing to do with his murder. We are unfortunately ... wretchedly ... despicably ... miserably ... innocent."

Realization dawned on Brian. "So your meeting here ... it's your alibi."

The Earl of Munderplast nodded slowly. He looked at the haft of the knife. He inspected it in the reflected light from the torches, frowning.

"Shall I kill him?" he asked the others.

A young knight shrugged. "Why not?" he said.

The earl nodded and stepped toward Brian.

Brian pulled back. He glanced at the wicked blade — then looked left, right, up, everywhere for a route out.

He felt hands grab his arms. Cup his elbows.

Push him forward.

The earl's breath was thick in the gloom. He raised the dagger.

"We'll bury your body here," said the earl. "After we drain it."

"Bad luck, old thing," said Gugs at Brian's ear.

The earl pressed the blade to Brian's neck. Brian gagged, started coughing. He felt the dull edge scrape his white flesh. He tried to pull away — and stammered, "Wait! Wait!"

The earl looked skeptically at him.

Brian said, "Wait! I know — I know — I can help you."

"Mmm?"

Brian held up his hands. "I have an idea."

"Help me? In what wise?"

"Win . . . you know . . . win the election."

The earl pulled the knife back.

"Doesn't seem very sporting," said Gugs. "Chigger really is giving the thing his full swing."

"Tell me," said the earl. "How could you help me win?"

"Because . . . because . . ." Brian thought quickly. "Because we don't know where Lord Dainsplint was the night of the murder."

"He had an alibi, thought I," said the earl.

Brian nodded eagerly. "He did! He told Gregory and me that he was with Gugs." Brian pointed. "They both said they were playing cards in the basement."

Gugs shrugged uneasily. "Well, deuce take it, so we did, for a while. Played for an hour or so. Before I bumped along to the Regicide Assassins meeting."

"So he was lying, wasn't he? And you were? You're Lord Dainsplint's alibi, and you're lying."

Gugs admitted, "It was a bit of a steamer. A corker. I couldn't very well say I'd been at a planning meeting for the assassination of the Regent. So when Chigger said he was with me at midnight, I said, 'Eh, true enough, lads.' It was not entirely the truth."

"So," said Brian, "where *was* he?"

Gugs looked angry. "I am not going to rat out Chiggs. Kill the kid, Mundy."

Brian flinched.

But the Earl of Munderplast looked at Gugs. He looked at him long and hard. "You may have to 'rat out,' as you say, Lord Dainsplint. I would find it very *useful* if you 'ratted him' thus 'out.'"

"I won't squeal. No, sir. Don't want you and your bloody old Melancholy Party to win the ruddy election."

"I don't know that you have any choice, Count Ffines-Whelter." The Earl of Munderplast jammed the knife back into his robe somewhere, stepped forward, and put his hands on Brian's shoulders. "You see, this darling child, this precious human cubling, this adorable, pallid little bairn — he can testify that you lied to hide Lord Dainsplint's true location at the time of the murder. And if Dainsplint cannot explain where he was when the Regent met his end all untimely, then I fear Dainsplint will be under investigation for assassination. He will have to withdraw from the election." The earl gave a gloomy smile. "Why, suddenly I feel the sun bursting through the clouds. It's a delightful feeling. I am feeling lucky, Count Ffines-Whelter. It is a happy day for melancholy."

"I won't tell you a thing," said Gugs.

"But you know?"

Gugs turned and walked away. The others looked nervously after him.

The Earl of Munderplast looked nothing but sly and triumphant.

"Come along, Brian Thatz," he said. "I am going to make you some hot chocolate. Tomorrow, we shall put, as they say, 'the squeeze' on Gugs. We shall consider what we may tell the investigating wizard, Thoth-Chumley. We will make some discreet inquiries as to where Lord Dainsplint might have been, if not playing poker or pinochle with his boon companion." Munderplast put his arm around Brian and led him out of the rough amphitheater. "In his chocolate, does the human boy," he asked, "prefer one marshmallow or two?"

TWENTY-FIVE

The Earl of Munderplast motioned for a drone to pour more chocolate. Brian, Gregory, and Gwynyfer were seated on an old sofa in Munderplast House just a few streets away from the palace. Brian and the earl had run into the other two kids near the Grand Hall, and Brian had asked the earl to invite them along. Gregory, after all, was another witness: He, too, had heard Chigger lie the other day and say he'd been playing cards with Gugs when midnight (and the killer) had struck.

Brian asked, "Do you think that Chigger really did kill the Regent?"

The earl waved his hand around. "Or, one hopes, something even more embarrassing. Who can say what he's hiding?"

Munderplast House was a narrow, ramshackle three-story place crammed with chipped gargoyles removed from Old Norumbega centuries before. The floors were slanted. They creaked whenever the drone shuffled in front of the piano.

"Is anyone going to go out and talk with the Mannequin Resistance?" Brian asked.

"It would be political death so to do. Whoever talks with them admits that one is weak, and that one is willing to negotiate with servants. The Court will accuse anyone who parleys with the Mannequin Resistance of being on the side of the windup toys. The mechanicals do not deserve the guerdon of our attention."

Gregory pointed out, "They'll get your attention pretty quick when they start blowing things up with those cannons. I kind of want to be out of the city by then."

"Once you provide your evidence that Lord Dainsplint lied," said the earl, "you may go as you will, I am sure. Leave. Retreat ye to the Scummy Marches, the Phlebotl Plains, the Lung of St. Eustace."

"We can't leave without our friends," Brian declared. "They're being held in the prison."

"Because, dear little wight, they are under investigation for assassination. They're not likely to be revived soon, unless it's for torture."

Brian, determined, said, "We're going to prove that they're innocent."

"Best of luck."

"And we're not leaving," Brian added, "until you tell us how to activate the Rules Keepers."

"Activate the Rules Keepers? . . . Yes, you've prated of it before. . . . Who remembers the Rules Keepers? Probably no one but Archbishop Darlmore, the Ex-Empress's brother. I recall that he spoke often of the Thusser and the need to keep watch upon them, lest they break the Rules."

233

"Archbishop Darlmore?" said Brian. "I haven't met him."

"He became so dull. So terribly, terribly dull. So awfully, despicably dull that he removed himself from our number and went to live as a hermit in the desert. The last I heard of him, he was off in the Wildwood. At the far end of the Dry Heart. He is probably mad by this point. Crazed. Wode as a jackrabbit in a sack. Why, I ask, would one leave all this?" The earl gestured at his sagging ceilings, his buckling walls, the broken stained-glass windows shoved into uneven spaces between the timber beams. He sighed. "True, true, verily; we are not what we once were. Our race was a proud race, and our dominion stretched from shore to shore, when mankind was but a pack animal scrounging in the bellies of dead pigs for sustenance."

Gwynyfer made desperate, secret signs with her eyes that the earl was about to become Melancholy and talk and talk and talk about how in the days of yore this fair folk had been the cat's pajamas.

"Well," said Gregory, "it was really nice of you to give us hot chocolate. We should probably go."

"A shame. Just when I was about to speak of our proud heritage in the days of yore. I have photographs."

Gwynyfer rose and curtsied. "The daughter of the Duke of the Globular Colon renders heartfelt thanks to the Earl of Munderplast for his hospitality."

"And thanks for not killing Brian," said Gregory. "That was really nice, too."

"Yeah," said Brian. "Thank you."

234

Gregory explained, "He hates being killed."

"So do we all," said the earl, sipping port wine.

Brian, Gregory, and Gwynyfer shuffled toward the door.

"Tomorrow morning," said Munderplast. "Tomorrow morning, after the funeral, we shall call out Lord Dainsplint and make him account for himself."

Brian nodded. The three kids all waved to the earl, said good-bye, and let themselves out.

As soon as they were on the street, Gregory started whispering to Brian. He told him about finding the little hidden microphone on the wall of the throne room. But he told him, also, that it hadn't been the one broadcasting to the radio Dr. Brundish had left behind.

"There must be *another* bug in the throne room somewhere," Gregory explained. "We think maybe one of the Council is carrying it."

Brian said, "I can't believe so many people were spying on the Regent."

"It does seem rather poor form," said Gwynyfer.

"But who could it be?" Brian asked.

They were walking through the Imperial Square, in front of the palace. It was mainly a crater. The guardhouse and several mansions were piles of rubble. They had to skirt the edge of the square, since the middle was a hole. In front of them, the wall of the palace was blackened from the blast.

"Why aren't people more upset about the deaths?" Brian asked.

"Because we aren't people," said Gwynyfer. "All your

worries seem very strange to us. We —" She stopped short. She was staring into the ruins of a mansion. Far back, one of the palace guards stood. His lamp was flashing on and off.

"Is he signaling at us?" Gregory asked.

The three stared into the darkness. The lamp flashed. Someone else was coming. The guard ducked and stepped back into the shadows. He covered the light.

"Let's see what he wants," said Brian. He tromped over the piles of rubble.

Gregory and Gwynyfer followed.

Unsteadily, they made their way across planks and broken furniture and chipped tissue. A few lone walls stood, where just that morning, one of the fanciest houses in the city had looked out on the Imperial Square.

The guard retreated back farther into the ruins.

"Hey!" Gregory called in a whisper. "What's up?"

The guard set down his lamp.

Too late, the boys saw he wore a black mask over his nose and mouth.

By that time, he had already raised what looked like a blunderbuss. He had pulled the trigger. And the ruins filled with smoke.

✳ ✳ ✳

It was some kind of gas gun. Huge billows of yellow smoke poured around Brian, Gregory, and Gwynyfer. They stumbled backward, eyes stinging, mouths burning.

They felt the smoke curl down their throats, parch their lungs.

Brian screamed to anyone who might be passing by. "Help! It's the killer! He has on his fake uniform!"

Screaming, however, turned out to be the wrong thing to do. Brian yelled and yelled — and then drew breath.

His lungs filled with poison. And he fell.

TWENTY-SIX

Gregory, scrambling forward, covering his face with his shirt, dimly saw Brian start choking. Brian's hands were around his neck. His eyes were wide. Gregory took two short, darting steps over the rubble toward his friend — and then saw the guard charging up the mound of debris toward them, his blunderbuss still spitting gas.

Gregory reacted by instinct. He closed his eyes and plunged toward the assassin, hand out. He half ran, half slid up and down the mound.

The killer was not expecting anyone to head toward him.

Gregory's hand slammed into the man's chest. The assassin raised his gun to batter Gregory's head — he swung it —

— and he would have sliced Gregory's skull right open if Gregory hadn't pushed the man, felt the man topple backward by two steps, arms swinging to right himself.

Gregory had his eyes clenched shut. He had his shirt and his hand over his nose and mouth. He couldn't see a thing. He felt the uniform. His hand crawled upward. He whapped the man's face. He tried to tear off the mask. He felt a strap and pulled. The assassin collapsed toward him, smacked him in the neck.

Gregory fell.

He gasped. The smoke filled his lungs. He saw stars. He coughed. He retched. The man was stumbling away. Gregory realized that he must have pulled the mask off. The assassin bellowed with sneezes. Gregory heard the bricks shift as the killer retreated.

The gas was still thick all around Gregory and he couldn't see Brian now. He had no idea where his friend was. He raised himself up on his elbows. He pulled himself forward.

A voice muttered something under Gregory's belly. He jumped.

Something was in Gregory's hand. Something he'd pulled off the assassin was talking.

He coughed and coughed. He was crawling down the slope, toward the square. Tears streamed down his face. He rubbed at his eyes wildly, but his hands were covered with grit. He sagged to the side and rolled before he could stop himself.

The gas was getting thinner.

Brian was there on his knees, next to a broken wall, whooping with the effort of drawing a breath. His hand was on his chest.

Gregory crawled toward him. He stooped and finally rose. He gagged.

"You okay?" he asked.

Brian nodded, his eyes bright red.

"I got this," Gregory said between wheezes. He held up the gadget he'd pulled off the assassin's head. He turned his head and coughed so hard his whole body spasmed.

Gwynyfer was sitting several feet away on the remains of a windowsill. She smiled, waved, and said, "Hey-ho."

Gregory stared at her.

A voice in his hand said, "Have you killed them?"

Gregory looked at the gadget in his hand. It was an old headset.

The voice asked, "Are they dead?"

He held the speaker up to his ear. Its sound was too metallic and distant for Gregory to be able to tell whether he knew the voice or not.

"No," he answered, speaking into the little horn on the mouthpiece. "We're not dead. We're angry."

"Who is this?"

"You tell me first."

"This headset is not your property."

"I'm sorry," said Gregory. "Your gas didn't kill us. It's no worse than my dog's."

There was a *click*, and the headset went dead.

Gregory shambled over the rest of the rubble to where Gwynyfer sat, looking as if she were perched on a split-rail fence in a field of wildflowers.

He couldn't believe she would just sit there and watch the two of them almost die of suffocation.

"What are you doing?" Gregory asked her.

"Oh . . . The haze adds such a very splendid golden tinge to evening's blue."

✳　✳　✳

When Brian and Gregory lay in their bunks, high up in the palace's rambling, rickety corridors, Gregory said, "So who do you think attacked us?"

"I don't know," said Brian. "There are two reasons that I can see for someone attacking us."

"My charm, your shoes?"

"Yeah. Right. Okay, first. First, it could be someone working for the Thusser. If they can hear everything that's going on in the throne room because of Dr. Brundish's device, then they know that we've been trying to get the Imperial Council to wake up the Rules Keepers and get the Thusser expelled from Old Norumbega."

"All right."

"Two: It could be Lord Dainsplint or someone working for him. He would want us dead before tomorrow so we couldn't help the Earl of Munderplast question him about where he was on the night of the murder. We're the ones who heard him lie about his alibi."

"And three."

"What's three?"

"People here think you're in league with the Thusser."

Brian shifted angrily in his cot. "How could they think that?"

"Because you keep mentioning the Thusser."

"But that's stupid! I keep mentioning them because we hate them."

"Well, I'm just telling you that everyone in that ballroom thought you were in league with the Thusser before you got out of there."

Brian sat grimly in the dark. Finally, he said, "And you didn't help much."

Gregory was genuinely taken aback. "What do you mean?"

"You didn't say anything! You just stepped back into the crowd when they accused me."

"What did you want me to do? Get burned at the stake along with you?"

"You could have said something. Or Gwynyfer could've."

Gregory turned onto his side. He buried his head in his pillow. "It was embarrassing," he said. "Everyone was staring at us."

Brian didn't say any more. He closed his eyes and thought furious thoughts about how Gregory hadn't really stood up for him.

It took a long time for both of them to get to sleep.

✳   ✳   ✳

Out in the darkness of the Dry Heart, the Mannequin Resistance inserted keys into one anothers' backs and wound each other up, so that they were ready for battle. They stared at a city that they did not truly see, a place of lights and spires and grand walls buckled with gatehouses. They stared through the night at the fairy lights and considered how best to apologize for the damage they were about to do.

✳ ✳ ✳

Deep within the gut, on endless seas of digestive sludge, men in dark overcoats trawled through the vast expanses in aluminum motorboats. Their faces were blue in the dim illumination of the veins above. Behind them slid large rafts, pulled by ranks and ranks of the seven-legged beasts of burden. On the rafts sat the Thusser army, hunched with their knees under their chins, their eyes open, their mouths frowning.

They sought the city of New Norumbega.

✳ ✳ ✳

In Gerenford, Vermont, at the edge of a wood, time quivered. Within Rumbling Elk Haven, time sped. Though only a week had passed in the outside world since Brian and Gregory had walked the softly curving streets and young lawns, within the suburb months had passed. Houses had ballooned into fibrous Thusser nests. Their skin of clapboards and brick had stripped away or turned wet and oozing, and now their supporting beams and studs were wound around with cotton-candy insulation

243

and shuddering walls of some alien wrap. Some of the houses were now on stilts, or sprawled across lawns infested with creatures that had scuttled from the Thusser's own world.

It was night there, too, and the streets were thronged with Thusser settlers greeting each other easily, helping the new folks move in. They stepped aside reverently for the military units that marched past, headed for the borders with the human world. Tanks on twenty or thirty armored legs rumbled past. A metal ship hung in the air. Construction equipment rumbled through ditches.

In each house, embedded in the walls or in the floor, hung humans, lost in folds of architecture like the wad of meat in a fried wonton. They dreamed uneasily, and the Thusser stalked their sleep. Curled up in their nests, slumbering themselves, the Thusser ate human dream, sucking gently at the imagination's teat.

In one of the houses, in a master chef kitchen that was warping into something inhuman, Prudence stared out of a wall. Across from her, Wee Sniggleping stared back. Their faces were terrified and frozen. They did not blink. The stove buckled and grew tendrils. The marble countertops sagged like hot Saran wrap. The room gradually shifted toward something that would cook the meals of the invader.

But the two faces did not shift at all. Their look of horror and shock never ceased.

Now, in the wood that marked off Thusser time from human, sudden jolts of movement burst through the trees. An army sped up, flowed to the barrier. The army stepped through into slower, human time.

There were hundreds of Thusser, wearing their long dark coats. They looked around outside their suburb. They growled reports into speaking-trumpets attached to backpacks. They listened for answers. They began to march.

Some marched along paved roads. Others followed dirt roads through the woods. They were followed by trains of construction equipment — bulldozers that blazed new paths as they rumbled forward.

One detachment reached a house — a double-wide trailer — with a little garden beside it. Among the flowers and vegetables stood cartoon rabbits and deer cut out of plywood.

A Thusser approached the house and knocked on the screen door.

A woman answered. "Yeah. Can I help you?" she said, not opening her door all the way.

"Humanite," said the Thusser, "be alerted that Rumbling Elk Haven has claimed your house and your land. We shall commence settling here."

"Ha!" said the woman. "Under what law's that?"

"We no longer require zoning laws, deeds, or permits. Please yield to me."

"You and what army?"

The Thusser smiled briefly. He stepped aside and gestured backward.

The woman looked out into the dark forest.

There she saw them, waiting in rows, glowering at her.

She was about to slam the door shut when the Thusser on her stoop thrust it open with his palm. The chain ripped off its fastening.

He stepped in.

She screamed.

For a long time, it was silent in the double-wide.

Then the Thusser commander stepped out. He beckoned to his Horde.

By the dawn, the little trailer home was surrounded by freshly dug cellar holes.

The woman, breathing raggedly, sat in a chair, her eyes vacant, a thick, goopy strand connecting the back of her head with the wall.

Through the night, the Thusser dominion was spreading.

TWENTY-SEVEN

*T*oday, thought Brian as he got up. *If we don't figure out who killed the Regent and tried to kill us, we need to give up and get out of here today. We need to find out as much as we can about the way to call the Rules Keepers, and we need to leave the city. We need to go out and find that bishop who's living out in the Wildwood and forget the Court and the assassin and all of these horrible people.*

That was what he thought as he got up, but after breakfast, he found himself sitting on the palace's great balcony with Gwynyfer and Gregory, watching an assault on the mannequins.

The Court was supposedly sending ambassadorial carts out of the city to speak with General Malark. In fact, these were the same carts that had met Dantsig several days before — carts fitted out with magnets strong enough to drive mannequins crazy and erase their memories forever.

"This is wrong," said Brian. "This is awful. You just need to leave them alone. You need to agree to let them live in their own territory. They just want to stay down in the gut." The carts rolled out along the main avenue. People watched from their roofs. "I don't want to be here," he said. "I can't watch this."

"I don't want to be here, either," said Gwynyfer. "It's frightfully hot out and I'm worried I'll burn." She rubbed her arms. She said to Gregory, "When they've been destroyed and the Fest has happened, we should all go away to my family's beach place out in the Organelles. You'd adore the Organelles. Everyone does. They have these crabbish things you can catch and roast, and the fluid is blue and warm. . . . Can you stay after the Fest?"

Brian watched Gregory sharply. Gregory looked at Brian, guilty, and said, "That would be great."

"But we can't," Brian interrupted.

"You've stayed here for days," said Gwynyfer. "Surely you're not in such a hurry."

"It looks like Thusser spies were responsible for the assassination," said Brian. "Once we prove it for sure, I think the Court will be much more interested in helping us defeat them."

"*In*-terested," Gwynyfer sighed. "*In*-terested. It takes a lot to interest us." She sagged in her deck chair.

The magnetic carts had pulled out of the city limits and were trundling across the desert. Brian watched them with anxiety.

Those poor automatons, Brian thought to himself. *When they reach the carts, the magnets will be switched on, and all the robots for an acre around will die.*

He couldn't take it. He stood up. He wanted to scream.

Gregory did not seem bothered. He looked a little nervous, but he was still reclined in a chair, drinking his orange juice out of a champagne glass.

Brian moved to the railing. It didn't help. He still wanted to yell warnings. He moved toward the door, as if he could bolt through the palace, down through the streets, and make it to the plains in time.

He closed his eyes. When he opened them, the automaton delegation had stopped, standing in formation, surrounded by guards. The carts were still approaching.

Brian raised his hand. Courtiers lounging on the deck turned to glare at him.

✳ ✳ ✳

Out in the granular sands, on the carts, Norumbegan soldiers prepared the magnets. They wore nothing metal. Knights sat in the carts, smirking, looking forward to the devastation they would shortly cause — the bodies crumpling, the active brains scrambling, these upstart machines with their dream of life torn from them, seeing the pitiless truth of Imperial dominance as they died.

The soldiers prepared switches.

"Not till we're close enough," said the knight in the seat of command. He looked out at the delegation. They stood, waiting for the carts to approach. "Junk-heap heroes," he muttered. "Come get death."

He raised one hand in greeting. He put the other hand on the toggle switch that would switch on the electromagnets.

And then he heard a whistling in the air.

✳   ✳   ✳

On the palace balcony, far above, the Court lazily watched the carts approach the mechanical enemy.

"Any minute now," said Gwynyfer, leaning forward. "You'll see them fall apart. They'll drop to the ground and bump up and down like dying ants." She smiled and interlaced her fingers, straining to see.

But instead, the Court watched as cannons spewed bombs toward the carts. They watched as the first bombs struck — and the desert spewed up smoke and flame.

Soldiers rushed from the wreckage, tiny, fleeing.

"How did they know?" The Duke of the Globular Colon muttered near Brian. "How did they know it was a trap?"

The Mannequin Resistance rushed past the flaming wreckage of the ceremonial carts. They quickly surrounded the soldiers. The action was tiny, indistinct. Smoke still rose through the morning air.

And Brian had an idea. He knew exactly how the Mannequin Resistance had known the carts were a trap: *They'd had the throne room bugged.* The listening device that Gregory had found must have belonged *to the mannequins.*

It all made sense to him now. *That* was what Dantsig was doing, the night of the murder. When he got the guard's uniform, he'd snuck into the palace to plant the bug. He'd crept into the throne room, stuck it to the wall, and slipped out.

He hadn't been in the palace to murder the Regent. He'd been in the palace so that the Mannequin Resistance would be informed of all of the Imperial Council's decisions and deliberations.

The bug was moved, now — in Gregory's pocket. General Malark might be hearing everything that was said near Gregory, if the sound wasn't muffled by jeans.

If there were two listening devices picking up sound in the Grand Hall, the other must be carried by the Thusser agent — the member of the Imperial Council who was probably the murderer.

Brian had faith that he and Gregory would figure it all out. Once Lord Dainsplint had been confronted, and Gugs had admitted he hadn't been playing cards with Chigger at midnight . . . then things would be clearer.

The answer was almost within their grasp.

The boy supported himself on the railing, stunned with this wave of realizations. He was sure he was right. He looked out at the triumphant mannequins leading their captives back toward their lines. He couldn't help but feel triumphant, too.

"Okay, boring," said Gwynyfer, rising. "Let's go play shuffleboard for a minute before I have to pop along and dress for the funeral."

TWENTY-EIGHT

A round lunchtime, the Court held the second state funeral Brian and Gregory had attended since they'd come to the city of the Norumbegans. It was in memory of Sir Pleckory Dither, the knight who'd been killed in the first mannequin bombing attack on the palace. Once again, the streets were thronged with people. Once again, vendors sold roast chestnuts and scoops of icy gelato. They sold balloons painted with faces like corpses.

Gregory and Brian stood near the Earl of Munderplast in a crowd of aristocrats as the parade began. Once again, the nobility of Norumbega were dressed in top hats and the face paint of mourning.

"After the requiem," said Munderplast, "I shall hold parley with Lord Dainsplint. I have no doubt that we shall discover he has been involved in something dastardly which shall add quite satisfactorily to my dismal opinion of what we've all become."

Brian said, "You could maybe search him, or get that wizard investigator, Thoth-Chumley, to search him. I think whoever is guilty of the murder might be wearing a secret transmitter that broadcasts everything to the Thusser. The Thusser are in communication with at least one person in the capital."

"And we think it's someone in the Imperial Council," Gregory said. "Whoever's responsible for the assassination must have one of those rings." He pointed at the signet ring on Lord Munderplast's finger. "He sealed a command to one of the servants with the Imperial mark on the day that the Regent was killed."

Munderplast held up his own ring and inspected it. "It's terribly exciting. One feels almost refreshed." He thought for a moment. "No," he corrected. "Not refreshed. But as if a new and more vigorous strain of rot and decay had taken over this old body." He smiled faintly and patted his own belly.

The Imperial band went past at the head of the parade. Behind them came dancers dressed as animals.

Gugs appeared at Munderplast's side. "I say," he said, "quite a ruckus."

Brian still couldn't believe that the Norumbegans were confronting an enemy army and attending the funeral of one of their own knights, and could only say things like "What a ruckus." Now he understood why, at the last funeral, Lord Dainsplint had talked about pinning the murder to Dantsig, whether Dantsig was guilty or not. Now Brian hoped it could just be proved easily that Dainsplint himself was guilty. Then Brian and Gregory could point the finger, get their mechanical friends revived, find a way out of this mess of a city, leave

Dantsig with the invading host, and head into the hills to find the hermit.

A band of musicians playing weird, wailing pipes walked past. A bagpipe with innumerable little horns was slumped on the shoulders of three men, all of whom blew and pumped its bellows.

Then came a choir, screeching a song in a high-pitched, unnatural voice, saying, "Alas! He has passed! He is out of the Great Body now! He is lost! He is tossed! He is . . ." They were gone down the street.

And then came the dancing girls, Gwynyfer among them.

She whirled along, doing the old dances of her people. Her eyes were sly and thin. This time, when Gregory waved, she nodded to him quickly before spinning by.

"You seem to much affect the daughter of the Duke of the Globular Colon," said the Earl of Munderplast. "One does so like to see young love. It reminds one faintly of when one had hope." He scratched his chin. "Faintly," he repeated.

"She's a grand gal," said Gregory. He could barely keep the giddiness out of his voice. He told Brian proudly, "Did you know her father is on the Imperial Council?"

Brian shook his head — then froze — and stared.

Gwynyfer Gwarnmore danced away, her hair shifting around her shoulders. Behind her came the young men of the Court, painted in blue woad, dancing on the mud of the road with their bare feet.

Brian felt tremendous alarm. "Her father?" he repeated.

"Yeah," said Gregory. "She told me yesterday. They're a really important family."

The Earl of Munderplast explained, "A decayed branch of the ancient royal line. Descended from King Durnwyth Gwarnmore the Navigator."

"Good blood, that," added Gugs. "Runs golden as honey. Clots when necessary."

"Clots?" said Gregory.

"Scabs," Gugs explained.

"Gregory," Brian interrupted, "her *father* is a *suspect*."

Gregory thought about it. "Well, yeah, okay, technically."

"*Not* technically!" Brian protested. "He really could have done it! And we've been telling Gwynyfer *everything*."

The rusted old automaton built to represent the Norumbegan Empire Herself, Grieving, rattled along the street, painted eyes blind, squirting tears. She threw flower petals. The petals were ground in the dirt of the avenue as the crowd surged forward and fell back.

Brian and Gregory weren't paying attention. Gregory challenged, "What are you saying?"

"That Gwynyfer could have been spying on us."

Gregory rolled his eyes. "Oh, sure."

"Yes, *sure*. And what about all those times she tried to convince us to stop investigating? Why do you think she did that?"

"She's one of *these* people," Gregory said, throwing his hand out toward the earl and Gugs with disgust. "You know they can't keep a thought in their heads for more than five minutes."

"I say," Gugs interjected. "That's a bit cheeky, old thing."

"Oh, come on." Gregory turned to Gugs. "You got to admit it. You people have the emotional lives of gnats."

Gugs shrugged. "Not entirely off the mark," he agreed. He looked anxiously over the shoulders of the mourners to see if the ice-cream man was out of banana gelato.

"Wasn't always like that," the Earl of Munderplast complained. "Once we wrote epic poems that made us cry for weeks." He pointed. "I say, look at this."

Brian didn't want to look at anything. He wanted to run after Gwynyfer and question her. She had disappeared, however, and clanking by was a set of three drones, all draped in black silk. Brian didn't care.

The Earl of Munderplast explained, "They'll be buried with Sir Pleckory Dither — in his tomb — to serve him in the afterlife. Time was, a member of the Norumbegan Court would have had ten or fifteen fully conscious mannequin servants entombed to accompany him to the next world. But, alas, if we had any mannequins now, we couldn't spare them. And imagine — now they're surrounding us. They're entombing *us*."

"Outrageous," said Gugs.

And Munderplast sighed. "Sad times. Sad times."

"You would *entomb* mannequins?" Brian said. "When they were *alive*?"

"They're never alive," replied Gugs.

"They *think* they're alive," Brian said.

257

"You're getting very emphatic," said Gugs.

"You would just force conscious automatons to walk into the tomb? And you'd seal them up in there?" Gugs nodded, bewildered. Brian asked, "What happened to them?"

Gugs shrugged. "'Spect they wound down. Unless someone left a key so they could wind each other up. Then maybe they'd last for a few years, keeping the tomb clean, till they decided the game was up, and they'd let themselves slow down and stop." He looked sadly at the disappearing drones. "When I was just a little lad, I was frightfully keen on being buried with a bevy of clockwork dancing girls. Thought they could do a little mourning polka."

Brian couldn't believe what he was hearing. *No wonder*, he thought, *the mannequins have formed the Resistance!*

"We're not finished with the Gwynyfer subject," Gregory said. "You're just paranoid."

"Her father is a suspect."

"You just don't like her."

"Why should I like her? She's —"

And Brian was just about to scream about everything that had been bothering him for days — all the snotty comments, the confusing talk, the mean lies, the cruel pronouncements, the insane evasions —

But then the screeching horn blew to announce the arrival of the dancer portraying Death.

"Look away! Look ye away!" the Earl of Munderplast demanded.

Brian and Gregory turned, along with the others. A great drum beat. Its sound thudded through the stone and sand. Brian could feel it in his skull, in the pads of his fingers.

There was a loud *bang*.

No one stirred, for fear of Death.

Except Gugs. He twisted his head to look.

Brian wondered what the bang had been. He thought it didn't sound much like the drum.

The crowd huddled in the square, facing away from the parade. They waited for the all clear.

But the all clear didn't come.

Gugs said something strange. It didn't sound like language. He bent down, looking for something on the ground.

Brian wondered if they were supposed to say a prayer or touch the dirt.

Then Gugs collapsed.

Brian yelped.

"Slungs," exclaimed the Earl of Munderplast.

Brian squatted at Gugs's side. The nobleman was lying facedown. "Help me flip him!" he said.

They heard the crowd exclaim — people were wondering what was going on. As he and Gregory heaved, Gregory gasped. "He's — it's a hole."

"Shot!" Brian said.

Gregory put his hand in front of Gugs's mouth. He held it there, feeling for breath. Brian watched Gregory's face. Gregory had gone white with terror.

Slowly, Gregory shook his head.

Brian stood up and, shielding his eyes so he wouldn't see Death, called out, "Count Galahad Ffines-Whelter has been shot in the back! Gugs is dead!"

The crowd roared. People pushed and shoved. Screaming. Panic.

And in the middle of it, the dancer costumed as Death scampered on its route, flinging out its arms — seen by many.

"We can see Death," said Gregory, delighted.

"Don't!" Brian called, grabbing his arm. "Don't forget these people *are* magic. Death *might* be fatal."

"Indeed," said the Earl of Munderplast. " 'Death might be fatal.' Such wisdom in one so young." The old man watched the Wizard Thoth-Chumley elbowing his way through the crowd. "Thoth-Chumley!" called Munderplast. He curled his hands around his mouth. "Seek Lord Dainsplint! Lord Dainsplint!"

Gregory asked, "You think Lord Dainsplint shot Gugs?"

"Of course. The late Gugs was living proof that Lord Dainsplint was lying about where he was at the time of the murder."

Brian didn't agree. He said, "But Gugs was Lord Dainsplint's best friend."

"Which is precisely why the fool Gugs doubtless told Dainsplint that I'd be questioning them about their alibi. And that is what sealed Gugs's doom. Dainsplint had to kill him once he knew that." The earl was waving again to Thoth-Chumley. He informed Gregory and Brian,

"There is nothing more deadly than a best friend. Who else do you let come so close? Who else may wield the dagger against you better?"

Gregory and Brian looked at each other.

Brian was thinking of Gwynyfer.

He wondered who Gregory was thinking of.

Far above, slim birdlike things lifted off the palace battlements and swarmed the air.

TWENTY-NINE

The crowds were clearing. The procession, interrupted, would not begin again. The dancers and bands who had been on parade were milling around, carrying their horns and trumpets and golden pikes. They inspected each other, suspicious, confused.

Down the avenue, the figurehead of the Norumbegan Empire Herself, Grieving, stood stupidly, grabbing handfuls of petals and hurling them mechanically at nothing as people walked past. Lurking in the gate of the palace was the ceremonial chair to which the corpse of Sir Pleckory Dither was bound. There had not been enough of him left together to sit upon the chair, so they had baked the pieces into a pastry that resembled him. It sat on the throne of death, garlanded with flowers. The egg-brushed pastry eyes goggled. His remains had been abandoned in the panic.

"I'm going to see how Gwynyfer's doing," said Gregory.

"Why?" Brian asked sharply. "Why?"

"Because she might be frightened."

"You know she might be our enemy. She might be working with the assassin."

Gregory grimaced. Waving his hands around in frustration, he said, "You are so — you are *so, so* paranoid."

Hotly, Brian said, "She's a suspect. Isn't that right? Don't you think so?"

"No. *You* think so."

"I know so."

"Oh. How does Sherlock know she's guilty?"

"I don't. I know she's a suspect."

"She has been nothing but cool with us from the beginning. She helped us. She risked her life for us."

"Maybe she knew she wasn't really risking her life," said Brian. "Maybe she knew Dr. Brundish wouldn't actually kill her. Maybe she knew whoever that was in the guard uniform with the smoke gun wouldn't actually kill her."

" 'Maybe she knew.' Is that all you can say?"

"She certainly didn't look very worried when we were attacked last night."

"You are such a jerk."

"*I'm* a jerk?" Brian protested. "What about *you*? You're a jerk! You're more worried about — about going on *dates* with the next Duchess of the Bulbous Colon than you're worried about saving millions of people from the Thusser!"

"Not 'Bulbous,' " said Gregory icily, his hands flexing at his sides. " 'Globular.' "

263

"I don't — I don't care what kind of colon she's from! I'm saying you're more interested in trying to make out with her than you are in trying to save your parents and my parents and all those kids stuck in the walls and all those families and —"

"You just can't handle that girls like me."

"I can't handle that all of New England is in danger and all you're doing is —" Brian couldn't come up with a mean enough thing to say. He wasn't used to arguing with Gregory. He wasn't used to speaking out — didn't like to argue — couldn't bear to see someone hurt.

"We're not talking about New England," Gregory said. "We're talking about Gwynyfer."

"Well? I'm right about her, aren't I? She didn't look very worried last night."

"You mean, when I saved you? When I saved your life?"

"That doesn't have anything to do with whether she's guilty."

"It has to do with whether you're a jerk."

"I'm trying to figure out what's going on here — who's probably a Thusser spy — so we can get someone at the Court to tell us how to activate the Rules. You — I don't know what you're doing. Waltzing in the grand ballroom. You love it! You love all these stupid jokes they make, and all the mean things they say, and —"

Gregory laughed. "You really hate that I'm popular, don't you?" he said. "I mean, ever since you won the Game, you've thought you were God's big, golden thumb sticking straight up. You think you're some genius, and I'm just your sidekick. Your funny sidekick. Look, Bri. I'm not going to be your comic talking horse. I *let* you win the Game."

"And ever since I won," Brian said — hardly knowing what he said, "ever since I won, you've been angry because for once, everything isn't all about you. I actually was doing something where people paid attention."

"And you've become a jerk as a result."

Brian just stared at him. He looked pale and sick. He said, "I don't believe you're saying this."

"Well, I don't believe you're saying Gwynyfer might be working with the murderer."

"Well, she might be!"

"Get lost," said Gregory. He turned and began to walk away.

The choristers who were going to sing the requiem mass were wandering past like a weird herd, their sheet music under their arms.

"Gregory!" Brian shouted. "Gregory!"

His friend didn't turn around.

Brian yelled, "Everything you're saying is probably being broadcast to the Mannequin Resistance! Through the bug you found! Gregory! It's a bug for the Mannequins!"

Gregory waved a hand angrily and kept on walking.

"Ah, friendship," said the Earl of Munderplast, his hands clasped in front of him. "Brightest bud of affection's rood."

Brian didn't feel good. He didn't know where to go. He looked around the square. The pastry corpse sat stiffly in its throne. The Wizard Thoth-Chumley was yelling orders to guards.

The Earl of Munderplast had turned away, and was speaking with reporters. "It is deeply shocking. Deeply, deeply. And galling," he declared, shaking his head. "What is particularly awful to consider is that it seems that the most likely perpetrator of this attack — this blasphemous and barbarous attack — is my worthy brother in the Council, Lord Dainsplint. I am told by the Wizard Thoth-Chumley that Lord Dainsplint has been sighted running through the lower city, as if trying to elude the dint and mickle might of justice. A sad, weepsome day it is, my friends. Of course, we must remain fair and never doubt my honorable colleague until he is proven guilty. I would not wish this incident to prejudice the Court as the election approaches. I am sure there is a perfectly, *perfectly* excellent explanation for why Lord Dainsplint should flee from the palace guards, as if guilty; and when he is dragged back to the palace keep in chains, I shall be the first to welcome him and clip him to my bosom and ask him many questions — many, many questions. Surely all of this proves what degenerate times we live in. Seek ye the past, my friends. Things shall only get worse. Here: a smile for the cameras." He put on a jaunty grin. They snapped photos. He bowed and walked toward Brian.

"My boy, by the wounds of the Dagda, it is a fine day for dolor."

Brian nodded. He felt more desolate than the leader of the Melancholy Party, who seemed positively chirpy.

The earl rubbed his dry hands together. "Let's along and watch Thoth-Chumley bring his man to bay. Lord Dainsplint cannot escape forever. The mannequins guard us all too closely."

Brian said nothing, but followed the earl sadly down the avenue.

A troupe of animal dancers walked past, their masks dangling in their hands. "Love some coffee," said a reindeer. A fox nodded, wiping the sweat from his cheeks.

Brian craned his neck to see if he could catch a glimpse of Gregory greeting Gwynyfer. He couldn't see the girls' dance troupe through all the clog of people.

The Earl of Munderplast was waving happily at palace guards who rushed past. "Godspeed!" he called to them. "May you find the killer! Whoever, of course, he may be!"

Brian had an idea. He ran forward a few steps so that he'd be next to the earl. "Sir," he said. "Sir?"

"Yes, child?"

"Do you think . . . is there any chance . . ." Brian thought again. He decided he should sound more forceful. Gregory clearly thought he sounded plenty forceful these days. He said, "You know what you should do? To really tie down the case against Lord Dainsplint?"

"Isn't it fascinating, the directions from which advice may come?"

Brian continued, "This is when you should order the two mannequins who were captured to be revived. Before the guards capture Lord Dainsplint. Because the mannequins are the main suspects, but we know now what they were doing in the palace. They were planting a bug in the throne room — the one that Gregory has now. If you'll just wake them up, they'll tell you that truthfully. That's what they were doing at the time of the murder. So they'll just make the case against Lord Dainsplint even worse."

"Better, you mean."

Brian thought about it. "Yes, sir," he said. "I meant better. They didn't do it. Someone just arranged the uniform for Dantsig so he'd be framed. Maybe it was Lord Dainsplint."

The Earl of Munderplast thought about this. He grew so deep in thought he stopped in his tracks. "So," said the earl, "it is possible that Lord Dainsplint is guilty not only of murder and of assassination, but also of freeing mannequins from where they were bound in prison?"

Brian nodded. "It's possible. If he wanted to kill the Regent, he could have gotten the two guard uniforms, kept one for himself, and given the other one to a servant anonymously, with a sealed note that said the Imperial Council wanted the uniform delivered to the prison. The servant went down and delivered the uniform, leaving it where Dantsig could easily find it. So Dantsig and Kalgrash got out. Dantsig put on the uniform and decided he would slip into the palace and stick the bug in the throne room. He must have had it concealed in a secret drawer in his body or something."

"Let us move swiftly over to the secret location," murmured the earl.

"Probably one of the things he expected to do when he was here exchanging us for the prisoners from Delge is stick it on the wall. So he headed into the palace with Kalgrash to do that. So the assassin —"

"'Twould be awful if it were Lord Dainsplint — though that, of course, is not out of the question."

"The assassin knew that Dantsig would be seen and would be suspected. So while he figured Dantsig was creeping around somewhere else, the assassin went into the Regent's room and killed him."

"All of this perhaps bearing upon Lord Dainsplint." The earl nodded. "Though God forbid, of course . . . God forbid . . ." He smiled. "My boy, let us go to the prison." He clapped. "It is time that we woke your friends up from their long nap."

THIRTY

When Gregory found Gwynyfer, she was leaning against a wall, talking to a girl dressed in wild, swooping pheasant feathers — one of the Ex-Empress's maids-in-waiting who'd danced some mortality mazurka in the procession. The girl's face was painted with black spirals on each cheek.

Gwynyfer saw Gregory and gave him a little curtsy. She excused herself to her friend ("Miss Gwynyfer bids a fond farewell to the dear Miss Rose. May the gods settle like butterflies upon her skirts."), pushed herself off the wall, and sauntered over to Gregory, wrapping her shoulders in a woven shawl.

"Are you okay?" Gregory asked.

She answered, "It's shiver-making."

Gregory nodded seriously. Coolly, as if he wasn't boasting, he said, "We were standing right next to Gugs when it happened."

"Poor Gugs," said Gwynyfer, shaking her head.

"We were right there. He just — it was weird. There was a bang, and he looked around, and then . . . We thought he was staring at the ground. But he was collapsing."

"That's awful. Dying in a crowd, surrounded by others — terrible. When I die, I want Death to print me a private invitation." She smirked at the tackiness of public collapse.

Gregory wanted to be able to laugh, but he was a little shocked. He just stared at her. It seemed like she was making a joke out of Gugs's brute fate. He tried to smile. He could tell it wasn't very convincing.

Gwynyfer looked around. "Where's your potty little friend?"

Suddenly, Gregory felt protective of Brian. He didn't want her to laugh at him, to despise him. He looked around on the street, hoping Brian wasn't following him. "He's busy," Gregory said. "Investigating."

"Of course," she said. "Always investigating. Danaan love a duck." She took Gregory's arm. He couldn't believe his luck. Her arm was so light. She was saying, "Have you heard they think it might be Lord Dainsplint?"

"It's . . . Oh, yeah. Yeah. They do think so. Because of, really, what we've been saying for the last couple of days. About who had an alibi. I mean, it's our investigation that's really made them suspect Lord Dainsplint."

She skipped a couple of steps, dragging his arm with her. "It is too, too very thrilling," she said. She sounded like one of the women of the Court, but her grin was a girl's.

Gregory didn't know what to think. He still felt the shock of Gugs's collapse — and couldn't believe Gwynyfer didn't feel it — but then again, there was her arm touching his, and people were looking at him with envy, and there she was herself — the descendant of a goddess, a fairy duchess wanting to walk out with him along the garbage-lined avenues of this elfin metropolis. It was like something from a daydream.

Guards ran past, blowing whistles.

Gwynyfer's striking eyes widened. "They've found him!" She grabbed Gregory's hand and ran.

There they were, he thought, holding hands, running through the crazy city. Weird, elephantine beasts of burden swayed in the streets, pulling carts. Cages full of chickens teetered in courtyards. She yanked him through a slim gate in a fence and over a piece of rough ground where ragged grass grew, littered with rusting cans. "Whoa, Nelly!" he said, almost tripping.

"Come on! Shortcut!" she cried. "The hunt's in full cry!"

She pulled him under a curtain hung in an arch — and ducking, he laughed, because she'd almost tangled him up and lost him. She laughed, too, tickling his knuckles — and he realized he was having a great time.

They slid down an embankment and clattered through a passageway, swerving to avoid men with a tub of steaming water. They heard the piercing whistles of the guards nearby.

They scampered down a stone staircase and ran through the shacks at the edge of the city. The air was filled with blue smoke. They tumbled across the main street, now looking left and right to see if they could catch the pursuit. The guards were nowhere to be seen.

They wandered down an alley.

Their hands were swinging between them now. There was no more dragging. Gregory loved the slenderness of her fingers. He loved that they were enjoying the same rhythm in their arms.

He didn't know when he'd felt better.

Until someone grabbed him by the collar and yanked him to the side.

Gregory stumbled — pulled Gwynyfer after him. She yelped.

Gregory saw the muzzle of the pistol before he saw who held it.

It was Lord Dainsplint. He held the gun near Gregory's temple. "Topping!" he said with slightly crazed and frantic good cheer. "Hostages!"

"I don't suppose that you're innocent," said Gregory, "and that we've made some kind of terrible mistake?"

"I fear that, no, I am guilty, and you may find it hard to keep your head wholish."

THIRTY-ONE

Brian, the Earl of Munderplast, and the Wizard Thoth-Chumley stood in a shed in the prison, surrounded by old machinery: sooty dynamos, decaying batteries, rattling fans. Everything was grimy with dust.

The wizard had laid Kalgrash and Dantsig face-down on a worktable. He had opened up their backs and attached wires.

"All right, okay," he said, chewing gum and flicking switches. "Yup. Yup. Voilà."

He turned a dial.

✳ ✳ ✳

— wouldn't let them shut him off! He would knock them all down! He would make a break for it! There was no —

Kalgrash blinked. He looked around, startled.

He was in a dark little room with lots of old machines. Brian was there, and an old guy in a black velvet tunic, and a wizard in a double-breasted suit.

"Uh, what happened to my fight scene?" he asked.

"Two days ago," said the wizard. "Move your left arm. Okay. Right arm. Okay. Left leg . . ."

While he flexed his limbs, Kalgrash asked Brian, "What's going on?"

The old man, the Earl of Munderplast, answered, "You, foul automaton, have been accused of assassinating the Imperial Regent of the Empire of the Innards. We have awakened you to see what you plead."

Kalgrash held up his hands. "Not guilty, not guilty, not guilty."

"So we suspected," said Munderplast. He told the wizard, "Now switch on the truth."

Kalgrash narrowed his eyes, but before he could speak, there was a jolt. He couldn't move. He could feel his voice like a little speaker lost in his throat.

The Wizard Thoth-Chumley took out a pad. "Explain your whereabouts the night you escaped from the prison."

Kalgrash heard himself explaining how he and Dantsig had crept out of their cell, found a uniform for Dantsig, and headed up to the palace. Helplessly, though he tried to be vague, he told them that he suspected Dantsig had planted a bug in the Imperial throne room. He told them that he had stopped by Brian and Gregory's room to talk.

275

"Did you, now?" said the Earl of Munderplast with withering interest. "After planting a bug in the throne room, you stopped to talk with this child here?" The earl looked with disgust at Brian and asked, "And you, my boy, are well-known to the automatons?"

Brian clearly didn't know how to answer.

The wizard kept asking Kalgrash questions. The clockwork troll couldn't help but answer.

✳ ✳ ✳

Carefully, Lord Dainsplint forced his two hostages along alleyways, stopping carefully at each cross street to make sure the "bobbies," as he called the guards, didn't spot him.

He was not alone, as it turned out. He had a girlfriend with him — a woman Gregory had never seen at Court — a blond woman whose hair looked too blond to be real and whose lips were too red to be fake. She wore a quiet, gray skirt suit of an old-fashioned cut.

"You shouldn't take them, Chigs," she said. "This is just going to get you into more trouble."

"Things have already gone rather wrong, darling of my heart — rather south." Chigger peered around a corner. "We need all the dashed help we can get."

"Maybe if you hadn't shot someone," said Gregory. "That might be where you went wrong."

"I didn't realize people would cotton on to Gugs's death so quickly," Chigger complained. "I should have shot your friend Brian first. He alerted all and sundry. Then people were looking around . . . and there I was . . ."

"I think letting us go would impress the jury," said Gregory.

"Keeping you with me will ensure there won't be a jury," said Chigger. "Nor a trial. Turn leftish and stay smart. No tricks."

Gregory felt desperate. He knew that Chigger — not just a criminal, but a Norumbegan, with no conscience to speak of — would feel no remorse for killing him. And they were getting farther and farther from the guards who might stop him. There was no way the soldiers he'd seen running about up above would ever find their way through this jumble of tiny streets. Rapidly, he tried to think of ways to alert someone as to where he was. . . .

Gwynyfer was inspecting the woman. "Who *are* you?" she asked. "I've never seen you before."

"Alice," said the woman. "Alice Nabb."

"Gwynyfer Gwarnmore, daughter of the Duke of the Globular Colon, greets Miss Nabb and wishes —"

"Oh, preserve me," said Lord Dainsplint. "We're not curtsying at an ice-cream social. More's the pity."

Gregory thought this was his chance to get in good with Chigger's girlfriend, to convince her she really didn't want him and Gwynyfer along for the ride. He said, "It's a pleasure to meet you. I'm Gregory." He held out his hand.

Gregory looked down and saw that Alice's hand was wrapped in a scarf. She'd been hit. There'd been gunplay.

"They got you," said Gregory.

She nodded, shrugged. Her arm moved clumsily. "They hit my hand," she said.

Gwynyfer still appraised the woman carefully. She repeated, "I've never seen you at Court."

Alice Nabb scowled. She gestured toward Chigger. "This one," she said, "wants to keep me hidden. It makes him nervous when I'm around."

"If the good lady would be so kind as to 'stow it,'" growled Chigger.

"Darling —"

"Don't."

They were on the outskirts of the city, creeping along a row of low shacks. A half mile away, across the granular sands, a set of four cannons faced the city, surrounded by automaton infantry.

And suddenly, Gregory had an idea. He knew how to get word of where Chigger was taking them. He thought of Brian's last words to him. He reached into his pocket.

"Keep moving," said Chigger, waving his gun. He yanked them into the next alley.

Gregory had the mannequins' little bug held loosely in his fist, concealed. Carefully, distinctly, he said, "I can't believe the Mannequin Resistance is so close. Did you see those four cannons?"

"Yes, I saw the four bloody cannons."

"This is crazy, Lord Dainsplint," said Gregory, trying to speak clearly enough so that the bug would transmit everything he was saying. "Kidnapping me and Gwynyfer Gwarnmore won't do you any good. You'd sure better hide well, so that the Court can't find you. Because if they captured you, it would mean a real embarrassment for the whole government. Complete confusion. (Which way here, on Magnolia? Left? Okay, left on Magnolia.) Imagine — one of the candidates for regent turning out to be a murderer — it's a real embarrassment for the whole of Norumbega. Very tough in a time of war. If they could actually find you and haul you in, they'd be able to prove that you murdered the last Regent and they'd —"

"Would you stop gabbling?" Chigger said.

"Right, here? On Goibniu Lane?"

"Please stop flapping your lips. My skull is splitting with a thousand headaches." The man threw open the door of a hut.

"In here? You want us to go into this hut?"

"Of course I wish you to go in. The gently applied pistol might be considered a wee hint."

"Gosh, those mannequins look pretty determined, don't they? It would be bad if they knew exactly where you were, too. They might try to capture you to disgrace the Court for all sorts of reasons."

"What is the purpose of your inane monologue?"

"I would really hate to be facing those mannequins we saw back there. Especially if I was the kind of person who had ever wanted the mannequins dead. I would be feeling really apologetic, right about now. Like, 'Whoa, mannequins, I am soooo sorry. I did not mean that "dead" thing at all.'"

"Are you suggesting," asked Lord Dainsplint, "that *I* murdered the Regent?"

"Of course," said Gregory. "Why else would you kill Gugs but to shut him up so he wouldn't say where you were on the night of the murder?"

Chigger gave a grim laugh. He looked pale and crazy. "If only," he said. "But no, my boy, I was nowhere near the palace that night. I was here in this hut. With Alice."

Alice looked sadly at the floor. Her face was filled with shame.

"She is my girl," said Chigger. "And has been for some years."

She sat, facing away from them, her face sorrowful. She unwound the wrap on her hand.

Gregory and Gwynyfer looked at Chigger in confusion.

"So why didn't you tell the Court where you were?" Gregory asked. "Why did you have to kill Gugs?"

Alice's hand was unwrapped. She held it out and inspected it. A bullet had taken off three fingers. Gears and rods were visible, poking out of the shattered skin.

"Because," said Lord Dainsplint, "I could recover my political career after a simple assassination. But no one would ever forgive me — let alone cast their vote for me — if they found out that my own true love is an automaton."

THIRTY-TWO

S o you see," said Brian, "it couldn't have been Dantsig or Kalgrash. It must have been one of the Imperial Council. Like Lord Dainsplint."

The Wizard Thoth-Chumley had forced both automatons to speak truthfully — and both had confirmed what Brian had guessed long before: that Dantsig had spent the evening peacefully bugging the throne room, and didn't even know where the Regent's bedchamber was in the maze of the palace. Now they sat in the prison — Thoth-Chumley, Kalgrash, the revived Dantsig, and the Earl of Munderplast — frowning at one another and wondering what to do next.

Reports occasionally came that the city guards had lost Lord Dainsplint's trail.

The earl said to Brian, "You claim it was a member of the Imperial Council. But most of us were either with the Ex-Empress and Ex-Emperor or were in the bowels of the palace, scheming — poor fools, we — to assassinate the Regent the next day at noon."

"But Lord Dainsplint wasn't either place."

"No . . . I discover, much to my delight."

The Wizard Thoth-Chumley flipped through his note-book. "I have a list, your lordship, of where all the members of the Council were at the time of the murder." He slid it toward the earl.

Brian read it, too, through eyes enchanted so they could understand the runic script of the Norumbegans.

It said:

Ex-Empress Elspeth F.	her own after-party
Ex-Emperor Randall F.	after-party, too
Earl of Munderplast	~~with his wife~~
	planning assassination
Lord Deft	after-party
Lord Attleborough-Stoughton	after-party
Lord Rafe "Chigger" Dainsplint	~~playing cards ???~~
Count Galahad Ffines-Whelter	~~playing cards~~
	planning assassination
Sir Beothach Drizzle	~~in bed~~
	planning assassination
Cardinal Gludge	~~chapel~~
	~~opium den~~
	planning assassination
Duke Gwarnmore	with his family

"As you may see, milord," said the wizard, "four were in the Ex-Empress and Ex-Emperor's suite, enjoying their hospitality after the tea dance. Four, though you all initially denied it, were in the basement, planning the Regent's assassination. One of you was at home, with his family, and one — Lord Dainsplint — has not yet explained his whereabouts."

"It is a sorry kind of time," mused the Earl of Munderplast, "when 'planning assassination' is the purest proof of one's innocence."

"So it seems, milord, that Lord Dainsplint is our man." The wizard went to the door that led into the prison courtyard and yelled for a guard. When one scurried over, Thoth-Chumley asked the man if there was any news of the fugitive Dainsplint.

Brian whispered to Kalgrash, "How are you feeling? Are you okay?"

"Oh, zippy. Swell." Kalgrash shook his armored arms. They rattled. "I can't believe they shut me off like that."

The Earl of Munderplast said sharply to Brian, "It is sweet that you take such an interest in the well-being of our enemy. Such compassion. I am moved verily to tears."

Dantsig stirred. His speech was still slurred and he still had the slow movements of someone just waking up. "The kid knows his friends. He knows —"

The Wizard Thoth-Chumley ran back into the room. "Game's afoot," he said. "Lord Dainsplint was seen a half an hour ago at the edge of the city with a woman and two hostages: Miss Gwynyfer Gwarnmore and your friend Gregory."

Brian felt his stomach drop.

"Let's go," said Thoth-Chumley. "We'll have to move quickly if we're going to save their lives."

✳　✳　✳

In the hut at the edge of town, Gregory and Gwynyfer sat on the floor, while Lord Dainsplint kept watch through the wooden shutters to see if anyone was coming. Alice Nabb, automaton, sat miserably on the sofa, which was decorated with a thin floral scarf, her little attempt to lighten up the house. Her oval-screened TV was on, though the sound was off. Norumbegan shows floated past in black and white without sense or reason: objects falling off of heights. Bushes slowly crawling up slopes. A man with a handkerchief sneezing and waving at someone offscreen.

"You're saying you didn't murder the Regent?" Gregory insisted. "You really pretend you didn't?"

"No, I don't pretend, you little wretch. I actually *didn't*. I was here dining with Alice. She whipped me up a pork chop and some crème brûlée." He said to Alice, "Now that tragedy has befallen us, my darling, I fear you never will master crème brûlée. For future reference, the crust is supposed to be baked only to a delicate golden-brown; yours was less amber than umber."

Alice turned away from him on the sofa. Her shoulders were low, and it looked like she would have cried, if tear ducts had been installed.

Gregory said, "So you killed Gugs — your own friend — because people would otherwise realize that you were going out with a mannequin?"

284

Alice flinched at the word *mannequin*.

Lord Dainsplint answered, "If people at Court had found out that Alice and I were mooning over each other, it would have ruined my career. Now, as it is, I guess I've bloody well seen to that myself. This shall not be a triumph for the House of Dainsplint and the Norumbegan Social Club." He frowned miserably.

"But if you didn't kill the Regent," Gregory insisted, "who *did*?"

He looked in bewilderment at Gwynyfer.

✳ ✳ ✳

Kalgrash and Dantsig had been sent in handcuffs up to the palace to await questioning at a meeting of the Imperial Council. Brian, the Earl of Munderplast, and the Wizard Thoth-Chumley were following guards through the alleys of New Norumbega, seeking Gregory and Gwynyfer before it was too late.

"There are hundreds of houses to search," grunted Thoth-Chumley.

They looked down a dinky track that led into the desert. A half mile away, the Mannequin Resistance watched them.

"These mannequins really are becoming intolerable," said the earl.

"So why don't you just free the ones you've captured," Brian suggested, "and promise to leave them all alone down in the guts?"

"You've been talking too much to your eggbeater,"

said the earl with distaste. "Your waffle iron. Your apple corer."

"It makes no sense!" Brian protested. "There's no reason to —"

A page boy was shouting and running toward them. He had a message in his hand. "Message for the Earl of Munderplast! Sir! Sir!"

It was a note from the Ex-Empress. The earl unsealed it, sliding his finger under the wax blob that held it closed, marked with the insignia of the Imperial Council. He surveyed the letter and then, without a word, swiveled it around and showed it to Thoth-Chumley and Brian.

The Ex-Empress wrote:

Malark from the Mannequin Resistance just called on the palace phone. I don't know when quite I've been so insulted and ill used. He says to pass on to any interested parties, this:

"It has come to the attention of the Mannequin Resistance that Lord Dainsplint, one of the two candidates for Norumbegan Regent, is holed up in a shack on Goibniu Lane with a gun, two hostages, and a mechanical named Alice Nabb. He claims to love Miss Nabb, though he treats her with the condescension common to all breathers. He was hidden away with her at the time of the assassination of the Stub's late Regent. Given that the governing Council of the Empire of the Innards is clearly unable to select its own leaders competently; given that its leadership is in a shambles;

given that the rulers of the Empire are obviously an embarrassment to the ancient, high honor of their race — given this, we, the Mannequin Resistance, humble servants of Norumbega, have no choice but to move in immediately and suspend the Imperial government until such time as kind, benevolent, and fair-minded rulers are chosen to continue the work of your august Empire. Yours with deep respect — General Malark."

Have you ever seen a thing so vexing? Never mind the impudence of the rotter. Just the thought of Chigger kissing a machine! The spittly appliance! One pictures the bower of love, and one wants to spew up one's brekkers.

Yours,

Ex-Empress Elspeth Fendritch

Brian looked up in astonishment. "Lord Dainsplint was there in that shack when the murder was committed?" His mind raced. "Then who killed the Regent?"

The earl smiled. "It pleases me in a small and humble way," he said, "to discover that Lord Dainsplint is not the assassin. I'm deeply gratified that, instead, he sought to hide something even shabbier."

"How could he not be the assassin?" Brian said. "He's the only one who doesn't have an alibi."

"True," said the earl, looking up and down alleys.

Brian thought back to Thoth-Chumley's list. Something stuck out. "Unless . . ." he said, "unless the Duke of the Globular Colon wasn't really with his family."

287

"You mean — you suspect the fair burde Gwynyfer of lying?"

Brian had considered it before. But it was awful to say it to these men.

"If," said Brian, and ran out of words. He tried, "She might have. Yeah. She might have lied to protect her father. She might have tried to stop us from finding out. She sometimes acted almost like . . . you know . . . like she had something to hide."

"Delicious," said the earl.

"Which would mean that right now Gregory is with three murderers."

"A lamentable plight."

"We have to get him out of that shack," said Brian.

"Easier said than done," commented Thoth-Chumley. "Let's move in." He nodded his head, and they all — earl, boy, mage, and guards — galloped off toward the hut on Goibniu Lane.

THIRTY-THREE

Out in the desert of salt, the Resistance was moving. Mechanical soldiers formed into rows. Whatever they had been trained to do — to cook, to clean — they had put it aside for warcraft. They were prepared to take the city — politely, if possible.

They wore uniforms woven from fibers peeled off the walls of alien lungs. They wore armor forged of metals extracted from cataracts of blood coursing through the Great Body's veins. They had come far to confront their former masters — to protect their masters, as they told themselves delicately — and they would not back off now.

The Mannequin Resistance, banners raised high, began to march on the city of New Norumbega.

✳ ✳ ✳

Thoth-Chumley glared down the alley of pastel-painted cabins. "Check all of them," he said. "Smash down the doors if need be."

289

"No!" Brian protested. "Lord Dainsplint might kill Gregory if —"

"Do it!" yelled Thoth-Chumley, swinging his hand.

There was dust in the air. Thoth-Chumley looked out between the houses at the edge of the city. He saw the first ranks of the Mannequin Resistance approaching.

"We have to drag Dainsplint back to the palace before they get here," he said, pointing scornfully at the clock-work infantry making their way over the plain.

"I," said the earl, bowing, "shall make my exit. This may be a moment of mickle hardship, and people may wish for a leader. I have a little thought of who might offer himself in that role." He gathered his robes about him and made off.

Guards were knocking violently on old doors, demanding to be let in. Brian felt sick with worry.

✳   ✳   ✳

Dainsplint, Alice, Gwynyfer, and Gregory could hear the guards approaching from each end of the alley, forcing their way into each hut in turn. At the crunch of every door kicked down, Lord Dainsplint's mouth quivered. He held his gun carefully.

"You can't win," said Gregory.

Dainsplint pointed his gun at the boy. "No, old top, *you* can't."

Gregory lost feeling in his feet and in his face. He stared at the barrel of the gun.

He kept quiet after that.

Brian watched the clockwork army approaching.

"If someone doesn't release those mannequin-head prisoners from Delge," said Brian, "those soldiers out there are going to destroy this city. They can blow us all up, if they want to."

"We leave these decisions to the heads of state," said Thoth-Chumley.

"Who are the heads of state? You don't have a Regent anymore. One of your candidates is in a hut on this street, holding my friend hostage." Brian was swept with panic and despair. *"There is no one in charge in this city!"* he cried.

✳ ✳ ✳

A shutter flew open.

"Blast it!" came Lord Dainsplint's voice. He screamed, "One more step toward this, my pretty little hovel, and I'll put holes in both the kids' heads!"

✳ ✳ ✳

Gregory and Gwynyfer stared at each other in horror. Gwynyfer reached out and took Gregory's hand. They squeezed each other's fingers tightly.

The television had been knocked down, but it still was on. Dim lights and shadows wriggled out from under it. Alice sat curled on the bed, her knees up against her face, her hair mussed over her eyes. Dainsplint sat with the shutters closed almost all the way — with just a slit so he could see anything that passed on the street. He pointed the gun at Gregory.

✳ ✳ ✳

Brian watched the guards creeping closer and closer to the house where Dainsplint was holed up. "You can't let them!" he said. "He'll kill Gregory if they get close!"

"We have to get Lord Dainsplint before the automatons arrive," the wizard insisted. "They can't take him prisoner. It would be a disaster." He shook his head. "Not on my beat."

Brian watched the guards slinking toward the little blue cabin. He looked out toward the approaching ranks.

There was no hope for escape anywhere.

✳ ✳ ✳

Inside Alice Nabb's cabin, they heard footsteps on the dirt.

"Keep off!" Dainsplint screamed, his eyes rolling toward the window. *"I'll bloody well take their heads off!"*

Gregory held his breath. He could almost feel his own pallor. He felt like he had no blood in him. He wondered if he was going to faint. Gwynyfer's mouth was open. She clutched Gregory's hand.

292

And then came the first slam into the door. Gregory heard Brian scream, distantly, in warning, in protest.

Dainsplint leveled the gun at Gregory. The man drew a deep breath, and —

Gregory watched Chigger whisper the Cantrip of Activation to trigger the gun. The lips moved as if in slow motion. Gregory could almost see the detonation curling out from the muzzle.

But Alice Nabb had thrown herself at Dainsplint a moment before. She landed on him hard, her metal bones yanking against his pliable elfin grip. The gun was pointed toward the wall when it went off — and the wall whickered with the force of the bullet.

Sunlight poured in through the hole.

The door thrashed as guards slammed against it.

Dainsplint fired the gun again, but Alice had forced it up and away. The ceiling rattled. She squeezed his forearm.

The gun fell.

She dragged him backward.

"Alice!" he yelped. "This isn't the time for the tender embrace and the cooing of dashed sweet nothings!"

She didn't speak to him. She simply held him. He struggled, belting out, "I say! Let me —"

The guards burst in.

✳ ✳ ✳

Brian saw the guards bundle Lord Dainsplint out onto the street, handcuffed. Behind him came a blond woman —

and Gwynyfer — and then Gregory, holding Gwynyfer's hand. Brian couldn't believe his friend was still alive.

"Come on!" yelled Thoth-Chumley. "The mannequins!" He pointed.

The infantry of the automaton army stood only twenty feet away — hundreds of them.

Brian staggered. There was no way any of them could run. The force ranged against them was overwhelming. They'd never make it back to the palace.

All he could hope for was that Gregory and he would be singled out by the mannequins and saved.

The guards cowered in the face of the army. They held Lord Dainsplint, uncertain of what to do.

Everyone froze.

They looked out between the houses.

The mannequins stared back.

And then a mechanical officer rode up on something armored that might have once been a horse, or a sea horse, or a six-legged industrial stapler. He was yelling a message of hope back to his troops.

"We are arrived," he declared through a mother-of-pearl bullhorn, "at the walls of New Norumbega. Though these walls be mighty — though they be the work of our masters — we can surmount them! Look at them in their glory — as they sparkle in the veinlight! We could never build such towers! But we can tear them down! With our masters' implicit permission!"

The army roared. They confronted an empty space where they believed a wall to be.

Thoth-Chumley chuckled, suddenly relaxed. "Such

morons," he said. "They can't even see we're undefended."
He shook his head.

The officer on the mechanical steed raised up a saber
and dropped it.

And cannons began to fire.

Huge explosions tore apart the ground, the houses, the
streets, the chimneys, the stoves, the dirt all around
Brian.

And everyone began pelting, pell-mell, back up toward
the palace.

THIRTY-FOUR

Scrambling through the streets, they felt the great heart rock with cannonades. Walls jumped around them. Gravel fell — who knew from where? People were surging through the streets, screaming. A fiery glow lit tenements and stores and bars.

Brian was running neck and neck with Gregory and Gwynyfer. As they ran, Brian studied the girl's face. She looked nothing but stern, glaring back down the slope at the mannequins who stood outside their ring of imaginary stone, waiting for invisible walls to tumble down. She set her eyes on the palace, slid them sideways at Brian, then ran past him, dragging Gregory by the hand.

Another round of explosions burst the city asunder.

Houses tore apart. Chunks of balcony hung on electrical lines, swaying, swinging. Wires fell, sparking along the street. Brian threw himself out of the way of one line that went striking past him like some demon worm.

Panicked wails went up from the citizens. The mannequins, trying to save the people, were destroying them.

Another shell hit — quite close — the detonation so loud they felt it in all their bodies.

Brian fell.

There was darkness — things were falling toward him: rocks, concrete, wood, metal roof.

He reached up, as if a soft hand could ward off tumbling stone —

He screamed once.

And the debris smacked into something invisible and slid to the side. Brian lay completely still — seeing the brick crowd the air, ready to pounce down on him. He didn't understand. He blinked.

Gwynyfer and Gregory were lying next to him. The Wizard Thoth-Chumley knelt near them, holding up his arms, quivering.

"Ski-Jack's Miraculous Bumbershoot," the mage explained, nodding toward the glow of his spell in the air. Charred beams slid off a force field above them.

When the trash had fallen, he dropped his hands. A few final things plunged down around them. He took a deep breath.

"Let's go," he said, and gave Brian a hand up.

The four of them fled toward the palace.

✳ ✳ ✳

The throne room smelled of frightened sweat. The folding doors were pulled aside, and across the Grand Hall, out the broken glass doors, the distant armies could be seen, massed by the city's edge.

297

The Ex-Emperor Randall Fendritch sat near his wife, looking white and weak. His clothes were too large for him and were cuffed and collared with smudges of dirt. The courtiers around him did not speak. They all were too aghast at the flames they saw reflected in the debris of the Grand Hall.

The Ex-Emperor spoke in a high, anxious voice, though no one listened. He said, "We don't fear anything. Not really, old top. We're Norumbegans. Hey-ho, anyone for a round of golf? A gent could exorcise his demons with a few choice chip shots right about now." A cannonball, trailing smoke, lofted past the windows. There was a loud crash somewhere in the tower. The floor shook. "I say," said the Ex-Emperor, blinking rapidly. "Speak of the devil. Looks like someone knows his niblick."

"Oh, do shut up, Randers," said his wife, bowing her head. "We none of us can understand a word you're saying."

The Earl of Munderplast cleared his throat. "This might be a moment for us to think solemnly of the past. Sadly recall the happy days of yesteryear. Stare straight forward. And prepare for the end, which shall come in the next few minutes, I wys."

Down at the end of Imperial Avenue, where it trailed off into the desert, the mannequins slung a real battering ram into a make-believe portcullis gate, waiting for it to fall.

298

And then, as Brian and his comrades jogged across the blasted Imperial Square, the bombing stopped.

It took them a moment to realize: The air no longer whistled. There was no longer a rhythm of detonations. They realized that all they still heard was flame and the calls of people rescuing other people. The Mannequin Resistance had ceased their attack for unknown reasons.

They looked at each other in amazement.

They had made it.

Slowly, they walked through the gates, into the palace.

They headed up the grand staircase toward the throne room.

✳ ✳ ✳

The Court sat gathered around the throne. The floor was covered in fragments of plaster. Everything sparkled with dust. Many of the Court were wounded, and bled on their silks. Hanks of their hair hung out of circlets and cloche hats. Women dressed in sharp pink suits stooped to pick broken glass out of their feet.

There were the Ex-Emperor and the Ex-Empress, the Stub beside them. There were the Earl of Munderplast and Lord Attleborough-Stoughton and the Duke and Duchess of the Globular Colon. There were Kalgrash, Dantsig, Chigger, and Alice, all of them in handcuffs, standing dutifully by the guards. There were maids-in-waiting, Knights of the Bath, governors from far-flung colonies in distant fringes of the circulatory system.

Everyone waited for someone else to speak. No one wanted to be first.

A wind blew in through the broken glass doors. It stirred the plaster dust, and people coughed.

Brian cleared his throat. He said, "Someone should . . . someone should organize rescue parties or something. Of guards. Maybe. Because people are looking for help out there."

Courtiers looked anxiously at one another. No one stirred.

"Who?" asked the Ex-Empress Elspeth as if she was wickedly and brilliantly scoring a point. "Who would you like to organize 'rescue parties'?"

"The Imperial Council," said Lord Dainsplint, stepping forward, his hands cuffed behind his back. (It gave him a keen debaters' kind of look.) "I hereby call the Imperial Council to order."

The Earl of Munderplast rolled his eyes. "My good wight, the Council is in shambles and cannot legally rule. We have no Regent and at least one of our Council members is an assassin who dinged down the previous Regent."

"I did not!" said Lord Dainsplint. "As I have said, I killed only Gugs."

The Ex-Empress said, "Yes, you're rather awful. I do believe he was quite fond of you. I suspect that later this evening we shall all decide to strip you naked and hurl you off the balcony." She spread her hand dramatically. "Splatters," she said.

"Then there must be another among us who is guilty

of the assassination," said the earl. "We cannot rule thus. The Council is riddled with vacancies, madmen, and murderers."

"I don't see," said Lord Dainsplint, "how that is any different than usual business, old man. You just want to sound off in the midst of crisis so the Melancholy Party gets the Regent's seat."

They glared at each other across the room. From outside, distantly, came the sound of fires.

"Um, hey," said Gregory, raising his hand. "Really, someone has to take charge here."

Ex-Emperor Randall said, "Well, why *not* Chigger? He seems awfully keen. The scepter in his eye and all."

Chigger bowed. "I should be glad to accept the charge to rule."

"All that are in favor?" said the Ex-Emperor, raising his hand.

The Earl of Munderplast swept forward and exclaimed, "I demand a full investigation of the Regent's murder before we put anything to a vote. We cannot allow the Council to be stocked with those who murdered His Excellency." He frowned. "As opposed to those who planned to, but — oh, night of rue — did not get the chance."

Everyone looked suspiciously at one another.

"Oh, very well," said the Ex-Empress Elspeth. "Let's clear all this up right now. Someone must know by now who punched the old Reejer's ticket." She looked around brightly. "Come along. Fess." She clapped.

No one confessed to the murder.

The earl said grandly, "I accuse Lord 'Chigger' Dainsplint of the assassination of the Regent."

"Utter rot," said Chigger. "All we need do is take ten minutes to force Alice to speak her memory and you'll see I was with her all that evening. I am not the guilty party."

The earl shifted uncomfortably. "There is one other," he said. He looked briefly at Brian, then at the throne. "Your Highness," he said, bowing to the Stub, "it may be that Lord Dainsplint, who was, we might well find, not present at the murder, was nonetheless involved with another on the Council who committed the very deed." He smiled secretively. "Would you not all fall back, astounded, if I revealed who this might be?" He paced back and forth.

Brian glanced at Gwynyfer. She cowered next to Gregory.

The earl said, "It has been brought to my attention that there is one other councillor whose alibi for that fateful night was not adequate. Most of us were with our own beloved and revered Ex-Empress and Ex-Emperor. A few of us were involved in some pleasant and convivial conversation in the basements of this palace. But one claims — one! — claims to have been 'with his family.' Yea, my friends — 'with his family.' Who are, therefore, the only witnesses that he was not dressed and bedight as a guard, creeping through the corridors of this palace — dirk in hand, murder in his heart — as he sought to kill our most gracious and beloved Regent in the flower of the man's youth."

The earl smiled harshly. "That man is . . . the Duke of the Globular —"

But before he could even finish, Gwynyfer had let forth a wail. She rushed forward to her father — mustached, sagging in his tux — and she threw her arms around him, saying, "No! Daddy! Daddy!"

Sadly, the man greeted his daughter, mumbling, "The Duke of the Globular Colon greets his daughter, Miss Gwynyfer Gwarnmore, upon this sorrowful day . . . and wishes —"

"Do you deny it?" cried the earl.

". . . and wishes that there shall be brighter days for his beloved daughter in years to come." The man looked up at the earl. "I, of course, deny it. I was at home with my family. We returned to our manor after the dance. You have no evidence."

"Do I not?" said the earl. He looked quickly at Brian. *"Do I not?"*

Brian was frozen to the spot, watching this unfold in front of him. He didn't know what to say. He wasn't ready to accuse anyone. He didn't know — couldn't figure out —

And now Gwynyfer faced him, tears running down her cheeks, and said, "Tell them — Brian — tell them what you've found. It couldn't be my father." She faced the whole Court and screamed, "It *can't*! You can't!"

Brian didn't know. Gregory looked at him angrily. The earl waited. The Court waited.

303

Gregory walked out in front of them. He glared at Brian, then began. "Lords, ladies," he said, "Your Highness." He bowed to the Stub. "The Duke of the Globular Colon could not have committed this murder. The murderer had to disguise himself as Dantsig. That was part of the plan: to make it look like Dantsig was guilty. Whoever it was stuck on a fake beard like Dantsig. So whoever it was *could not have had a white mustache, too — as the duke does!*" He pointed furiously at the duke.

"I say," said the duke. "No need to point at my 'stache."

"By the breath of the Morrigan!" the Ex-Empress swore. *"It must have been one of you on the Council! Will someone simply accuse someone else who can't make excuses? So we can be done with it?"*

The Wizard Thoth-Chumley did not look comfortable. He stared down at his notebook and scribbled something.

Meanwhile, Brian had just realized something. He had just thought about the murder in a way he'd never thought about it before. He'd just realized one thing that had blinded him all along. He looked around wildly: noble faces strained and confused; chalky dust lit with shafts of sunlight; the Stub, his eye wheeling wildly; battered drones clanking forward with sandwiches. He saw things he'd never seen before.

He said, "Excuse me. Excuse me." He walked to Gregory's side. "I think I know who killed the Regent, and why."

THIRTY-FIVE

Well?" demanded the Ex-Empress.

Brian thought for a minute. He said haltingly, "Now...we know it's someone on the Council, because only someone with a councillor's ring could have sealed the order for a spare uniform to be left where Dantsig would find it. Right?"

The Ex-Empress sighed and held out her skeletal hands. "I have no earthly idea," she said.

Brian had too many thoughts crowding his head... too many ideas swarming all over one another...and it wasn't easy to think with all the courtiers staring at him in confusion, boredom, and anger. He needed time. He looked up and said, "The servant who received that letter was named Mr. Gwestin, and he was sent down to the dung furnace after we spoke to him. I would like to call him as a witness and ask him a few questions."

The Ex-Empress waved her hand, and a servant bustled off to draw Gwestin away from his dung shovel.

"So . . . ?" the Ex-Empress said.

Brian hesitated. He wanted a minute to collect his thoughts. Gregory and Gwynyfer looked at him expectantly — with suspicion, but with relief and gratitude. She didn't realize that he'd been the one who had suspected her of aiding her father with the murder.

So many things to think about . . . so many people watching one another, and commenting on one another . . .

Brian looked up. "If I tell you who murdered the Regent — and why — then Dantsig and Kalgrash will be proved innocent, right?"

The earl looked with distaste at the two mannequins. "That would seem to be the case. Except that they are still prisoners of war. And, moreover, they are Norumbegan property. We may install them or deinstall them as is our august will."

"If I tell you who murdered the Regent," Brian repeated, "if I prove that there was a dangerous conspiracy right within the palace walls — then you owe me something, don't you? You owe me a favor, like the release of these prisoners and information on how to activate the Rules Keepers and stop the Thusser."

"You cannot bargain, boy," said the earl.

The Ex-Empress added, "If we wish, we can just strip you and throw you over the balcony, too, when we're done hurling Chigger." She looked around. "Or is that no longer on the menu?"

Brian would not give up.

"When I tell you what has been going on . . ."

Brian said. "What I *think* has been going on ... you're going to —"

At this point, Gwestin appeared. He bowed before the Stub. "Your Imperial Highness," he said, "may the herons call your name. May you hunt down the gods and bring them to bay. I am your lowliest servant: waitron and dung slinger."

"Rise," said the Earl of Munderplast. He gestured impatiently with his hand.

Gwestin looked to the Stub, as if for approval, and stood.

Brian moved forward. He was so nervous there was sweat on his shirt. He could tell everyone saw it. He did not feel very sure of himself. He couldn't imagine what would happen when he accused someone.

"Mr. ... Mr. Gwestin," said Brian. "You are a servant of the Imperial palace, isn't that right?" Gwestin nodded. Brian continued, "You received a note — *signed with the Council's seal* — two nights ago, the night we arrived in the palace. Isn't that right?"

Gwestin assented.

"And what did that note tell you to do?"

"Your Imperial Highness, your lordships, it told me to take a palace guard uniform down to the prison, ask to be let in to see the two mannequins, and to leave the uniform where they'd find it."

"Did it say why?"

"Your Imperial Highness, your lordships, my betters do not need to explain themselves to me. I do what I am commanded."

307

Brian nodded. He felt giddy with anxiousness.

"UNLESS," he said. "UNLESS."

"You're rather leaking under the arms," said the Ex-Empress.

The Ex-Emperor said, "Someone should fetch him a chamois."

Brian's rhythm was broken. It took him a second to get up his courage again. "UNLESS," he insisted, "you never received a note at all, Mr. Gwestin."

The Court gaped.

"You told us that the note was destroyed before we saw it. Maybe it never existed in the first place. Maybe *you* stole those two uniforms from the guardhouse. Maybe you kept one for yourself, and took the other one down to the prison. You told the guard on duty that the Council had ordered you to deliver a message to Kalgrash and Dantsig. No one was going to disbelieve you. They knew you worked at the palace. They knew your face.

"Or at least," said Brian, feeling a weird kind of triumph suddenly, "at least they knew who you were — *until, a few hours later, when you put on a false goatee and the other uniform, and went and murdered the Regent.*"

Gwestin showed signs of panic — and then he quelled them. He crossed his arms. "I did it," he said, "for the glory of the Empire. I serve the Imperial House of Norumbega. The dog Telliol-Bornwythe had to die."

The Court craned in to look at him. The Ex-Empress demanded he be spun around so everyone could see him. They all wanted to touch him, wanted to pluck at him.

There were hands all around him. He didn't wince as they pinched him. Eyes stared into his eyes. He stood firm.

Gregory was at Brian's side, mystified. "So who was . . . I don't get it. . . . Who was that voice, the night he attacked us? It must have been him who attacked us, with the gas?"

"It was him," said Brian. "I think."

"Who was the voice over the intercom? Who was telling him to kill us?" Gregory was perplexed. "I thought it was the Thusser."

Brian nodded. His brain was racing. "It was," he said. "In a way." He looked at the Ex-Empress, hoping she'd shush everyone, so he could explain. He said, louder, "IN A WAY, it WAS the THUSSER."

She was busy poking at Gwestin, giggling at the purple spots on his arms where he'd been pinched. The Court gadded around him, grinning.

"The Thusser?" said Lord Dainsplint, who couldn't pinch, since his hands were handcuffed behind his back. He stood nearby, interested in what Brian had to say.

"Yes," said Brian. "The Thusser."

"Hush!" cried Lord Dainsplint. "The boy says the Thusser are involved, too! Hush!"

The Court quieted down. They drew away from their victim. Gwestin staggered as they stepped back. His hair was twisted from where they'd pulled it. He had little nip marks on his shoulders, and pinch marks on his arms.

"You were an agent for the Thusser, Gwestin?" asked Lord Dainsplint. "That doesn't ruddy well seem like a good way to support and sustain the old Empire."

Gwestin, for the first time, looked angry. "The Thusser? I would not serve those wolves! Those animals! I serve only the Imperial House."

Brian said, "That's what you thought. But . . ."

He looked around. It was now or never. Everyone stared at him expectantly. If he didn't get this right — if he couldn't prove it — there was some chance the pinching would descend on him, the dragging, the hurling — *splatters*.

"Mr. Gwestin, you thought you were serving the House of Norumbega. But you weren't." He shook his head. "You were —"

"A dupe?" suggested Lord Dainsplint. "A patsy?"

Gwestin looked deeply disturbed at the idea. Clearly, he hated the Horde. "I would never submit to the Thusser! My orders come from the highest authority! I listen only to him — only to . . ." — he bowed deeply, his voice catching with emotion — "Your Imperial Highness the Stub."

"He tells you what to do?" Brian asked.

Gwestin bowed.

"The Stub?" Dainsplint protested. "That's a bit rum. I mean, he's an excellent chap, if you go in for eye rolling, but he's not one of your great talkers, the Stub."

"He spoke to *me*. His servant."

Several women of the Court smiled behind torn fans. They thought he was crazy.

Brian said, "Ex-Empress Elspeth, do you know Dr. Brundish?"

"I do, of course. Lumpish fellow. Recently went walkers."

"You know him well?"

"He has been my MD since olden times."

Brian nodded gravely. "Dr. Brundish was a Thusser spy. He had a two-way radio that could pick up signals and transmit. He could listen, and he could broadcast reports to the world of the Thusser. He could whisper orders, Mr. Gwestin, and you'd hear them in your headset. And he had a powerful antenna that let him do this. A bug that let him hear everything that went on in the throne room." Brian paused and breathed deeply. "That bug," he said, "that antenna . . . it is . . . the Stub himself."

At this, the Court approached Brian. They had their fingers out, ready for pinching. They seemed like they'd delight in it. "The Stub?" — "He accuses the Stub?" — "The Imperial Stub?"

"No! Truly! Your Highness! Ex-Empress! Didn't Dr. Brundish help you when you were pregnant?"

"I don't like the direction this conversation is taking," the Ex-Empress said.

"Didn't he? And . . . and . . ." The courtiers were almost upon him. "And Ex-Emperor Fendritch, Your Highness, didn't your uncle, the last Emperor, complain because his kids all came out as spirals and sand and things, because of a Thusser curse?"

The Ex-Emperor shrugged. "My uncle complained about a great, great number of things."

The fingers reached Brian. They began to squeeze.

311

Fingers were locked in Brian's black hair. They pulled, they twisted — only lightly for the moment, nipping.

"Ex-Empress Elspeth!" Brian called. "Ex-Empress, *is it possible that Dr. Brundish injected you with something, or cast some kind of curse or spell over you — so that you gave birth to something that wasn't Norumbegan?*"

The Ex-Empress thought. The Court paused in their torment. The Ex-Empress said, "There were the injections, obviously. And the pentagrams. All strictly necessary to provide good fortune for an Imperial child. Pull the organs of the Great Body into alignment. Bring luck."

Brian crouched, surrounded by stooping figures in gauze and old lace and silk, reaching forward, ready to torture him.

He said, *"That is not your son! He was built in you! Planted!"*

Gwestin wailed, "My Lord! Your Highness! Your Imperial Highness!" and threw himself down before the Stub. He sobbed. "Speak to them! Tell them these are lies!"

"The Stub talked to you out loud at first, didn't it?" Brian said. "It saw that you were loyal. It told you things."

"He did! Your Highness!" The man was prostrate before the plug of a king.

"It wasn't the Stub's voice. It was Dr. Brundish's. He could hear everything that was going on with the Council. He reported everything back to the Magister of the

Thusser Horde. Whenever he needed something done, he'd speak to you. He'd pretend to be the voice of the Stub. He gave you that headset, I bet."

"Dr. Brundish was a loyal . . . He was a servant of the one, true Norumbegan Emperor," said Gwestin, crying.

"So, see? He heard that the Regent was going to oppose the Thusser, and he needed him killed quickly. He had you do it. He told you how. Then he heard me speaking out against the Thusser, and saying that we needed to wake up the Rules Keepers, and he ordered you to kill me. You're the one who put that little . . . little . . . death beetle in my hamburger. You're the one who tried to poison us with gas. On the Stub's orders. On Dr. Brundish's orders. You see?"

The Court was shocked. They stood, almost uninterested in the prospect of harm. They held their fingers poised, at the ready, but did not swoop in to grab at Brian.

Until Gregory said, "Wait . . . but by the time Gwestin tried to gas us . . . when we heard the voice in the headset . . . Dr. Brundish was already gone. And we had his radio."

"That's impossible," said Brian. "Unless . . . unless there was another Thusser with a radio somewhere in the Great Body who could transmit to —"

But the Court no longer wanted to hear what he had to say. They didn't want to hear their sovereign Stub insulted. They moved in for torment.

Men in pinstripes, women in silk, they all moved in to

313

harass Brian in their cruel and elfin way, and he saw peering down at him the chiseled faces of grannies and leering men of business, daughters of the nobility, knights, all of them grabbing at him, pinching, twisting, plucking: gray hands, pearl buttons, a black cuff.

He struggled. The crowd was too thick. Gregory waded toward him.

They were all over Brian — sharp darts of pain — roiling like insects in some gruesome hive, ripped away from a wall and revealed piling near their queen. His legs quivered and shot up with new, sharp snaps. His arms were twisted. His shirt sagged.

He couldn't breathe to scream. They were dragging — he could almost see, through the crowd of scuffed brogues and dancing pumps — they were dragging him toward the balcony.

His hair — he felt shocks of his hair pulled out like kernels off the cob. Across the floor . . . he grabbed at things he felt . . . but they were just a litter of plasterboard . . . slipped through his fingers. His arm jolted as someone dug their thumbs into the joint of his elbow.

"For the glory of the Stub!" they hissed. "Our Imperial Majesty the Stub!"

He flipped over, kicked at them. Gregory was at his side, shoving, screaming, "No!"

And Brian found himself being heaved up.

He was outside. On the balcony. Above the city.

The hot wind from fires blew across his face. Light was red. The city burned.

Arms lifted him, tearing at his clothes.

He swung out — facedown — the crater of the square below him — eight stories below — He screamed.

They held him.

He struggled.

They still held him fast.

They prepared to drop him.

Gregory hoarsely yelled. He lunged. They forced him back.

Brian wheeled his hands in the empty air.

And then, just as they were about to drop him, a voice said, "Excuse me. Lords, ladies, is this the Imperial Council of Norumbega?"

The elfin rout halted, intrigued.

They all looked back into the Grand Hall. It was a beautiful youth with golden, feathered locks. He was dressed in a white flag of truce. He held his head on a platter. "I have been sent by the Mannequin Resistance." Awkwardly, he explained, "Your phone is out of order." The youth's head on the platter, it appeared, was attached by a few wires to his shoulders. This youth, the messenger of the armies that had ceased their fire, announced, "Your lordships, your ladyships, I bring dire news. The Thusser Horde are in the Great Body."

He said, "They have taken Pflundt."

And at that, the Stub began to make a noise.

THIRTY-SIX

The hum was low but loud. It made the floor of the throne room vibrate. Courtiers turned from the messenger to the Stub, and saw their monarch gazing at them with an intelligence he had never shown before.

The regal plug's gaze swung across each face there, as if inspecting them for the last time. Then the pupil rolled up in the socket. It faded like a good-luck message in a Magic 8 Ball.

The eye was blank and white. The hum got louder.

"He's going to detonate!" Gwynyfer yelled, and she bolted toward the exit, waving for others to follow her.

Gregory grabbed Brian's wrist, dragged him out of a clump of stunned viscounts, and headed for the great staircase. "She's right," said Gregory. "I can feel it. Something's up."

Ex-Empress Elspeth was staring at the Stub as if waking from a dream. "Not my son," she said. And again, but this time more triumphantly: "Not my son! He's not!"

She even began to smile. "No. No, he isn't. He's a bomb. And a radio. And a very bad boy."

She took her feckless husband's hand. "Come along, Randers," she said to him. "Let's leave the thing to pout. Think about what he's done."

The eye of the Stub had grown milky gray.

The courtiers stumbled and pushed on the stairs. There were too many now — too many to fit, and they were shoving and screaming at each other. They were gasping:

"Servants' stairs — use the servants' stairs!"

"*You* use the servants' stairs!"

"I wouldn't *deign*." (Shrieks as people fell, as people were stepped on.) "This is the absolute crush of the season, darling. Everyone will be watching. Get your hand out of my face. You're smearing my dimples."

Back in the empty throne room, the Stub sat upon his throne. His eye was black and glittering.

On the floor in front of him, Gwestin lay spread in subservience. His shirt was off. His head was bowed. His lips kissed the plaster dust. "I am Your Majesty's last servant," he said. "I served you better than all the others. All the others have fled. I am Your Majesty's true protector. May Your Imperial Majesty live long and be vaulted into godhood when you pass on. May Your Imperial Majesty inherit not only the Empire of the Innards, but the space of mouths undiscovered, and eyes that might lie above, and the Great Body's hands or tentacles, and may you thrive always, with this Great Body to serve where you lack even a torso of

317

your own, O most mighty Stub, most glorious monarch, most —"

And then his king exploded.

＊　＊　＊

Out in the desert, where General Malark sat in a wooden conning tower built atop three slow beasts, he saw the palace erupt. He saw its side blow out. He saw the burning junk rain down.

＊　＊　＊

Hurled to the side, Gregory couldn't catch his breath. The staircase had buckled. He heard groaning.

It was not animal groaning, he realized. He was in a wooden gantry attached to the side of the palace, and it was sagging. Courtiers crawled around him. Brian, shaking, was sitting next to him. Gwynyfer pulled herself toward him. He held out his hand for her.

"Hold on!" Gregory said. "Hold on to . . . a railing or something. We're tipping. We're tipping!"

Some strut cracked. The gantry wobbled free of the wall and swung.

Gregory and the others clung to banisters. They were looking down at the trash heap fifteen feet below.

Another wooden buttress snapped.

They were heading right into the junk.

They screamed.

The gantry fell.

They hit, curling their bodies as the staircase slewed into the trash.

Flaming debris still drifted down around them.

A huge, ragged hole in the palace wall smoked. The air was almost unbreathable.

Gregory, Brian, and Gwynyfer kicked their way to the surface. Courtiers around them moaned and crawled through old drapes and discarded shoes. The kids gave them a hand.

The palace sagged. Two of its turrets had fallen off. Fires still clearly raged inside.

"The palace!" Gwynyfer choked.

Gregory looked grimly up at the hole that disgorged thick smoke into the newly polluted haze of the Dry Heart.

When Gwynyfer was off a few paces, helping the Mistress of the Robes disentangle herself from some heating ducts, Gregory muttered to Brian, "I guess this is what they get for crowning a candy corn their king."

✳ ✳ ✳

No one seemed to notice that Kalgrash and Dantsig, having snapped the chains off their handcuffs, were helping people up out of the rubble. In fact, many people took it for granted. They were mechanicals, after all.

No one questioned that the Empress Elspeth was now in charge, no longer Ex; or that the Earl of Munderplast, candidate for the Melancholy Party, would act as her Grand Chamberlain and Prime Minister.

No one protested — except Lord Dainsplint himself —

319

when the Empress decreed, in a voice dead with exhaustion, that he should be exiled into the desert.

No one argued when Brian and Gregory said that they had to leave and seek the Empress's brother, Archbishop Darlmore, where he lived as a hermit. No one complained when they said they needed backpacks with food and water and maybe a map. No one, now, believed that they should delay in their quest to waken the Rules Keepers and halt the Thusser Horde from their inevitable march.

No one was particularly surprised when the mannequin messenger, his head held under his arm (his platter had been lost in the blast), requested a grand parley and a truce between the Mannequin Resistance and the Norumbegan overlords.

"The mannequins offer their aid and help to Your Imperial Highness," he said to the Empress, bowing his head (with his free hand). "We have a common enemy that shall destroy us all," he said. "They have already taken our capital, Pflundt. None of us were there to repel them. We recommend, therefore, that we put aside our differences and join forces to protect the integrity of the Empire."

"Good show," said the Empress.

The headless youth indicated the burning city. "Here in this magnificent capital, massed safely behind your impregnable walls, we shall withstand a siege until the humans can awaken the Rules Keepers."

"Our impregnable walls," the Earl of Munderplast repeated desolately, looking at the ragged line of candy-colored huts that marked the edge of New Norumbega. He muttered, "By the sacred rood of Woden."

"If we are joined together," the youth said with a bright smile on his face (under his arm), "who can defeat us?"

The Empress said, "Jolly thought, that." And to her anxious subjects: "We'll work out the finer details later." She wriggled her fingers vaguely.

Kalgrash raised his armored hand. "No," he said loudly. "Work out the details now." He looked at Dantsig's hard face. "The mechanicals won't fight unless you grant them freedom."

The Empress scowled. "I see."

"And then give up Three-Gut and the mannequin-held entrails."

The Empress smiled to herself. "Does one mean a territory currently held by the Thusser? You wish me to grant it to you?"

"Yup," said Kalgrash. "Because it's not going to be held by the Thusser for long. We're going to get it back. And it's only fair: If we fight for it, if we win it, we own it. Simple, simple, simple."

No one spoke out while the Empress, with irritation in her eyes, considered the demand. No one needed to point to the armies already ringed around the smoking city. And so she said, "Granted. If you successfully protect New Norumbega from the Thusser invasion, we shall declare Three-Gut and the mannequin-held entrails to be your own sovereign state. Your own kingdom or republic or theocracy or what have you. To protect as you will. If you can." She waved her hand. "Congratters."

She did not seem happy about it. Neither did the rest of the Court.

321

But Dantsig laughed and clapped once. He looked like he wanted to do a little dance, but couldn't, standing on the rubble and before the Empress of the Innards.

Kalgrash had a satisfied smile on his face.

Out in the plains, beneath the slow, soaring shadows of bubbles in the veins, the mannequins waited for news. They did not know it, but they had a home now. It was a home occupied by the Thusser, but still, it was a kingdom for windup citizens, a place where they could turn the key in one anothers' backs without a blue-blooded Norumbegan hand to knock it away.

In the rubble, the irritable Empress turned to Brian and Gregory. "Well, boys, you did chivvy out the assassin, as promised. I rather think that's the last we'll be seeing of old Gwestin. Except perhaps when we dust. He's in a million bits."

"We want to leave the city as soon as possible," Brian said.

"You want me to thank you, don't you?"

Brian shrugged. He didn't really want her to thank him. He didn't care what she did, as long as she let him go.

"Well, I don't need to thank a human," she said. "I don't."

Brian nodded.

But then Gwynyfer Gwarnmore stepped forward. "But I want to thank him," she said. "And I want to go with them." She turned to her father. "Gwynyfer Gwarnmore presents the Duke with the following petition: *Requested*, that she be allowed to accompany the human boys on their quest to find Archbishop Darlmore. *Requested*, that she be given money and mounts for the expedition. *Requested,* that her parents continue in their affection for her until she returns home, at which point they may assess her success and decide whether praise or scorn would best greet her efforts."

Her father granted her petition.

And so, first thing the next morning, a procession of five-footed beasts set off into the saline deserts of the Dry Heart. Brian rode on one, Gregory and Gwynyfer on another, and a third was stocked with their tents and much of their water.

Kalgrash and Dantsig did not go with them. They remained behind to assist in the new alliance between mannequin and breather. Kalgrash was the only mechanical who wasn't programmed to see a city of clean stone and white marble in place of the real squalor of New Norumbega, the garbage pits, the hovels painted like fine mansions. So he hugged Brian and shook hands with Gregory and Gwynyfer, and he watched the three of them on their steeds lumber away from the crumpled palace.

They passed down the great avenue of the city. No one else paid them any heed. The Norumbegans were too busy clearing away the rubble from a day of bombing.

The three beasts passed between the ranks of the Mannequin Resistance. The automatons were already preparing to march into the city gates (which they still believed stood as before). They made preparations to repel the Thusser, whenever the Thusser arrived. They carried their banners through the heat, calling out orders.

Into the bright morning of the Dry Heart the three

323

beasts rode, and Brian, for the first time in days, was happy. Gregory was contented, riding with Gwynyfer. Gwynyfer was clearly thrilled to be part of something that would take her beyond the courtesies of the shattered palace.

Brian was leaving behind the murk and confusion, the backstabbing and the political lies of the Court. It had only been a few days, but it felt like forever.

Still, he thought, he was glad it had all happened. He and Gregory had seen things and noticed things that the adults around them had not. He and Gregory, two humans, had proved themselves as smart — or at least less lazy — than the elfin race who despised them. And now they were on their way to save the world.

He felt good again. Sure of his purpose. He smiled at the dazzling granules around him.

So they made their way across one chamber of one heart in a cluster of hearts, hanging in a net of ropy veins; while at the verge of one stomach, in the fortress of Pflundt, the Thusser scurried along the narrow corridors, preparing to launch their attack; and elsewhere, farmers tilled the rich soil of livers, and miners drilled into fats, and the wings of twelve lungs unfolded from a central stem, and people surged through veins in submarines and made their way on flightless birds through the labyrinthine tripe; and all of the Great Body, ancient as it was, prepared for its next convulsion.